Shades of a Warrior

CALUMET EDITIONS

Minneapolis

Shades of a Warrior

Robert Saxton

CALUMET EDITIONS

Minneapolis

For Tommy

Author's Note

This story is about an area that I have loved and appreciated my entire life: the north shore of Lake Superior, Minnesota. Although the physical descriptions of the places between Grand Marais and the Canadian border are close to reality and will be familiar to many, I have made many alterations. The people, names, and events in the book are entirely imagined.

Chapter One

BJ blinked at the middle finger. In fourteen years, he'd observed his share of them. He'd seen them reaching out of the car window way down in Minneapolis. He'd seen them in the stands of high school hockey games. The Native kids at school were particularly skilled at the gesture. Until today, though, he'd never seen one in the clouds. But there it was, as clear as a spring morning in May, fluffy white fingers flipping off the entire world. Sometimes, you had to use your imagination to see something in the clouds. It could be an elephant or a hat. But this time, there was zero doubt. BJ was puzzling this when two bronze faces appeared, staring down at him.

"Is he alive?"

"He's fine."

"Think he'll have brain damage?"

"Like we'll ever know."

Laughter.

BJ realized that he was lying in the middle of the school playground. What had happened?

"MAKI!" A third face appeared, this one with lighter skin and a louder voice. "Keep your eyes open!" BJ felt a warm glob of tobacco goo strike him in the temple and run down the side of his head. "In I-rak, the quickest way into a body bag was to daydream! Eyes. OPEN!" He spun and disappeared. BJ sat up and watched his gym teacher stomp away. Bud Davis ran class like he did boot camp for the army, barking in his Boston brogue, chewing tobacco like it was his worst enemy, leaving little brown spots scattered across the ground in his wake. BJ wiped the spit from his temple and turned his face to the lake. He saw a taconite barge far out, low in the water, loaded with ore. It would be headed to Sault Ste. Marie.

His mind hopped all over the town. Gentle waves washed onto the beach, melting into the smooth, penny and golf ball-sized rocks, the color of deer hair in November. A mud-encrusted Ford truck stopped in the middle of the road while an elderly woman crossed with nine movements of her walker. A dog tied outside the post office barked twice, paused, then barked twice more.

"Johnson got you," said Tony, helping BJ to his feet. "The girl can throw. I think I'm in love! She dropped you like a rock." *Oh yeah*, thought BJ. *Dodgeball*. That's what they were doing. BJ hated dodgeball.

David grinned, his big white teeth juxtaposed against the mess of sherbet-orange and green hair. "Could of been worse, Niichi. Tony got one in the nuts."

They all winced.

"You were just staring out at the lake when she hit you," said Tony.

"Seagulls," BJ lied. The middle finger was strange enough, but if he told them what else he had seen, they'd think he was crazy. "I was looking at a flock of seagulls in the air."

"There's a flock of balls in the air, too, Nature Boy!" shouted Mr. Davis. "Eyes OPEN!" He shot a brown stream onto the ground and blew his whistle.

Ninety-six lockers, twenty-four stairs, and seventeen floor tiles later, BJ arrived at US History. There, he slumped into his seat, his mind clutching onto another number: four. Four more days until summer vacation.

Notebook on desk. Pencil on notebook. Hand on cheek. Hailey

Jensen breezed into the room and walked down BJ's aisle as if she were floating. BJ kept his gaze down. Hailey took her seat behind BJ, then sniffed at the air. *Oh no...* "Hey," she whispered, "are you wearing perfume?" BJ shook his head, annoyed. "You know it's Mom's oils. Shut up."

"You smell like a girl."

"Shut up, Hailey."

She poked his shoulder and whispered, "Little bitch."

He swatted at Hailey's hand without looking back because Mrs. Heikela was entering the classroom, her blond hair pulled into a tight bun and wearing a loose green dress, which exposed her chubby arms and neck. Her heels tapped sharply as she strode past the steely gazes of early US presidents towards the too-tall lectern. Nancy Heikela was, like the Makis, of Finnish descent and whose ancestry on the north shore of Lake Superior went back no further than three generations. She had been teaching World and U.S. History for more than twenty years and ran a tight ship. She was married to the county sheriff. "We will do a quick review of chapter one before Wednesday's final," she announced. "Please open your books to page fourteen."

BJ wondered why the review was necessary. It had, he recalled, been straightforward: Pilgrims meet Indians, America fights for freedom, then builds a nation and all that. He flipped to the end of chapter one, where there was a list of twelve important summary points. "We will take turns reading the summaries and discuss, if necessary," said Mrs. Heikela. BJ judged that the level of energy in the room would make this quite unnecessary. "Hailey, why don't you start?"

Hailey cleared her throat and read. "Soon after Columbus discovered America, modern weapons, tools, and clothing began to make their way across the continent." BJ was half listening—until he realized that this was not what summary number one said on his page. In BJ's book, it said this: *Soon after Columbus stumbled upon America, disease, slavery, and genocide made their way across the continent.*

BJ flinched. He glanced at the books around him. Maybe he was on the wrong page. "Page fourteen," confirmed Mrs. Heikela, noticing him. BJ nodded and looked down again, just as Soren Knutsen began to read. "Guns were prized by the Indians."

A Native archer could shoot fifteen arrows in the time it took a white man to reload a black powder rifle. What the...?

"The Constitution enumerated numerous ideals," read another student.

Many of these were learned from the Haudenosaunee People, said BJ's summary number three.

"Life was difficult for the Indians before..."

They had a four-hour workday, slept in warm beds, and could build a fire by hand in two minutes.

"Westward expansion into open country..."

Westward invasion into populated country...

"Treaties were signed..."

Treaties were broken...

"Settlers..."

Invaders...

"Built..."

Destroyed...

BJ was sweating. He didn't remember reading any of this earlier. None of the other students gave any indication that their books were acting strangely. Had he sustained a concussion in dodgeball? The next paragraph in BJ's book nearly caused him to fall out of his seat. It said:

Find the warrior with the red hand. Before the summer is out. Your family is in danger. Your community is in danger. Find the warrior! Oh, and look up. Your teacher is talking to you.

Mrs. Heikela was staring at BJ expectantly. "Go ahead."

A rather large stone landed in the pit of BJ's stomach. "What?"

"I said," Mrs. Heikela spoke slowly, as if to a young child, "Please read the final summary point."

"Little bitch," whispered a voice behind him.

BJ rubbed his fingers through the dark cowlick above his right eye and felt it spring back into place, as always. He looked down, bracing for the worst. But the sentences he had just read were gone. The words on the page matched exactly what the other kids in class had been reading. And the final summary point, the sentence BJ was to read, looked harmless. Boring, even. BJ breathed a sigh of relief and read: "Eventually, the United States was built on the principles of freedom and democracy by men of valor and conviction. Women played a role as well, raising children, toiling in the fields, and, when necessary, leveling a gun. None of them, however, was as smoking hot as Nancy Heikela, who I'd love to take out on a date and… and…"

A ringing silence followed. A solitary fly buzzed around and between students with open mouths. Mrs. Heikela stood rigid and pale as if she had been slapped across the face. There was nothing for BJ to say. There was nothing he could say. She pointed at the door. BJ gathered his things and headed out.

Minutes later, BJ was sitting at a heavy oak desk and counting the stripes of an impressive lake trout mounted on the wall behind the principal, whose knuckles were white as he gripped the phone and listened. His right eye twitched. Ryan Olafson was a pear-shaped man with receding blond hair and a small mustache. All in all, he was a decent principal and an extremely good fisherman, which earned him general respect from most of the students. BJ liked Ryan. After one minute, he hung up the phone and sighed as he rubbed his eyes with one hand. "Smoking hot? Really, BJ?"

BJ shifted in his seat. He didn't know what to say.

Mr. Olafson leaned forward, then stopped and sniffed at the air. "Say, are you wearing—?"

"No. No," he repeated more firmly. "It's my mom's…"

5

Ryan held up a hand to stop him. "Sorry. Forgot." He sat back in his seat and began tapping a pencil against his mustache. "So, did your mom get into the oils after she started managing the co-op?"

"No, she's always had them around."

"Is she using them to address your attention issues?"

"Yup."

"Are they having any effect?"

"Making me smell like a girl, apparently."

Ryan's eyes narrowed, then softened. "I see."

BJ leaned forward. "Would you tell her they worked and to stop rubbing these damned..."

"Language, BJ!"

"Sorry. I'm just sick of them!"

"I'm not sure I want to butt heads with your mother again. She's a wonderful woman, Molly, but she's been a firecracker since she was little. Did you know she got kicked out of daycare?"

"Yeah." BJ had heard the story. "She bit someone."

"She sure did," said Ryan, pointing to his left forearm. "Right there."

"Oh, it was you!" BJ smiled.

"Look, I'll call your mom and try to bring it up without her taking my head off, alright? As for the thing with Mrs. Heikela..."

"I'll apologize to her," blurted BJ. "I don't know what came over me. I just... I don't know."

"Okay then," said Ryan. "Honestly, you're a kind soul, and you've had a very good year..."

"Better than my sister."

Ryan's eye resumed twitching. He stood and pulled a red-and-white handkerchief from his shirt pocket, wiped his brow, folded it, and began to clean the dust from the fins of the lake trout. "Are there"—he blew on the tail—" any subjects that you feel you're good at or something that makes you special?"

BJ didn't remember what he answered the last time Ryan had asked him this. He thought for a moment. He was getting pretty good at cross-country running and skiing, though still nothing like his mother. He'd been able to sing pretty well until his voice began cracking in eighth grade. His grades were good, especially in math. He was an advanced rock-skipper. The final bell rang. BJ stood and walked to the door. When he opened it, the noise flowed in and around them like water pouring through a broken dam.

"Well, what is it? Hello, BJ?"

"What's what?"

"A subject you like or something you're good at?"

BJ looked at the floor. What was he good at? Was there anything that made him special? Mr. Olafson tapped his right shoe on the floor one, two, three, four times. BJ met his eyes and said, "I'm good at counting." Ryan Olafson blinked. BJ stepped into the river of students and was swept away.

BJ floated with the stream of students until he reached the fourth-grade classroom. Charley was there, wearing a violent-pink T-shirt, a green denim skirt, polka-dot stockings, and Wizard of Oz ruby slippers. What was left of this morning's pigtails hung in wild strands around her ears. Fiery blue eyes in a sea of dark freckles flashed a hello to her brother. Together, they headed towards the east exit. Charley popped a piece of bubble gum in her mouth and began humming the theme song from *Legally Blonde* (the school had put on the play that spring).

The exit door was in sight, and so was a large pack of hockey players blocking the door. BJ pulled a black ball cap from his bag and snugged it over his head. Most of the hockey kids reminded him of the chimps he had seen in the Como Zoo in St. Paul. He imagined them throwing turds at each other. They waded through the boisterous group and had nearly reached the door when the hat was yanked from BJ's head. He stopped and spun, finding himself

7

staring at the broad chest of Eddie Sourmeister. Eddie was a year older than BJ but had been held back a grade. He was a gifted hockey player; his father had coached (and yelled at) him since he could walk. He had been an asshole since BJ could remember. Eddie looked at the hat, then down at BJ. "What's 'AIM'?"

"Give it back!" said BJ, trying and failing to grab it. "It's David's, and I have no idea."

"David Beaulieu?" shot Eddie, studying the letters. "Expel. Indian. Men." He said, then guffawed at his joke.

BJ glanced to the side, then back to Eddie. "Expel is with an 'e'."

"Don't sass off to me!" blared Eddie. "Maybe I'll keep it."

"Give my brother back his hat," said a voice nearby. As soon as these words were spoken, the atmosphere in the hallway shifted. Phones were put away. Backpacks were set down. Whispering ceased. BJ rubbed his cowlick and cleared his throat to speak, but Charley squared her feet and repeated her demand. "Give it back."

BJ felt himself breathing quickly, in short bursts. He needed to get Charley outside. Nothing would cap off a crappy day like having your little sister stick up for you. "Keep the hat!" he said to Eddie. "Come on, Charley!" BJ grabbed her by the hand and pulled, but Charley leaned back like a stubborn dog. There was more laughter. BJ could feel his face burning hot. Even Hailey Jensen was there, grinning.

Eddie turned his attention to Charley. "He says I can keep it."

Charley's face lost all expression, and the hair on the back of BJ's neck stood on end. She yanked her hand from BJ's grasp, plucked the gum from her mouth, stuck it on the end of her finger, and pointed at Eddie. "Give it back. Now."

Eddie's smile disappeared. For a moment, BJ thought he would do it. He would hand back the cap, and all of them could go home. But that's not what he did. Instead, he leaned into Charley's face and said, "Make me."

Charley inhaled, and BJ covered his ears. "Give. It. BAAAAAAAAAAAAAAAAAACK!"

Eddie stumbled backward into the lockers, his cheeks rippling like a skydiver. BJ knew this scream. He had experienced the "Blast" several times over the years, but never at this decibel level. Even as a toddler, Charley's yell could make his head throb. When she began school, their mother had made BJ promise to keep an eye on her. To help her get through the day without incident. Most of the time, he succeeded at this, but the distance between "sweet" and "attack" was a very short one on Charley's dial. When the horns of battle were blown, Charlotte Maki would fix her bayonet and charge down the hill, opposing numbers be damned. Usually, a yell, a shove, or a punch was enough, but on a couple of occasions, BJ had seen his little sister come close to unleashing something else. Something wild. Something powerful. BJ called it the "Wolverine." He knew it was there, lurking just beneath Charley's cuddly surface. If the Wolverine was ever unleashed, there would be blood. Maybe body parts.

Eddie's eyes were clammed shut, his shoulders hunched, and his teeth clenched. He raised his hands to block the sound waves, but this gave Charley the opening for the final part of her assault. Quick as a rattlesnake, she socked him in the nuts. The hat flew up. Eddie slid down. Charley snatched the cap in midair and tossed it to BJ. She popped the gum back into her mouth and strode from the building, humming *Legally Blonde*—just where she'd left off.

Chapter Two

BJ jogged past the playground and northeast on the sidewalk until he caught up with Charley. He was sure he would be back in the principal's office the following morning, struggling to explain the latest disaster. Even though Eddie was the one who had been destroyed, BJ still felt humiliated. Who else lets their little sister do their fighting for them? Not the Red Head Warrior, he supposed. Or was it the Red Hand Warrior? He walked alongside his sister for a few paces, then said, "You didn't have to let him have it that hard, you know."

"It wasn't that hard," said Charley. They arrived at a little square set at the top of the beach with picnic benches and two fifteen-foot statues of Paul Bunyan and his blue ox, Babe. An elderly Ojibwe woman in a red shawl and white tennis shoes was sitting on the bench nearest the statues, tossing grain to a handful of very excited pigeons. "Hi, Audrey!" chirped Charley, sounding like a chickadee, one note high and one low. Audrey brushed the seeds from her dark, leathery hand, picked a flat gray stone off the bench, and held it out to the kids. BJ picked it up and inspected it. Their mother had always said to look for skipping stones the size of a Kennedy half-dollar. This one was close to a Kennedy. Really close. Maybe BJ could get a twenty with this one. Twenty skips across the water were what separated the men from the boys in the skipping world. BJ nearly pocketed it, then remembered that Audrey had already given him a stone the previous week. He handed this one to Charley. She grinned at him in thanks. Audrey nodded her approval, then squinted up at the statue of Paul Bunyan. "He's got a nice butt." Charley giggled and covered her mouth.

BJ considered the statue. The impish expression. The plaid shirt. The thin pipe protruding from the corner of his mouth. It was said that Paul Bunyan and his trusty blue ox, Babe, came to this country during the logging era, that he could clear an entire forest in a day with his giant two-headed axe, and that he was so big his footprints made the lakes. Babe could haul a sled of logs half a mile high. "I never really noticed his butt before," said BJ.

"It's a nice butt."

They continued walking up the sidewalk that led away from the beach and into the downtown business neighborhood, which included a diner, a shoe store, a bank, and Ida's Bakery, where they paused to admire the goodies. Moist cakes, gleaming fritters, and every kind of donut imaginable were laid out the way BJ imagined a Parisian patisserie would be. Charley studied a particularly fine wedge of carrot cake on the other side of the window while BJ counted donuts: fifteen chocolate, eight cream-filled, eleven powdered sugar, five sprinkled ones, and three apple strudels. Ida Richardson made four strudels every day, but by the time school let out, there were always three left. The reason was Ralph Kern, the retired postmaster, who came to the bakery each morning for coffee and a strudel. Mr. Kern was part of BJ and Charley's morning routine. They always waved at him on their way to school.

They crossed the street diagonally towards Rusty's Bait and Tackle at the corner of Main and Kalevala. Rusty's was in an old building with wavy pine siding and a cedar shingle roof. Two bay windows—one facing each street—displayed a dazzling array of fishing lures of all shapes and colors. At the corner entrance, four Adirondack-style chairs—three regular-sized and one extra-large—

sat on the sidewalk in front of a sturdy red door. Above the chair, and easily the coolest part of the building, was a fish—a walleye, to be exact—built into the overhang, leering down towards the sidewalk with jaws agape as if ready to swallow anybody who lingered below. Charley stood beneath the fish to listen to the lyrics issuing from a speaker inside its mouth. She tilted her head like a puppy at the words. "That's California Girls!"

BJ looked up at the fish. "What are you talking about?"

"Hey!" growled a voice as deep as a canyon and as rich as maple syrup. "You kids, get away from my store!"

In the doorway or, rather, filling the doorway, was an enormous, bearded man in a fish-belly-white apron, scowling. Callused and scarred chestnut-colored arms as thick and knotty as beams of ironwood were crossed over a barrel chest. The jet-black beard covering his face looked rough enough to scour a frying pan. If BJ and Charley hadn't known him, the sound of his voice might have sent them—or any grown man, for that matter—scurrying for the hills. But they did know him almost as well as they knew their own parents. Charley wrapped her arms around one leg. "Hi, Uncle Russ!"

Russ wasn't their real uncle, but he had been named Charley's godfather due to the unusual circumstances of her birth. Although his complexion was darker, his physical stature and beard meant that he sometimes dressed up as Paul Bunyan for festivals or parades. Russ would sign autographs for out-of-town tourists. He rubbed a dinner-plate-sized hand on Charley's back. "How's my little warrior?"

"She nearly killed a hockey player today," offered BJ.

"We can spare a few." Russ looked down into Charley's bright blue eyes. "Did he deserve it?" Charley nodded. "Sourmeister?" She nodded again, and Russ grunted. "Eddie's old man is still ticked at your dad for busting him for too many walleye a few years ago. Say, did I ever tell you about the time your dad arrested Troy Gustafson?" BJ shook his head. Russ was a true storyteller, and BJ had heard many of his tales, but not this one. He had only been vaguely aware

13

of Troy Gustafson. All BJ knew was that his father had received a law enforcement commendation.

Russ scooped Charley up with one arm and settled into the big chair. It creaked menacingly, and BJ braced himself for an explosion of wood and splinters, but it never came. An elderly couple wearing broad, white sun hats, likely part of the first wave of summer tourists, crossed the street towards them. They stared at the walleye for a few moments, then went through the door into the store. A minute later, the man poked his head back out. "We're ready to buy a lure."

"The owner's in the basement," said Russ. "He's a bit hard of hearing, so ring that bell on the counter a few times, and he should show up." The man disappeared inside. *Ding, ding!* went the little bell.

BJ gave Russ a shrewd look. "You don't have a basement."

"Nope."

How Russ managed to stay in business sending customers on wild goose chases like this was beyond BJ. Russ had once made a middle-aged couple dance the tango in the store before he would sell them a fishing rod. BJ supposed the bait-and-tackle business could sometimes be boring, so maybe he was just keeping himself amused. BJ felt a little buzz in his pocket and pulled out his Blackberry. It was a note from his mother: *Almost ready.* He stood and motioned for Charley to come along. "We gotta go. See you later, Russ."

Russ raised his hand to wave goodbye, then looked up sharply at the fish, which had begun to sing a snappy, pop tune. "That's... not Lenny Kravitz," he said aloud to himself, then pulled out his iPhone and began punching a thick finger at the screen.

"Charlie watched Russ for a moment before turning around and walking with BJ. "Who's Lenny Kravitz?"

"No idea. Russ's phone is connected to the speaker in George's mouth, and it's not playing what he wants, I guess."

"Like last summer, when we were here with Dad, and those camp counselors were cracking up at the fish?"

"Right," said BJ. "Some guy named George Carlin was coming out its mouth, and he was saying seven really dirty words."

"Yeah," said Charley, "but I wasn't close enough to hear. What words was he saying?"

"You wish." There was no way BJ was going to be held responsible for a salty expansion of his sister's vocabulary.

"Good thing Mom didn't hear it," said Charley.

BJ nodded.

"So that's when Dad started calling him George?" said Charley.

"Yep."

Charley walked quietly for a while, then said, "I like George."

They arrived at a parking lot and walked across diagonally towards a shiny red barn with a large mural of an Ojibwe woman holding a basket of blueberries. They walked through the yellow doors and beneath the words "GM Co-op." Inside, they waved at Keanu, the lanky, dreadlocked cashier, and walked back to the kitchen where their mother, humming to herself, was making sandwiches. Tall, lean, and athletic, Molly Maki wore her frizzy black hair down her back in one thick braid. She had dark eyes like BJ. Charley had inherited the freckles. "Hi, guys!" she called. "Ready for summer vacation?"

"God, yes!" said BJ.

Charley pointed at the sandwich. "What's that?"

"Hummus and bean sprout on rye!" said Molly. "It's got lots of fiber. Good for your digestion!"

"My digression?"

"Are you changing subjects?" said Molly.

"Huh?"

"Just stay on topic, Charlotte," pressed Molly. BJ shook his head. Honestly, half the time, he didn't understand a thing his mother was saying. "Want one?" said Molly, indicating a sandwich. They both declined. BJ didn't care how good they were for his digression. Molly looked around. "How about these?" She held up

15

a bag of little green balls. BJ eyed them with suspicion. "Dried and salted peas! They're delicious!"

BJ's lip curled. "Seriously? Mom, I don't even like peas when they're wet!"

"Try them, Mr. Picky. They're better for you than mac and cheese—and they're chock full of antioxidants!"

"Ants and oxy dents?" said Charley.

"Never mind," shot BJ. He reached into the bag, wishing that, just for once, they could have a plain-old hamburger or pepperoni pizza or a tater tot. Eating at the Maki house was always interesting—in the sort of way a car crash could be interesting. This was because their mother was both a vegetarian and a distractible cook, which meant lots of burnt tofu. BJ chewed on one of the peas, thankful that his classmates weren't there to see him. More than once, David and Tony had looked at his sack lunch and asked if his mother was trying to kill him. He never had a solid answer for this.

Charley ate one, smacked her lips, and pronounced herself full. "Are we driving Keanu home today?"

"He still doesn't have a car?" said BJ.

"He's only been in town a few weeks," explained Molly, removing her apron and hanging it on a bronze hook. "Your father's giving him a ride home. You two head on out while I clean up here."

At the front of the store, Keanu was putting pricing labels on bags, the anti-war and anti-oil buttons jingling on his tie-dye T-shirt as he worked. "Excited for summer break?" he said. BJ nodded, officially tired of the question. Keanu pointed at one of the bags on the counter. It was full of familiar-looking green. "You want to try a new product? Just got them in to—hey, where are you going?"

Two minutes later, Molly met the kids at their little red Civic carrying three produce-laden hemp bags, and they rattled and clunked their way up Highway 61. A few minutes into the drive, Molly wiped a frizzy strand of hair behind one ear. "So I had a conversation with Ryan Olafson."

"I really didn't mean to!" blurted BJ.

"Look," said Molly, "When boys reach your age, it's normal to have new urges and feelings..."

"Mom, it's not puberty, and I was not hitting on my teacher! She's, like, over twenty, Jesus!"

"Language!"

"Sorry!" BJ thought quickly. "I got hit in the head in dodgeball today in gym class, and maybe it made me confused or weird or something. I'm totally going to apologize to her tomorrow."

"Dodgeball!" cried Molly. "Good grief, BJ, kids have gotten knocked out playing that game!"

"Really?" BJ croaked.

"Totally! Make sure you pay attention. Maybe some lavender oil..."

BJ let his mother talk, grateful his blow to the head distracted her. He looked out on the lake for a while, then turned his gaze north towards the hills of the Superior National Forest. He began counting the trees, rocks, and springs on the hillside. *One, two, three. Boulder, stream, cedar branch, crack, eyes, bould—what??*

There had been a pair of eyes staring out of the last crack in the wall. BJ twisted around, but the car was well past that spot, and he could no longer see inside. BJ faced forward and rubbed his cowlick. What was wrong with him? He didn't feel sick. His head didn't hurt. Could someone have shoved a mask into the crack as a prank? After all, eyes did not appear in solid rock. History books did not go crazy. And, thought BJ, wolves did not stand on top of the misty surface of Lake Superior and stare at you during gym class.

Chapter Three

BJ's shoes pounded the face of the forest as he ran after the man with long dark hair. The same branches that let the stranger pass by as if he were made of smoke seemed to reach out and catch BJ's shirt, pulling at him. BJ swung at them, annoyed, then tripped over a birch log and fell, narrowly missing a moss-covered boulder. "Keep your head up!" laughed the man. BJ scrambled back up and continued after him. He didn't know who the man was or, for that matter, why he needed to catch him.

Concentric waves of birds flew up and away as he stumbled towards a dark tangle of cedar and spruce. BJ awoke with a start as the car groaned up Man Gun Road towards their house. BJ tried to hold onto the dream, but it was like trying to grasp a cloud, and it faded, leaving blurred images of a birch log and a mossy boulder. The road flattened out, and an old house with peeling yellow paint and a collection of vehicles came into view. Molly stopped the car at the first driveway. There, a Native man in his sixties, wearing flannel and a Twins cap, was collecting his mail. He walked around to the driver's side to greet Molly.

"Hi, Elmer!" she said in the same happy tones used by Charley.

"Mauer had a great game last night."

"That's our Minnesota boy," said Molly. "He'll be in the Hall of Fame for sure one day." BJ's mother had spent many hours listening to Twins games with her father when she was young and still paid attention to the team out of habit.

"I'm making a fire tonight." He leaned down to look at Charley, who was out cold, her face pressed against the window. Her nose was stretched like a rubber ball on the glass. "Gonna have marshmallows."

"Sounds like an invitation," said Molly. "The kids can make it, but I'll be out running. Thanks!"

Elmer nodded and headed back into his yard. Molly drove the Civic another fifty yards into their driveway, past a little log home to a single bay garage with pine shiplap siding. She parked in front of the garage, hopped out, grabbed two of the hemp bags from the trunk, and, in a flash was across the deck. BJ opened the car door and was met with a giant wet tongue across his face. "Aaarg! Get off, Max!" He shoved the Labrador away, fetched the remaining groceries, and headed towards the door, giving a little tap on the big iron triangle hanging on a post. Charley wrapped her arms around the dog, then wandered to the bird feeder in the middle of the yard and sat down.

The Maki house was a simple two-bedroom, two-story building. It was tight but cheap enough for a young conservation officer and co-op manager to afford when they decided to settle down. It had previously belonged to the supervisor of the Superior National Forest. It sat on the far end of the plateau, just before the mountain resumed climbing upwards towards one million acres of trees, rivers, and lakes. In addition to the house and garage, the yard had enough room for a little woodshed, a sauna, and, to the left of the driveway, a set of raised-bed gardens full of recently planted seeds and hope.

Inside, BJ kicked off his sandals and walked straight down the hallway to the living room bay windows. He looked out onto the lake below for a moment, thinking about the wolf he'd seen.

"How's your head?" Molly was standing next to him.

"Fine, I guess." Molly rubbed his hair and took the remaining bag past the dining table and into the kitchen. The sound of clinking plates, glasses, and silverware filled the air. BJ turned back to the lake.

The screen door opened. "I'm going for a walk!" shouted Charley.

"Your brother wants to go with you," said Molly.

"No, I don't."

"No, he doesn't!" said Charley.

"Maybe tomorrow," said BJ.

"There is no tomorrow," said Molly, then poked her head out of the kitchen. "There's only now." BJ mustered a confused look, and his mother said, "I read it in a fortune cookie. Your sister wants you to come with."

"No, I don't!" shouted Charley.

"No, she doesn't," said BJ.

The phone rang. Molly answered. "Again? Wait, what homes? Oh no, what did they take?" Molly's expression looked serious. "Okay, we'll see you whenever you get home." She hung up. "A bunch of cabins were broken into up on Reservation Road," she explained. BJ flinched. He had never heard of break-ins around Grand Marais. "Listen," she said firmly, "I want you to go with your sister. I'll ring the dinner bell when supper's ready." Her tone was such that there would be no further debate on the matter. "Charley, do not ditch your brother!"

BJ headed back down the hallway, lips pursed. Charley was definitely old enough to go out without him. Honestly, just because he let her get away once and she spent the night in the woods, you'd think he had let her get kidnapped or something. Charley was at the bird feeder, arms crossed, when he came outside. As soon as the door closed behind him, she ran up the little slope in the backyard, skirted around a gray boulder the size of a small car, and disappeared into the woods.

BJ chased after her, trying to keep her in sight as she darted in and out of fiddlehead ferns, wildflowers, spruce, and pine. The sounds and smells of spring were everywhere. Soon—too soon— the mosquitoes would join them, and everything would change. The "mountain," as they called it, was really a set of hills sloping up from the shore of Lake Superior. Fairly high by Minnesota standards, they were full of lakes and shallow rivers that ran cold and fast across ancient red and gray granite down to the shore. In some places, the water-filled pools, sometimes ten or fifteen feet deep, were perfect for swimming or even diving if you knew where the rocks were. Grand Marais had been a logging town, then a mining town. It has since reinvented itself as a tourism and vacation destination. People came here from all around the country, renting cabins, hiking, fishing, and exploring. Once they got a taste of the place, many spoke of retiring to the area.

Charley pointed at a pair of dead fir, whose naked branches stretched out like thin, skeletal fingers: "Ghost trees!" Recently, their neighbor, Elmer, accompanied Charley on a walk and taught her an old trick the Ojibwe used to avoid getting lost. As BJ understood it, they were supposed to pick out a series of distinct features and name them. A large rock. A fallen tree. A clump of brightly colored bushes. Anything that was semi-permanent. Charley had picked out a series of landmarks and named them herself, all the way to a pretty spot along the river, about a third of a mile into the forest. Today was only the second time BJ had taken this trail, but the landmark game worked so well that he remembered all of them. The first landmark was, of course, the boulder at the top of their yard, which Charley had decided to name Cannonball Rock because of its smooth, rounded shape. BJ had argued for Potato Rock, but teen logic was trounced by youthful persistence.

Charley paused now and then to inspect a new spring flower or wave at a bird perched in a tree. BJ looked back to see if the ghost trees were still visible. He thought he recalled Charley saying that they needed to be able to see the next landmark before the previous one was out of sight. "X-Men!" she yelled. They were at a pair of poplar trees that leaned past one another in the form of an X. Next was a birch snag covered with mushrooms, which they dubbed the Fungi

Tree, a large red pine, a low, wet area full of cattails, the turned-over root ball of a big spruce they called the Treasure Stump and, finally, a slab of granite near the river. Charley called this the Tabletop.

As she had taught BJ, the storyline went like this: Once upon a time, the Cannonball Rock shot into some trees, killing them. The ghost trees joined the X-Men, who were Fun Guys. They told a bad joke, making the red pine blush, and then they all picked some cattails and dug into a Treasure Stump for some sharp rocks to cut them into small pieces, which they ate on the Tabletop. BJ thought the story was pretty dumb, but he couldn't think of an alternative, so that's the way it stayed. This weirdness, it turned out, actually helped him remember the story and, therefore, the route. It was not easy to forget the image of dead ghost trees or a blushing pine.

"Lookit!" said Charley. About four feet up the trunk of a large poplar was a hole, about the size and shape of a big loaf of bread. "Do you think there's anything in there?"

"Doubt it," said BJ authoritatively, then realized that he would have to establish this. He stood on his tiptoes and peered in the hole—and found himself nose-to-nose with a man. "Hi!" said the face. BJ sprang from the tree like he had been electrocuted, landing hard in the wet moss below. "There's a—" he gasped. "In the tree... there's..."

"A squirrel!" finished Charley. A furry red blur had exploded from the hole and scrambled up the trunk. It stopped at the first branch and scolded BJ roundly.

BJ pointed at the hole. "There was a GUY in there!"

"Really?" Charley grabbed the edge of the hole and pulled herself up to peer in. "Nobody in there now!"

BJ shoved her from the tree and looked in. Nothing but a hollow tree. BJ rounded on his sister. "Charley, there was a man in the tree, and he spoke to me!"

"What did he say?"

"He said—wait, what do you mean 'what did he say'? There's not supposed to be a man inside a tree, Charley!"

"Okay. But what did he say?"

BJ blinked. "He said… well, he said, 'Hi.'"

A chickadee flew down from an overhead branch, flapped near Charley's nose, and then landed in an adjacent tree. "Well, you should have just said 'Hi' back then." She spun and continued along her trail, the little black-and-white bird following in the branches above.

BJ stared after his sister. *What is happening to me? And why did Charley not even care?* He hustled to catch up. *Don't lose Charley!* Honestly, though, his sister would probably do better without him here at all. When Charley walked through the forest, she was not so much a visitor as an inhabitant. She belonged there among the deer, the birds, and the trees. BJ had never felt like this. Until recently, he had assumed that being outside was just, you know, outside. You go out, then you come back in. The more he watched Charley, however, the more he realized that this was not her experience. Charlotte Maki was a person of the present, perfectly at ease in the natural world. And for that, BJ envied her.

BJ was too distracted to notice the final three landmarks, and before he knew it, they had arrived at the Tabletop. Charley sat on the granite and tucked her knees in her arms. BJ lay on his belly beside her, his chin on his hands. The granite was cold. A mist from the rushing water swirled into the air in front of them, creating a little rainbow each time the sun peered from behind the clouds. Slowly, the sound of the water began to scrub the thoughts of a crazy history book and faces in trees from his mind like grease from a frying pan. After a while, there was only the sound of water. The smell of wet rock. The boom-boom-boom of his heartbeat.

Charley began humming a new tune, one BJ didn't know.

BJ's eyelids drooped. He drifted into a half-sleep state where he felt as if he were connected to the river as if he were part of it. The water wasn't just flowing past him. It was flowing through him, pushed by the pumping of his own heart. BJ was barely aware of this sensation, and he let it linger without thought or distraction. *Boom-boom, boom-boom.*

This went on until BJ realized that something strange was happening: the beating sound he was feeling was coming from somewhere else. He pushed himself up and listened. "Can you hear that, Charley?"

"Hear what?"

BJ cocked his head. "There's, like, drumming somewhere."

"Like a grouse?" said Charley. It was, after all, spring, and the males would be strutting back and forth on logs, beating their wings hard to attract mates. They sometimes sounded like tractors trying to start. But this was a continuous drumbeat—no pauses—coming from across the river, out of a cluster of tall pine trees. They removed their shoes and socks and waded into the water, holding hands. It was less than a foot deep but slippery and frigid. It felt like icicles stabbed into his feet. Once across and shivering, BJ jogged on numb feet toward the pines.

"Hold on!" said Charley. "We need a landmark."

She was right. They shouldn't head into unknown parts of the forest without identifying landmarks to help navigate their way back to the river. BJ surveyed the area. A balsam fir had snapped off some fifteen feet up but remained attached at the break. The tip had tilted to the ground, giving it an unusual formation. "Arrow tree?" suggested BJ.

"Triangle tree," countered Charley.

"Fine." The name hardly mattered, and BJ wanted to find the source of the drumming, which was definitely coming from the other side of the little knoll. "Can you hear it now?" Charley shook her head. BJ couldn't understand why he was hearing something that his sister wasn't. If they didn't find anything, he would seriously begin to wonder about that blow to the head in gym. The cluster of pines grew near the top of the hill, maybe fifteen feet up from where they stood. Somewhere on the other side, someone beat a drum. They scrambled up the slope around thick roots and slippery moss.

Halfway up, BJ stopped to listen. Voices! People were singing with the drumming, like a Native group at a pow-wow! Why was there a drumming group in the middle of the woods? A sharp gust of wind blew through the trees, adding a flute-like note to the drumming and the singing. The skin on BJ's neck tingled as they took the last few steps. At the top, BJ and Charley saw that they had climbed to the lip of a little crater, maybe forty or fifty feet in diameter. Down below was a small room-like space with a moss-and-needle-covered floor. The branches of the white pines, growing inward and overlapping, served as a ceiling, concealing the little "room." BJ had never seen or imagined anything like this place. The drumming was still there but muffled, and it seemed to BJ that it was coming from inside the hill. He took a few steps down to the other side, then felt his left foot step into a void. He barely managed to catch himself before falling further.

Charley hustled to him. "Are you okay?"

BJ was fine, but his leg was dangling in midair beneath him. He pulled himself up and pointed in the hole. "It's hollow down there."

Charley's eyes grew wide. "A cave!" They took turns poking their heads through the opening and squinting into the darkness. "Echo!" yelled Charley. "Echo!" Although there was not enough light for detail, they could clearly see a floor—maybe ten feet down. It was a cave. A hidden room inside a hidden room!

"Let's go in," said Charley, poking a foot through the hole.

"Wait!" BJ seized her by the arm, his mother's warnings fresh in his mind. Furthermore, he remembered a tragic story of two boys who had died from lack of oxygen while exploring a cave in St. Paul a few years earlier. But that cave was deep, and those boys had gone too far. BJ could see the bottom of this one just fine. "Charley, do you mind if I check it out first and make sure it's safe before you go?"

Charley rolled her eyes. "Fine. Hey, you're shivering."

"My clothes are wet."

"Well, take them off."

"Um, well, you're here."

"I'm not helping you."

"No, I mean..." BJ pointed down to the mossy area below. "Just go down there and don't look, okay?" Charley did so as BJ peeled off his clothing and placed them on the warm, sunny rock. Then he put his Blackberry in his mouth and slipped through the hole. With care, BJ climbed down, making sure he had a good handhold before he moved his feet and a good foothold before he moved his hands. He was a good climber. He should have mentioned that to Mr. Olafson. In a few short moves, he was standing on the dirt floor. He pulled the phone from his mouth and shouted, "I made it!" Then he wished he hadn't because the echo off the walls hurt his ears.

"Okay!" came a muffled response.

BJ pressed a button to get the screen to light up and began to look around. His nose filled with the scent of rock and dust. A heavy silence pressed against his ears. The cave, shaped roughly like a banana, mirrored the curvature of the hill outside. He explored one of the corners, finding only dust and rocks. He turned to go check out the other corner, but something on the wall caught his eye: four lines. Four... wavy lines. BJ held the phone close. A drawing? He lowered the phone, and the light landed on the figure of a bear. BJ raised the phone again and saw a circle above the lines. Now, there was no doubt. Indian paintings! Real Indian paintings! He squatted back down to look at the lines. BJ had only seen a handful of like images on cliff walls during canoe trips, and this bear was at least as good as those. What a lucky break! Wait until Charley sees this!

In the time he'd been staring at the bear, his eyes had better adjusted to the weak light of the blackberry. Now, he could see what had been there the whole time: The wall before him was covered from end to end with paintings. BJ let out a long, slow breath as he moved his phone across dozens of images of people, animals, canoes, shelters, trees, and birds. Scenes of travel, hunting, and war. The sun. The stars. Abstract images that baffled him. And, down low to the left, as crisp and clear as if it had been made that very morning, was an image that froze BJ for a very long time: a single red hand.

27

Chapter Four

Was this the warrior? The Red Hand Warrior? *Find him before the summer is out...* BJ examined the image carefully. The little bend in the ring finger. The knuckle of the thumb. Even the folds in the skin. Here was part of a real, tangible person. Not a large or, he presumed, very tall person. What was his name? How old was he? What was the world like when he dipped his hand into ink and pressed it against this rock? Were the glaciers here? Mammoths? Was he really a warrior? Maybe it was a girl? BJ felt a kinship with the maker of this print as if a thread connected the two of them, and he had a sudden desire to know more about him, about his life and his world. He raised his hand and let it hover over the red mark, then let it rest on the print, his fingertips gently pressing the rock, wishing to see. Wishing to know.

A sensation, sudden and sharp, shot through BJ's stomach, like the feeling one gets when an elevator takes off. It felt like the wall was shaking. An earthquake? A sinkhole? It lasted for a second or two, then stopped. BJ's knees buckled slightly, and he staggered backward. When he looked again at the wall, he gasped.

The handprint had vanished.

BJ looked at his palm, expecting to find flecks of red paint. It was clean. He scanned the wall again. The handprint was nowhere to be found. It had been right under the painting of a moose, which was still there. Below it, there was a blank space on the wall. In fact, there were many blank spaces that had not been there moments earlier. The shapeshifter was gone. Half of the drawings had disappeared. BJ rubbed his eyes and looked again, but the images in front of him did not change back to the way they were before. Before what? BJ's first thought was to take a picture of the newly changed wall, but his phone had also disappeared. What on earth had happened? BJ climbed up and out of the hole as quickly as he could.

Once outside, he saw that the hill had changed. Instead of a ring of white pines with their branches growing inward, there was—where Charley had been lying minutes earlier—one giant and ancient tree whose trunk rose up like a skyscraper and whose branches stretched out and over the hill like a tremendous parasol. "Charley, hey Charley!" BJ scrambled down to the mossy floor, which was now mostly filled with tree trunks. Where was she? Did she go home? Either way, he thought, how did this tree get here? "Charley!" BJ scrambled back up and over the crater and looked around. He was completely disoriented. There was no Triangle Tree. BJ turned in a slow circle, rubbing his cowlick. "This cannot be!" And where were his clothes? A quick search proved fruitless. Setting his jaw, he walked gingerly in the direction of the river.

The river was there as always, water gurgling down towards the great lake. BJ's relief was short-lived. Though he found the Tabletop, crack and all, both his shoes and those of his sister were gone. And every living thing seemed to have changed. BJ was no longer standing in the middle of a forest of poplar, fir, and birch but rather in a stand of very large pine trees, three, maybe four feet in diameter. This was old growth. BJ was reminded of the Lost 40, near Northome, where his father had once taken the family on a Saturday in May. The Lost 40 was a tract of forest that had been slated for a timber harvest a century earlier, but due to a surveying error, the loggers never found it. To this day, it is one of the few pre-colonial stands of trees in the state. Trees with massive trunks and spaced out so that you could nearly drive a car between them.

The forest floor was a thick, soft blanket of rusty red and brown needles. This is what BJ saw in every direction, and it made absolutely no sense. He knew where he was. The river and the Tabletop were right there! But, like a disoriented hunter within shouting distance of his own truck, he felt lost. It was now that BJ thought of the advice his father had drilled into him and Charley over the years: panic equals death. So BJ sat his bare bottom on the granite slab and took some deep breaths. The wind whistled above. The water gurgled below. Slowly, the pounding in his chest lessened, and his breathing returned to normal. After a few minutes, BJ's mind began to clear. *Let's keep it simple,* he thought. *The landmarks are gone, so I'll follow the river back to the house. Everybody will be there—including Charley. Mom will give me a charred grilled cheese, and Dad will explain the new landscape thing. Probably a weird mutation from a nuclear plant leak or something.*

BJ stood and headed down along the edge of the river. Walking barefoot—not to mention bare everything—was new to BJ, and this forced him to slow down significantly to avoid scraping sensitive places. The thick needle duff felt good on his bare feet and sent a tingle of pleasure up through his body. Different sounds and smells were registering in his mind, but he set these aside for the moment. He was partway down a slope when, all at once, he was covered in darkness. Instinctively, he ducked as if reacting to a falling object. The sky was shimmering like a dark blanket being shaken free of dust. Birds, by the thousand, maybe tens of thousands, were passing overhead. BJ stared, mouth agape, until the river of birds reached its end, and the light reached the forest floor once again. BJ had never seen such a thing. He could not even tell what kind of birds they were.

He continued on, picking his way through a flat, wet area dotted with cattail and alder. Mud squished up between his toes as he moved. Something brushed past his hair, making him flinch. A bird?

Another whooshed by. Then a third, but this time it struck the cedar tree, not three inches from BJ's nose, its wooden shaft quivering from the impact. An arrow! Before BJ could touch it, there was a shout from the other side of the river. Two bare-chested men with long black hair were charging full speed through the woods. Their faces were streaked in red and black. They each carried a bow.

They were running right towards him.

Chapter Five

Charley lay on her belly and focused on one piece of moss. She imagined herself a tiny ant, climbing up the dark green trunk and exploring out onto the moist, green, feathery branches. She could feel the cool surface beneath her six feet as she moved back down towards the ground where great pine needles lay at all angles like trees felled by a windstorm. For a while, she allowed herself to live in the ant world, then came back to herself and pressed her face into the softness and inhaled deeply. Somewhere in the distance, a fox on the hunt was being scolded by a winter wren. Probably the same fox Charley had seen at the top of their yard an hour after sunrise. The chickadees in the pines above her paused to listen, then resumed their chatter, pecking away for tiny seeds or bugs within the grooves of the branches. One minuscule flake of bark landed in the moss just beyond Charley's nose and she smiled at this. What would an ant think of such a thing falling from the sky? Charley didn't know how long BJ would play in the cave, but it didn't matter. She was not alone. In the forest, she never was.

Chapter Six

For a fleeting instant, BJ thought he had stumbled into some type of reenactment. It wasn't all that unusual for members of the Gichigami Band of Ojibwe to dress up for holidays or powwows in the summer months. But something about the body language of the two men triggered an instinctive reaction in him and he dropped to his belly. The men were two steps into the water when they flinched violently. One of them dropped his bow with a cry and fled, a feathered shaft protruding from his left shoulder. The other staggered forward and fell face-first into the shallow water. Two arrows were buried deep in his back.

"Holy shit!" BJ launched himself deep into the alder bushes, tucked his knees under his arms, and sat, trembling, like a rabbit. A moment later, a group of five men stood at the edge of the creek, three of them with bows. After a brief pause, all but one ran through the water in pursuit of the injured man. The fifth, a lean elder with gray hair at his temples, stood still, surveying the scene. "Mawinazh!" he yelled after his companions, then began studying the ground. He tilted his head back and forth a few times, then got down on all fours, placed his cheek to the earth, and closed one eye. He was reading the tracks.

BJ held his breath. *Don't look this way. Not this way!* The elder stood and frowned. The injured man and his pursuers had run west. But the elder was interested in something else. He grunted to himself

Robert Saxton

and headed north—towards the cave. "Holy shit!" BJ said under his breath. None of this could be real. It had to be a dream. Maybe he was asleep in the cave? "Wake up!" BJ rubbed his cowlick furiously. "You need to wake up! You're in a dream!" BJ closed his eyes and then opened them, but the warrior's body was still there, being lifted up and down in gentle rhythmic movements by the water flowing around him. *Why can't I have a dream about flying or winning the Stanley Cup?* "What do I do?" he said aloud.

"You find that warrior and bring him back." A buckskin-clad man with a braid of jet-black hair, handsome walnut skin, and penetrating eyes was in the bushes with him.

BJ was so shocked, his scream turned into a choked gurgle. The only thing that kept him from charging out of the bushes and fleeing was the expression on the stranger's face, which could only be described as one of mild amusement. "Who are... how... where... what is this?"

"Some might call it a vision," said the stranger.

"A vision? What are you talking about? There's a dead guy there!" he croaked, pointing at the body. "What do you mean vision?" BJ realized he was practically yelling and lowered his voice again. "A vision like a dream or whatever? Isn't that an Indian thing?"

"It's a human being thing," said the man, waving at a mosquito. "It is everyone's birthright to have a vision. Some have them and don't realize it. Other people choose to ignore their visions. Some visions require lots of hard work. Some are subtle and take years to figure out. Others"—he indicated the scene around them—" are big and scary."

BJ still felt as if he were in a dream. "Do I get to wake up?"

"That's the idea."

"Huh?"

"Find the warrior and bring him home."

"The—what? Wait, are you the one that made my history book go nuts?" BJ held up his hands, palms out. "Mister, honestly, I just

36

want to find my sister, start summer vacation, and maybe go fishing. Why don't you find him?"

"That's your job."

BJ nearly pulled his cowlick from his head. "And how am I supposed to find someone I don't know?"

"Watching and learning, mostly. If you do it right, he'll find you. First things first. Gid-ojibwem ina?" BJ sat silent. "Didn't think so," the man said. "Well, I can help out with communication. For this vision, you get four visits. Four trips through the cave." The man belched, smacked his lips, then reached into a decorated bag hanging at his side and pulled out a piece of soft, brown leather. "Also, you'll want to keep your privates from getting sunburned." He tossed a piece of leather to BJ. "Your butt is brighter than the snow in March."

BJ had forgotten that he was stark naked. "Who are you?"

The man flashed a grin so white and wide that BJ felt like he was in the middle of a great practical joke.

The four men were back and began pulling the dead warrior from the water. They rolled him over onto the ground. One of the men, tall with powerful arms, jutted his chin towards the dead man's face. "Ni-gikenimaa!" BJ had a very strange sensation as the man spoke. His words were still there, ringing in the air, but somehow BJ understood the meaning as if this was a language BJ knew by heart. "I know him!" was what the man had said. He spoke again, and once more, BJ understood: "He tried to steal my pipe during the gathering last fall!"

"I remember that!" said a young, broad-shouldered boy with straight bangs. "The other guy was interested in our bows as well. You whipped him pretty good, Strong Hand! I guess he still wanted it."

"Well," said Strong Hand, "it is a good pipe!"

The others smiled grimly. The elder arrived and was informed of the dead warrior's identity. "Did you catch the other one?" he asked. They nodded. "So, there were two of them?" More nods. "Then we have a problem."

The boy said, "What do you mean, Grandfather?"

The man called Grandfather jutted his head and puckered his lips at the ground. "There are," he said, "tracks of not two but *three* strangers here." A thick silence landed on the group. BJ's heart began to pound so hard in his chest, he was sure they would hear it. The stranger who had been in the bushes with BJ had disappeared. BJ was alone—and naked.

The elder and the other four men studied the ground. In unison, their eyes moved from where BJ had walked to where he had dropped to the ground to where he had scooted into the bushes. They were going to find him. As their gazes reached his hiding place, they raised their bows and crept forward with the man called Grandfather in the lead. He reached out and parted the branches. BJ found himself staring into a pair of dark, penetrating eyes. They showed a flash of surprise, then a moment of keen study. He had an L-shaped scar on his forehead. His jaw was strong, and his cheekbones sharp. We have a boy," he announced to the group. "He has no weapons. In fact, he has no clothes."

The tension in the group dropped as quickly as it had risen. Two of the men lowered their bows, but the third, a thin, wiry man, did not. "Red Fox," admonished Grandfather, "you would shoot your own brother. Relax." Red Fox un-knocked his arrow and lowered his bow. Grandfather straightened up and motioned at BJ. "Come here."

BJ crawled out, careful to keep the leather cloth over his privates.

"Where are you from?" said Grandfather. BJ wasn't sure how to answer this. "Did you come from the cave?" BJ's mouth parted involuntarily, and he thought he saw a moment of understanding from Grandfather. There were murmurs among the others. Grandfather lowered his head in thought. After what seemed like a long time, he looked up and said, "I will need to council with the other elders." He jutted his chin at BJ. "Come with us." BJ held the leather over his crotch, not wanting to move. "Are you going to wear that," said Grandfather, "or are you going to carry it?" So that's what

38

it was, a breechcloth. BJ had never worn one, of course. He unfolded it, contorting himself to keep his privates private. A leather thong or rope fell from the bundle.

"What is wrong with him?" said Strong Hand. "Does he not know how to get dressed?"

"His skin is disgusting. He is very white."

"Except below the elbows and knees. Maybe he is sick or has been bleeding."

"He smells like a flower."

BJ fumbled like an idiot for a minute, then decided to just wrap the rectangle-shaped cloth around his waist. He would figure out the proper method later. The instant he moved it around to his rear, the men got their first view of his crotch, and they reeled.

"Did you see that?"

"What is wrong with it?"

"I have never seen one like that!" said the broad-shouldered boy. He pointed at BJ's crotch. "Show us again!"

BJ shook his head violently.

"What happened to the tip?" said Red Fox.

"Maybe," said Grandfather, turning to leave, "he put it somewhere he shouldn't have, and it got bitten."

The broad-shouldered boy, Strong Hand, and the third man snorted, then joined Grandfather, heading down the trail.

"Like in the hole of a tree, maybe?" said Strong Hand.

"Who would be so foolish to do something like that?" asked the broad-shouldered boy.

Red Fox launched after them. "I was eight!" he shouted. "And besides, how was *I* supposed to know there was a squirrel in there!" The four others burst out laughing, their voices echoing off the great pines around them.

BJ followed along in a daze. In spite of all that he had seen and experienced—the paintings, the new trees, the dead warrior, all of it—his brain still insisted that there was a simple answer, that he was dreaming or that he was in some type of grand practical joke. As he made his way towards what he knew was his home, he convinced himself that Charley would be there, waiting for him. His mother would rub some essential oil into his temples, which would be good for hallucinations.

Maybe the guys ahead of him would reveal their prank and head back into town or to the rez. Maybe they were friends of Elmer. The Cannonball Rock came into view, and BJ breathed a sigh of relief. A familiar landmark. An anchor. A wisp of smoke rose beyond the boulder, and BJ knew his mother was happily burning their lunch. Maybe pine nuts. Tonight, he would even eat those! Everything would be set straight. Everything would be explained. Everything would be back to normal.

He was wrong.

The smoke, it turned out, did not come from his kitchen window but from a small campfire. Down where his garage should have been, down where the dog house, the sauna, and his home *should* have been, was a primitive village, complete with birchbark wigwams, fire pits, piles of wood, canoes, drying racks—and people. People of all ages and sizes ranged across the little plateau, working on projects, cooking food, or playing. Dogs barked. Food was being prepared. BJ's entire world had evaporated like the spring snow. No more Mom, Dad, or Charley. No more house. Even the town of Grand Marais would be gone. Faced with the disappearance of everything he knew and loved, BJ did what any normal fourteen-year-old would do.

He fainted.

Chapter Seven

BJ lay on his side, feeling the world spinning.

"What is wrong with this boy?"

He felt a hand touch his forehead. "I think he has fainted. Do you remember Sleeping Woman, from my sister's village to the north? She did this whenever she was startled or frightened. It never lasted long."

"Dad?" he said. "I had the weirdest dream. I couldn't find Charley, and everything was different, and these guys got killed and… and…" The world came into focus, and he was nose-to-nose with the man called Grandfather. "Aaaarrgh!"

The group of men rolled their eyes and walked down the slope from the Cannonball Rock and into the village. There, they were greeted by a crowd of people asking about the attackers and gesturing at BJ. Grandfather spoke to them for a minute, then seemed to send them away. They all retreated, with many glances at BJ and murmuring in low voices. By now, BJ was on his feet and following in Grandfather's wake as he strode around eight birchbark wigwams, seven fire pits, and five large drying racks holding every sort of meat and fish. He saw an infant in a little wooden cradle, hanging from a branch, swinging back and forth as the mother sat nearby, working on a piece of leather and rocking the child with a little string she had attached to her toe. A very old man with one arm sat on a log, watching. Multiple dogs ran in and out of buildings, too numerous and too quick to count.

As they moved, BJ became aware of a bubble of silence that followed them with each step. As they neared anyone in the village, conversations halted, and they were met with silent stares. When they had walked past, whispering resumed. Beyond this bubble, however, BJ could hear a continuous chirping of children's voices, but, like spring peepers, they remained unseen.

They walked past a group of women scraping and stretching hides on wooden racks, then a pair of gray-haired elders laughing near a small campfire. Beyond them, a young man was using a small stone to shape what appeared to be an arrow shaft. He held the shaft up, examined it for straightness, and continued. Eleven finished shafts lay in a pile near his feet. The number of new sights and sounds was dizzying, and, like a drunken man using a wall for support, BJ struggled to find familiar objects to lean on: Lake Superior, the river, and, of course, the Cannonball Rock. These were BJ's landmarks, and they were still here, unchanged. But everything else was new. Or was it old? Nothing bombarded BJ's senses more than the smells: Smoke, rock, musk, sweat, and rancid odors were all there, whirling and swirling through the air. BJ felt like his dog, Max, with his head out the car window.

At the southwest end of the camp, roughly where Elmer's house should have been, they reached a small fire being tended by a white-haired woman in a dark-brown shawl and dress. Blue and red rings danced back and forth in her earlobes as she stirred a clay pot full of steaming beige liquid. Her thin, wrinkled eyes opened wide when they arrived, then narrowed to slits. "Hmmph!" she said to Grandfather, "what did you find?"

"He has come from the cave."

She considered BJ. "He looks sick."

"You haven't seen the half of it," quipped Grandfather, sitting on a stump and motioning for BJ to do the same. A long

42

and uncomfortable silence followed. The old woman watched the pot. Grandfather watched BJ. BJ watched everything. Eventually, Grandfather said, "I am called Running Wolf. I am of the Wolf clan. My people have been here for some years but came from far to the east."

The strange sensation BJ had early on at hearing one language and understanding another had been dissipating. He understood everything he heard but wasn't sure which language was being spoken.

"You came through the cave."

BJ nodded.

"Do you know why you are here?"

BJ opened his mouth, then closed it.

"Where are you from?"

BJ cleared his throat. What should he say to that? He was from right about where they were sitting, actually. He decided on a different answer: "My name is BJ." BJ spoke in English, but he heard another language come out of his mouth. "BJ izhinikaaz." BJ's hand shot to his mouth.

"What is your clan?"

"Er..." BJ was afraid to speak.

Running Wolf motioned at the old woman. She was holding out a bowl of steaming liquid. BJ took it and offered it to Running Wolf, who said, "That is for you." BJ felt the hand of the old woman on his shoulder and saw that she wanted to add something. He held out his bowl, and she sprinkled a pinch of brown crumbles into the liquid, then used her finger to stir it. BJ managed, barely, to avoid reacting to this last bit and held the bowl to his nose, then sipped. Pine and maple. "Miigwech," he heard himself say. It was a tea, both warm and relaxing. BJ told Running Wolf about the appearance of the strange man. "He said that I was supposed to watch and learn and that I was supposed to find a red-hand warrior."

"A red hand warrior?" said Running Wolf.

"Er, yeah."

"What does that mean?" said Running Wolf.

"I was kind of hoping you might know," admitted BJ.

Running Wolf shook his head. "I don't know this person."

BJ felt his heart sink. He had been sent on a wild goose chase. "He said if I watched and learned, the warrior might come to me."

Running Wolf stared at BJ in silence for a long time. The woman handed BJ a plate of food. He tried to pass it to Running Wolf, who said, "Why do you keep giving me your food? Eat!"

BJ popped a piece of smoked fish in his mouth. It was salty and oily. As he chewed, his eyes followed a broad-shouldered man as he limped up the hill toward their fire. He had a prominent scar running from his ear to his chin and a nose that had been misshaped from an accident or a fight. When he saw BJ, he dropped his basket in surprise, spilling green leaves and stems across the ground. Running Wolf went to him, placed his hand on the man's shoulder, and said, "I will explain later. It is time for me to council." The man looked as if he wanted to say something but collected his harvest and left.

"Come," said Running Wolf, striding back across the village. BJ scrambled after him, and the bubble of silence resumed. They had just passed the arrow-maker when Running Wolf stopped and spun around. "What are you counting?" he demanded.

"I... what? What do you mean?"

"You just said 'thirteen.'"

"I did?" BJ supposed he had been counting the arrow shafts and said so. "Sometimes I like to count," he explained.

"You said 'eleven' before." BJ had not remembered doing this, but Running Wolf clearly did. "Do you count fast?"

"I don't know. It's not like I'm a math genius," said BJ. "Sometimes I notice numbers and shapes and things."

"What else do you notice?"

"I don't know, all sorts of stuff." BJ felt like he was talking to Mr. Olafson. "Nothing important, though."

They arrived at a long birchbark-covered lodge on the east end of the village. The entrance was covered with a large animal skin. Adjacent to the long lodge was a smaller round wigwam, a pile of stones, a log, and a fire pit. Next to this, a skinny and tall wigwam. Three gray-haired men and two women were lingering at the entrance to the big lodge. Running Wolf said to BJ, "You stay here," then ducked through the entrance with the others.

Once more, BJ was alone. What now? He shivered and tried to shove his hands into nonexistent pockets. A big pine log lay perpendicular to the lodge, so he sat down and began to wait, feeling a little bit like he was in the dentist's office. No magazines to read, though. No blackberry to look at. When was his mother going to get him an iPhone anyway? Was he ever going to be able to go home? The stranger had said he would have four visits, so maybe he can go back and forth? How would he do this? BJ thought back to the red handprint and his desire to meet that person. Something about that wish, that desire, had sent him back in time. Could he wish to go forward in time? BJ scanned around for someone with a red hand, feeling dumb. Even Running Wolf didn't know what he was talking about. Maybe it was someone from another village?

Watch and learn, and he will come to you.

BJ twisted in place. No one was around. What is there to learn when there is nothing to watch? Running Wolf's voice crept through the birchbark walls to BJ's ears: "It seems that the Spirit Cave has spoken to us again. The boy is looking for a warrior." BJ scooted across the log and leaned in to listen.

"I have dreamed about this," said an old voice. "During the sugar moon, I dreamed a visitor would come to learn. I think this boy is probably that visitor."

BJ scratched his ankle, then turned when he thought he heard a noise, but nothing was there.

"What is he supposed to learn?" said a woman.

"Probably," said a new voice, "how to eat. He is too skinny."

45

There were some chuckles.

I'm not that skinny!

"He is too white. Maybe he is sick."

I'm too what?

"No," said Running Wolf, "I have been watching him, and he is not sick. Do you remember the prophecy of the light-skinned people coming from the east? I wonder if he is of that tribe."

"Maybe they live underground."

"They need to be in the sun more."

BJ snorted.

"What of the two invaders?"

Running Wolf reported the results of the battle.

"How far did they travel?" asked one voice.

"They are from the big lake five days paddle to the northwest," said Running Wolf. He told of their interest in Strong Hand's pipe.

"They are like the Windigo," said a woman. "Never satisfied."

"I have had dreams of Windigos as well," said the voice of the old man.

"I hope they were only dreams," said Running Wolf.

"So do I."

A silence followed, and then Running Wolf said, "I think I have an idea how to proceed."

There were words about the teachings of the birds and animals, and "clumsy," and "gift of observation," but BJ understood little of it. His neck began to stiffen, so he shifted his position and arched his back. High cirrus clouds stretched into thin, wavy lines above him, and a whisky jack hopped from branch to branch, issuing murmurs of inquiry. An uneasy feeling tried to nag at BJ, to pierce his fog of distraction, to tell him something. But he was bored and tired, and he wished he had something to fidget with—a phone, a piece of paper, a book.

Where was everyone anyway?

Chapter Eight

The elders filed out of the lodge and headed off in various directions without so much as a glance at BJ. Running Wolf appeared last. He stretched and squinted at the sky. He walked stiffly to BJ and said, "Do you count children like you count arrows?"

BJ shifted his weight on the log. Counting children? He hadn't seen a single kid in… now that he thought about it, he hadn't even heard one since the council began. He stood and looked around. "Where are they?"

Running Wolf fixed him with a look. "You cannot count if you cannot see."

It was clear that BJ was missing something, but he didn't know what. "Grandfather, er, I mean Running Wolf, how do I count them if they are not here?" Running Wolf laughed so suddenly that BJ flinched. A hearty laugh. A deep laugh. It came easily and made his eyes crinkle and the crow's feet at their corners deepen. BJ was reminded of Russ. And then a chorus of laughter arose from the rocks, the dirt, and the woods around them. Giggling. Chuckling. Wheezing. Before BJ knew it, a dozen children had materialized, covered with leaves and mud and bearing shiny, white smiles. BJ was too stunned to speak. They seemed to have sprung from the earth around him. How had they been so close without him realizing it? One boy had been lying almost at his feet. Another was sitting on a branch in the white pine above him, an arm's length away. BJ felt both amazed and vulnerable. The kids had stalked him like they would a deer. He had been completely and utterly unaware of it.

Then they gathered in close, laughing and smiling, and the mood was light. Indeed, it was hard not to smile along with them. They reached out to touch, rub, and poke at BJ as if he were a new puppy. Running Wolf watched, amused, his hand on the shoulder of a girl in a sleeveless buckskin dress with big brown eyes. A streak of mud ran from her forehead down to her right cheek. A large basswood leaf sat on her head. BJ was struck by her. So much, in fact, that he didn't notice the cool breeze suddenly blowing across his midsection. When the girl's eyes grew large in surprise, BJ looked down to see that a tiny bundle of curiosity had lifted BJ's breechcloth in a thorough, if poorly timed, inspection. BJ's privates had, once more, become quite public. He shrieked and pulled his outfit back in place amidst the stunned faces.

"Did you see that?"

"What happened to him?"

"Maybe he tried to catch a fish with it."

"He put it somewhere he shouldn't have, like Red Fox."

BJ wanted to crawl into a hole and disappear.

Running Wolf, mercifully, interrupted them. "Children! This evening, I will tell you a story!"

A cheer arose from the group. "But Grandfather," said a tall boy with delicate features and penetrating eyes, "the ice is melted."

"Yes, Shines Bright, it is unusual for a long story this time of year. But this is an unusual time. Go fill your stomachs and come back to my fire," he looked into the sky, "when the sun is four fingers from the horizon." Running Wolf put his arm around the girl with the big brown eyes and left with her. The children scattered like squirrels—all except a broad-shouldered boy with bangs and the boy named Shines Bright. BJ recognized the first boy as one of the fighters that had pursued the invaders. "Do you need help with your breechcloth?" asked Shines Bright. BJ nodded, feeling stupid.

Shines Bright reached out and untied BJ's sloppily fastened strap. He held this out for the other boy to hold. "Unwrap it," he said to BJ. BJ did so, watching for any reaction when they saw his privates. The boys gave each other a glance, but that was all, and BJ was grateful for this. "Here." Shines Bright took the breechcloth from BJ and spread it on the ground so that BJ was standing at one end, looking down its length. "Now straddle this in the middle." BJ stepped forward and put each foot next to the middle of the cloth. "Stalking Bear, give him back his strap, and then you grab the back part, and I'll grab the front." BJ held the strap while the two boys lifted the cloth until it was up to his crotch. They took a step towards BJ, holding the ends in the air. "Now," said Shines Bright, "tie the strap around your waist." BJ quickly realized how it worked. After tying the strap, the boys let down their ends, which folded over the belt and draped about halfway down his thighs. It felt awkward, and his privates were much freer than he was accustomed to, but it was adjustable. And it sure beat a miniskirt.

BJ spent the next hour fending off herds of tiny children, most of them naked, all of them interested in lifting up his breechcloth. He got to the point where he could bat away a curious hand without even looking at it. Stalking Bear gave him a tour of the village, pointing out relatives, members of his clan, and friends. Most adults acknowledged BJ, then turned back to their work or resumed their business. Every size, shape, and age of person there, with one exception: no one was what he would call overweight. All looked strong and fit. Some had scars or injuries. It was a medley of humanity. Many of the women were topless, and it was all BJ could do not to stare. Other than accidentally meeting his mother as she came into the bathroom once, a trauma from which he was just recovering, BJ had never seen a pair of breasts. Now, they were everywhere, as varied in size and shape as the people themselves.

A crowd was already at Running Wolf's fire when they arrived. BJ sat on the log as he had earlier and tried to settle his mind. Running Wolf was sitting opposite, cross-legged, on a small red-and-black blanket, along with a bowl and a bundle of sage. Eventually, when he'd decided enough people had arrived, he grasped the bowl in one hand and the pipe stem in the other. He seemed to wait for a minute, then said "Children, has it been so long since I have told you a story?" Shines Bright leaped up and, using his left hand, offered Running Wolf a palmful of dried herbs. Running Wolf accepted these with his left hand, nodded, then leaned forward and tossed the herbs into the fire. Then he began: "In the way back time, when the Anishinaabe began to form villages in the east, they had great difficulty finding food and spent much of their time wandering the forest looking for animals to hunt or plants to harvest. Sometimes, they would stumble across hunters from other tribes and get into fights with them. It was a dangerous time. The people would often get caught off guard by their enemies. The tribe suffered. There was a boy who felt the pain of his village. He was not strong or fast like some other children, but he had great love for his people. One day, he climbed to the top of a hill above their lodges and sat on an exposed rock. He prayed to the Creator for help. For four days, he stayed there, listening to his mother cry out his name far below. His heart ached.

"When your prayer to Creator is heartfelt," Running Wolf reminded the children, "and your need is truly great, the spirit world will respond. On the fourth day," he continued, "when the sky was gray, and the boy was tired from lack of food and sleep, he had a vision. A voice said to him, 'Follow the light, and you will find help.' He opened his eyes to see a ray of sunlight shining through the thick clouds, striking the base of a large red pine. This was the only spot of light that the boy could see, so he took this as a sign, and he walked to the tree and sat in this beam of light. As soon as he did this, he knew that he had done the right thing. He knew that he had found a Sacred Place. He sat there for a long time before returning to his village down the hill.

"The boy's parents were greatly relieved that he was safe. When they asked him where he had been, he said, 'I was praying for help to keep our people safe.' They were proud of him but knew that he could do nothing since he was not big or strong. But he returned again and again to the place where the light had shone. Every day he went. Sometimes in the dark. Sometimes in the rain. He waited for a warrior to come. Sometimes, when he was very quiet, he thought he saw a glimpse of a shadowy figure. One day, a robin landed at his feet. The next day, a deer walked by so close he could have reached out and touched it. He watched them in silence. Sometimes, he grew restless, and he built things or played games or climbed trees. Other times, he slept. But he never gave up. Over time, he glimpsed the shadow more and more often. The boy could sense that a warrior was going to arrive, and he sang a thanksgiving song each morning as he waited.

"Day after day, he did this. Month after month. Year after year. Then one day, he awoke with a start. A young warrior was standing before him. Strong, sharp, alert. He led the boy through the forest for two days until they arrived near a hidden camp of six men. 'They are going to attack your village,' said the warrior. Together, the boy and the warrior followed the men, moving when they moved, on silent feet. They learned their strengths and their weaknesses. They saw how aware the men were, who the leader was, and, most importantly, how hard they slept. On the third night, when the men were dreaming of war and glory, the warrior slipped into their camp like a shadow and took all their belongings. When the men awoke in the morning, absolutely everything they had was gone—their bows, their food, their fire-making tools, even their clothes!"

A few giggles sounded around the fire.

Running Wolf smiled. "The enemies could not believe that it was possible for someone to sneak into their camp without waking them up. Only a Manitou could have done such a thing, and this frightened them. They returned, naked, to their own village and told their people that they should leave the Anishinaabe alone because they were protected by the spirits. The young man brought the warrior back to the village and gave a full report to the elders. They were so impressed and grateful that they held a celebration for the boy and the warrior, whom they honored with a new name."

"Shadow Walker!" shouted a child.

"Yes, this was Shadow Walker, the greatest of all scouts." There were smiles and nods around the campfire. Running Wolf rolled up the blanket. He had finished.

The kids burst out in chatter like a flock of chickadees: "Have you heard that story before? Did you know that was how Shadow Walker became a scout? Do you think that is a true story?"

That night, BJ dreamed of running naked through the forest, leaping over the rotten birch, and skirting around the mossy boulder. His father was lying face down on the ground, a dark wolf looming over him. The wolf stepped in between Mark and BJ, its yellow eyes glowing like beads of amber.

BJ awoke with a start, breathing hard. He had fallen asleep on the ground. Someone had placed an animal skin over him. A robin sang a full-throated greeting to the morning somewhere high in a birch tree. Indigo blue shone on the eastern horizon. A wisp of smoke rose from the remains of the fire. It was still early. Through the wigwams, BJ saw a few figures moving about on the east end of the camp. He rubbed his cowlick and thought about the wolf. Why was he dreaming about a wolf? The image of his dad lying on the ground haunted him. This was not his first nightmare about his dad getting hurt. Conservation officers had dangerous jobs, after all. What if the dream was some type of warning? A week earlier, BJ would have written off such a dream as, well, just a dream. But now… was it a message? Was his dad in danger? BJ tried to clear his head. He put his palm to the ground and felt the coolness of the earth to double-check that everything was still real, that he had actually been transported to this place or time. It was.

Find the warrior with the red hand. Watch and learn. He will come to you.

For the moment, the dream stirred in BJ a desire to be home with his family. He stood and looked towards the Cannonball Rock. Four visits. If he returned home, he would have three more to find the warrior. BJ stood and stole out of camp. He followed the river to the Tabletop, and from there to the great white pine in the center of the little hill. BJ climbed into the cave and stood before the paintings. He found the spot where the red hand had been and stood still for a few moments. How did this work? Could the cave read his mind? It occurred to BJ that he should probably leave the breechcloth there. He would definitely want it if he returned. He had shown his dick to quite enough people, thank you very much. He folded it and placed it in a dark corner. BJ returned, naked, to the open spot on the wall and pressed his hand onto the rock. He closed his eyes and wished to see his sister.

Quickly, he felt the elevator-like sensation strike. His stomach lurched. BJ opened his eyes. There was the red hand, along with the rest of the original paintings. His Blackberry was on the ground at his feet. Was he back? Had it been a dream? It sure didn't feel like it. BJ seized the phone and scrambled up and through the hole. The sky was blue. His underwear was on the rock near the cave entrance. Far in the distance, he could hear his mother clanging loudly, insistently, on the triangle for the kids to come home. And, down below, Charley lay on her side, her head resting on one outstretched arm. A chickadee sat perched on her shoulder.

Chapter Nine

The creature's eyes opened in the darkness. For a while, it lay still, listening, its stomach twisting at the sound of the dinner bell. It wondered if it would be safe to prowl and hunt along the edge of the villages or if their protector still be there. It stretched ancient limbs and began to creep through the tangle of dead, twisted wood, and into the open. It squinted against the sunlight.

The cool morning breeze blew off the vast, endless lake, mixing with the warmer air on the hill, swirling through the pine branches, sounding like notes on a flute. The birds who had been singing in harmony with the wind, fell silent and watched, still as stones. Good. The trees, it noted, were younger, their bark thin and branches slender. They, too, were silent. The earth-memory in the forest was strong. It would be the same with the great lake and the hills of granite. And The People? Would they remember? The creature sensed that it had slept for a long time. Had the people survived the arrival of the forest-killers who had come in numbers too high to count? There had been chaos and misery, and it might have continued to prey on them but for the presence of the protector.

The pain in the creature's stomach forced it to begin moving down the mountain, cautiously at first but gaining confidence with each step. As it advanced, it noted the new smells in the air. Gone were the scents of wood fire, fish, and tallow, replaced by acrid, oily things. New sounds, loud and sharp, emanated from below. This was a new world. It had been a long time, indeed. But if the creature had awakened at this moment, there must be a reason. Perhaps the dangers had passed. Perhaps there were new opportunities to feed and to take. "Yes," it said to itself. "You will know my name." It would take its time. It would watch. And it would learn. And it would kill once more.

Chapter Ten

BJ threw on his underwear, seized his shirt and pants, and scrambled down the little slope. "Charley, Mom's ringing the bell! We gotta go! She's got to be freaking out!" The chickadee perched on Charley's shoulder flitted up into the trees as she sat up. A glob of green-brown moss was stuck in her left nostril. BJ began to shove his legs into his still-moist jeans and fell over into the moss. Charley lifted one eyebrow at him. "Why would Mom freak out? We go on hikes all the time."

BJ rolled onto his back, still struggling into his pants. "Yeah, but not for a whole day and night!"

"What are you talking about?"

"Charley, I've been gone for… I've been gone…" He finished putting on his pants and stood up to look around. The sky was robin egg blue. The sun was in the same position as when he'd first climbed into the cave. His clothes were still wet. Charley was just where he had left her. "How long," he said, "was I in there?"

"I don't know. A few minutes, maybe."

BJ rubbed his cowlick and squeezed his eyes closed. He had just experienced a full twenty-four hours, but for Charley, it had been mere minutes. Did he dream all of it? Was it the dodgeball injury to his brain? Or had he really been gone and experienced some kind of time warp? He began to put his T-shirt on, and by the time his head popped through, Charley was disappearing into the cave hole. "Wow!" she said from inside. "Wow!" Then, a long silence. BJ held his breath. Was she still there? Would she go back in time as he had? A minute went by. Then two. He ran to the hole and peered in just as Charley's face was coming out. "Hi!" she said, sending BJ backward and onto his rear. Charley climbed out and headed down the backside of the hill. BJ scrambled after her.

"Those are awesome!" said Charley.

"Did you go anywhere?" he said.

Charley gave him a funny look. "Yeah, I went into the cave."

"Yeah, but did you go anywhere else?" he pressed.

"Where else is there to go?" she said. "I looked at the paintings and came out. They are super cool. I like the shapeshitter."

"SHIFTER!"

"Oops. Right."

Charley's time in the cave appeared to be without incident. On the way home, BJ related everything, from the story of the battle to the strange man, to Running Wolf and the kids, even the tale of Shadow Walker.

"Cool!" said Charley, skirting around the ghost trees.

"So, Charley, I went back in time!" he emphasized. "Like five hundred years or something back in time!"

"Cool!" she repeated.

BJ wanted to scream. How was his sister accepting the entire story without a single "Holy crap!" or "Oh my God!" Didn't she know how incredible it all was? Didn't she know it was impossible? They arrived at the Cannonball Rock. There, BJ stopped to survey his home with new eyes: the garage, the garden, the sauna, and their house. Max was there, too, lying spread-eagle, sunning his balls in the driveway. Since the time of Running Wolf, the trees had grown back, filling in the plateau. Their yard and Elmer's place were the only clearings now. Same place. Different world. BJ knew it would never look the same.

Charley sniffed at the air. "Mom burned something again." No sooner had she said this than the kitchen windows began opening faster than the petals of a morning dandelion. A tall man with neatly combed blond hair and a maroon and yellow Department of Natural Resources uniform burst out the back door and hurled a frying pan into the yard where it lay, smoldering.

BJ could hear the pan sizzling in the grass. "I wonder what's for supper?"

Charley skipped down the hill and around the smoking ruin to greet her father, who scooped her into his arms. "Hey, beautiful!" he coughed.

BJ studied the charred black bits in the frying pan. "So what was it?"

"Not sure," said Mark. "Better ask your mother. On second thought, don't ask. Let's just go in and make the best of it."

Charley touched noses with her father, forcing both of them to cross their eyes. "Daddy, can you count my freckles?"

Mark leaned back. "Let's see…" He began to touch Charley's nose and cheeks again and again with his index finger, all the while counting in a barely audible whisper. BJ headed inside. "85, 86, 87… 88!" he heard his father say as he walked inside. "That's more than last time—they're growing!"

At supper, BJ set a family record for distractedness. When his father asked him to pass the salt, he gave him the water pitcher. When his mother reminded him to put his napkin in his lap, he passed Charley the tofu. "How was your hike?" asked Molly.

"Huh?" Charley suppressed a grin, but barely.

Molly put her fork down on her plate. "How. Was. Your. Hike?"

"Oh, fine! Fine." BJ took a swig of milk.

"See any magical places?" asked their father.

Milk exploded from BJ's mouth, sending white spray across the table.

Mark jumped up from his chair. "What the—"

BJ coughed and sputtered, white foam dripping from his nose. "Magic? (cough) What do you mean (hack) by 'magic'?"

Mark wiped his shirt and face with a napkin, then sat back down. "Well, I don't know. I wasn't being serious." He looked to Molly for support.

Molly set down her fork again—BJ hated it when she set down her fork—and smiled patiently. "You know, BJ, when boys are your age—"

"Mom, it's not puberty."

"BJ, there's no need to be embarrassed. Every boy—"

"Mom, listen to me!" If he heard the puberty talk one more time, he was going to lose his mind for real. He glanced at Charley. He had to tell his parents. He had to let them know. Maybe it was important for them to know. Maybe the Red Hand Warrior or whatever could help his dad track down the wolf. They would believe him.

So he told them.

About the battle and the dead warrior. About the village. About Running Wolf and Stalking Bear and the man with the limp and the story of Shadow Walker and falling asleep, then returning to the cave. He told them everything, knowing in his heart that they would believe him, knowing that, this time, his mother would not send him to a therapist or make him go jogging or, God forbid, rub some stupid oil into him to make him stop having delusions.

The lavender oil, it turned out, didn't smell all that bad. And the scalp massage was kind of nice, too. Molly finished, then ran her fingers through his hair one last time. "Goodnight, kiddo. Get some sleep and let your brain rest from that dodgeball."

"Goodnight, Mom." BJ wasn't mad. Annoyed but not mad. Not really. A few weeks earlier, he wouldn't have believed any of it himself. At least his parents hadn't freaked out and restricted his time in the woods. He could go back to the cave. He should go back. Molly leaned down below the top bunk, and BJ heard her kiss Charley. She left the room. The door latch made a soft "click." The hoot of a barred owl echoed through the woods, and a lone mosquito bounced furiously against the window screen. Far away, a wolf howled.

"Were there any girls there?" said Charley.

"Where?"

"In the Ojibwe village."

"Yeah, there were girls."

"Did they paint their toenails?"

"I don't think so."

"Maybe you could bring them some nail polish."

BJ contemplated the image.

"Do they wear underpants?"

"Nope."

There was a pause. "I wonder if they're circumscribed."

BJ leaned over the bed. "What?"

"You know, that operation that some boys get when they're babies."

"You mean *circumcised?*" BJ rolled back and covered his face with a pillow. Then he laughed, a full-on belly laugh. The bed shook.

"What's so funny?"

BJ removed the pillow. "Actually, Charley, I happen to know the answer to that: definitely not."

"Okay."

BJ heard her roll over, and within minutes, she was breathing steadily in a peaceful sleep. BJ chuckled to himself as his eyes drooped. No wonder the people in the village had been shocked when his breechcloth had been lifted. Honestly, he couldn't blame them at all.

Chapter Eleven

Sunday mornings meant comics, pancakes, and hot chocolate. Molly was at the kitchen table, still in her running clothes, sipping coffee and answering the quiz on public radio, when BJ came into the kitchen, still rubbing his eyes. "Protuberance," she said to the radio.

Charley stirred her cereal. "What's exuberance?"

"You, mostly. Protuberance is your brother if he doesn't zip his fly."

BJ zipped his fly. "Smells good."

"In the oven," said Molly. "Procrastinate."

"Procrastinate?" said Charley.

"I'll tell you later."

BJ shook his head and poured himself some hot chocolate. He opened the oven door and recoiled at what looked for all the world like a plate of hockey pucks. "No, they're not burned," said Molly, "they're buckwheat. Darker flour. Extra protein." BJ put three on his plate, closed the oven door, and sat down next to Charley. Black pancakes. Oh well. Nothing that can't be cured with extra maple syrup. He seized the Ball jar and poured with abandon.

After breakfast, Molly drove BJ and his sister into town. As was often the case, Mark worked weekends, so they would likely not see him until evening. BJ suspected that his mother wanted them to come into town while she did some work at the co-op so that they wouldn't run off into the woods and come back with wild stories again. Anyway, he figured he would go in the cave later in the week, and he sort of felt like he needed a few days to think about all that had happened.

Halfway to town, they spied Audrey Giizis walking along the side of the road in jeans and flannel. Molly pulled over in front of her and opened the passenger door. The old lady climbed in with a grunt. She smelled of smoke and leather. They pulled back onto the highway and continued towards town. BJ turned to wave at Audrey, then faced forward and thought about her thick gray braid and her deep, dark wrinkles and reckoned she would blend in seamlessly with Running Wolf's village. He wondered who in that tribe she was related to. At the edge of town, Molly said, "Where to, Audrey?"

The old woman tucked a strand of gray hair behind one ear. "Gonna go see my boyfriend, he-he!"

"You going to the statues or to visit Russ directly?" Molly teased. BJ wondered if Audrey had ever directly complimented Russ on his butt.

"By the lake is good," said Audrey. "Russ has been playing hard to get, but I'll win him over one of these days, he-he!" They looped around, past the school, then dropped her off at the statues. Molly drove another block to let BJ and Charley hop out at the bait shop and continued to the co-op. George was singing a very catchy French-Canadian tune as they arrived:

Oh Marie Malurette, nous cueillons
dés aujourd'hui, les fruits de notre bonheur!

The big red door creaked open, and a dark beard appeared. "Is she gone?"

BJ said, "Who?"

"Audrey!"

Charley pointed down the street, where the elder was sitting on a bench. Russ opened the door all the way and stepped out, holding a poster for the Walleye Daze Summer Festival in his hand and smelling like fish. He looked up at George and listened for a moment. "I like that. Don't know what it is, but I like it." Russ went back inside and put the poster in the window above the "Closed" sign, then strode to the counter. The kids followed, BJ turning the sign from "Closed" to "Open."

"Coffee's on!" grunted Russ from somewhere below the counter. Russ had been offering the kids coffee since they could walk. Not once had they accepted the offer or even hinted that they would consider drinking coffee, but he kept at it in an almost ritual fashion. By now, BJ would be insulted if he didn't. Charley was at the back of the store, pressing her nose against the side of a bait tank to watch shiners, ciscoes, and fatheads swim back and forth in little schools. There were always a few fuzzy, stiff, dead ones that would fall, get pushed back up to the top by the aerator bubbles, and then sink back down again. Russ continued his work beneath the counter while BJ admired the huge, antique double-bladed axe hanging on the wall. Russ sometimes carried it for photo ops during festivals when he dressed as Paul Bunyan. The handle was painted yellow, blue, and red with markings near the blade. In the wrong hands, BJ reckoned, it could do some serious damage.

A large Suburban with Wisconsin plates and pulling a shiny fiberglass boat pulled up in front of the store. Two broad-chested middle-aged men with goatees and sunglasses got out of the car and swaggered inside. "Morning!" belted one of the men, speaking around a large, unlit cigar. BJ allowed a small wave. The men began perusing the tackle in one of the aisles. Outside, George began to sing "Big Shot" by Billy Joel.

BJ turned his attention back to the wall of photos and artifacts. An old ash basket hanging on the wall prompted him to ask a question he had been pondering: "Russ, how did the Indians catch fish in the old days?"

"They did lots of netting, especially in summer. Still do on some lakes. Sometimes, they used hooks made from bone and line made from cedar bark, basswood bark, or sinew. In the winter, they speared. I've done that with some friends from the Rez a number of times. I've also helped your dad and the guys from fisheries do some sample netting, which is lots of fun."

"I bet you can catch a lot of fish with a big net."

"Too many!" said the man with the cigar, dropping a bag of chartreuse jigs with a heavy clunk. "Damn Indians are fishing out all the good lakes." His friend, still in sunglasses, came to his side, nodding. "Why don't they play by the rules like everybody else?" the cigar man continued.

"The DNR lets wolves take all the deer, and the Indians take all the fish," added his friend.

BJ glanced at his sister, who looked as if she'd just eaten something very bitter. The men were clearly looking for approval of their comments. BJ figured they were used to throwing their weight and opinions around without being contradicted in other bait shops. The silence from behind the counter, however, told BJ that these men had just made a big mistake.

"Indians need to get over it," continued cigar man. "Those treaties are two hundred years old and—" He stopped mid-sentence.

The scowling bearded face of Russ had appeared from behind the counter and was growing slowly and menacingly. With each inch he rose, the man's cigar fell, bit by bit, until Russ towered over him like a redwood before a sapling. The cigar hung limply from a pair of colorless lips. Russ placed two dinner-plate-size hands on the counter and leaned forward. "The Indians," he said calmly, "got every right to fish and hunt on their land the way they've been doing since long before the colonists showed up. What do you have against that?"

The men shrunk like a pair of scolded dogs. "Well…" Sunglasses man swallowed. "It's not fair."

Russ smiled at him. It was not a smile anyone would want directed at them. "You know what's not fair?" His voice rose a bit, but it was more than enough. "Waging war against them, hooking them on alcohol, giving them diseases on purpose, making them sign treaties they didn't understand, logging off every pine tree, trapping every beaver, tearing children away from families and shoving them into boarding schools where they were punished for speaking their own language. Genocide," he summed up, "isn't fair. You bring your shiny suburban and $100,000 fishing rig to a place where most of the Indians are living in trailer houses and scraping by for gas money, and you want to talk fair?"

The only sound was the tick-tock-tick-tock from the clock in the rear of the store. Limp-cigar man reached out and touched the packet of jigs with one finger as if fearing it would explode.

"We're closed," said Russ.

"But… but your sign says…"

Russ held up a fist, then raised one bratwurst-sized finger, then another and began to count ominously, "One Mississippi… two Mississippi…" Both men fled from the store, leaped into their vehicle, and drove away with screeching tires. Russ turned to BJ and winked.

"That looked 'fair' to me," said Charley.

"RIGHT!" Russ boomed, pounding the counter with his fist and causing the entire building to shake. "Who wants a milkshake?" BJ and Charley each shot a hand in the air. Russ handed BJ a ten-dollar bill and pointed out the door. Half an hour later, the three of them were out in front, listening to George sing and watching locals and out-of-towners stroll by. Russ sipped coffee from a large mug while Charley sat on his lap, sucking on her strawberry shake. BJ nursed a chocolate shake from his chair and silently counted pedestrians. Almost all of them walked with their faces towards the two-legged solar panels, like recharging their batteries after a long and dark winter. The scent of cut grass and warm asphalt mixed in with coffee and fish. Summer had arrived.

Russ said to Charley, "Did I ever tell you about the time you were born?"

About a million times, thought BJ.

"Tell it again!" said Charley.

Russ took a sip of coffee and began. "We were in the middle of a *huge* snowstorm, twenty inches and counting." (BJ was sure it had been "fifteen inches" last time). "Gas stations and restaurants were closing. Your gramma was here to watch BJ because your dad was somewhere on assignment."

"He was in Hibbing," offered BJ. He knew the story by heart.

"Right, right, over on the Iron Range." Russ took a sip. "Anyway, I had just returned with my sled dogs from checking my traplines and was about to unhook them when I heard the phone ring in the house."

"Mommy!" cried Charley.

"Right! She was in labor and stuck at home. The ambulance couldn't get out of town, so she called me to see if I could help. I turned the dogs around and drove them down to your house. Took me about thirty minutes."

A couple of young men wearing St. Cloud State sweatshirts stopped to listen to George sing. "Store's open," said Russ. "Owner's in there somewhere. Grab the tambourine on the counter and start shaking it. He should show up." They exchanged looks and went inside. Soon, a timid jingling could be heard. "Anyway," continued Russ, "your mom and gramma met me at the door. Molly was sure breathing hard. She looked at me and said—well, I won't tell you what she said—but we got moving fast! The dogs were great! Moving in fresh snow is really hard, but they could tell it was an important mission, and they pulled to beat the band! I spent half the time running behind and helping push the sled, hoping we wouldn't have a baby on the trail! All of a sudden"—Russ set the mug on his armrest—" we came around a bend and saw, standing there, in the moonlight..." He paused for effect even though both kids knew what was coming. "...a pack of timber wolves in the middle of the trail!"

BJ hugged his knees tight and grinned. He loved this part.

Russ continued, "My first thought was, 'oh, please, no fight, no fight!' but when we got closer, the wolves scattered to either side of the trail, and I'll be a two-tailed walleye if they didn't start running right along beside us! The dogs were yapping and running as hard as they could through the powder, and I could see two or three wolves moving in and out of the trees, their tongues lolling, looking like they were having the time of their lives!"

Russ took another sip of coffee and considered George, who'd begun to sing "Born To Be Wild" by Steppenwolf. "Anyway, we charged down the trail with your mother huffing and puffing all the way into town." Russ's imitation of their mother's puffed-out cheeks made both kids laugh hard. "The trail goes right by the hospital, and so we popped into the parking lot and headed towards the main entrance. Now…" Russ set his mug back down, which he did each time he wanted to emphasize a point. "Ever since that night, folks like to tell this story like I meant the next part to happen, but that's not the way it was."

"My dad says you did it on purpose," chided BJ.

"Absolutely not!" countered Russ. "As we were heading towards the entrance, I was looking back for the wolves and so didn't notice when we got up to the doors. They opened automatically, and we all went right in—dogs, sled, your mother, and me. Down the hallway, past the screaming receptionist, and, as it happens, right up to the delivery room!" Russ slapped his leg at the memory and laughed a laugh that was as deep and heavy as Lake Superior itself, and BJ could feel his own chair vibrate. "Margie Schmidt bolted out of the room, hollering, but your mother stood right up on her own and said to her—well, I won't tell you what she said—but she got herself into the room quick as a wink. I turned around to right my sled, and the next thing I knew, I almost got knocked over by the sound of *your voice!*"

Charley's blue eyes sparkled. "My voice?"

"Yes! You came out hollering so loud, you scared the dogs right back out of the building! 'BAM, CRASH, BANG!' They charged down the hallway and out the door. What a mess! I had my hands full unscrambling them, then tying 'em up. When I came back in to check on your mom, there you were—lying on her belly and mad as a bull moose in October. I was sorry your dad wasn't there, but I was glad to help."

"She still sounds like that," offered BJ.

Charley stuck her tongue out at him.

"So I've heard!" said Russ, beaming down at her. "I'm glad she hasn't used her yell on me! Well, that's the absolute truth—as I remember it, anyway." Russ gave Charley a squeeze. "You were kind of famous for a while after that. The story made it all the way into the *Star Tribune* in Minneapolis!"

For a while, the only sounds on the street were from a pair of gulls fighting for space on a lamppost and the jingle of a tambourine inside the store.

"What was the name of that lead dog again?" said BJ, thinking how proud Russ had been of that husky.

"Thunder! Great dog. He ran the sled until he was nine. Then he retired."

An image of the dog playing golf in Florida flashed through BJ's mind. "Where did he go?"

Russ rubbed his beard. "Well, I tried to let him in the house— figured he deserved it after all those years of work. But, uh, that didn't pan out."

"What'd he do?" asked Charley.

"Ate the cat." Both kids cracked up.

The story of the wolves reminded BJ of his dad's predicament. "Russ, do you think one of those wolves, or I mean, a wolf—any wolf—would kill a cow?"

"Nope."

BJ had not expected such a quick answer. "Why not?"

"Just don't," said Russ, and that was that.

Audrey Giizis appeared across the street. Russ stiffened slightly as their eyes met. She blew him a kiss.

"Hi, Audrey," said Russ flatly.

"See you later, Paul Bunyan!"

Russ waited for her to disappear, then sighed.

"I believe she likes your butt," said BJ.

"BJ!" scolded Charley.

"Just sayin'." He shrugged.

Above them, George sang, "Put a rock in your butt... put some fleas in your butt, put a tin can in your butt...!" BJ and Charley stared, dumbfounded, at the fish. What on earth kind of song was that? Russ pulled out his iPhone and began stabbing at it with a forefinger. "Where the hell is Lenny Kravitz?"

Put a little tiny man in your butt, put a little tiny man in your butt, put me in your butt... put your boogie in your butt, in your butt!

Chapter Twelve

Monday and Tuesday were pretend school days. The teachers pretended to teach, and the kids pretended to learn. Everybody knew the idea was to tick off the remaining two days on the school calendar and get the hell out of there. After the final bell of the year on Tuesday, all of the students burst out of the school doors and into summer freedom. BJ was invited for a sleepover at Tony's, so they met at the statues and waited until a large white SUV pulled up, then climbed in. Tony's mother, still talking on her phone, waved at them with one hand, then pulled out into the road and headed north out of town. The car smelled of clean leather and Drakkar Noir perfume. A mile out of town, she hung up and said, "Happy summer, boys! You glad to be done with school?" Angie spoke with a slight Mexican accent, placing a soft 'j' at the beginning of "you." She glanced in the rearview mirror at the boys. "I'm sure your teachers will miss you."

"Not mine!" said BJ.

"Oh yes, they will," she countered. "You're a great kid! I would have loved having you in my class when I was teaching!"

BJ felt a warm tickle in his chest. He tried to imagine having a teacher like Angie. Her long auburn hair, pearly white smile, lips as red as a summer tomato, and big brown eyes had always managed to make BJ forget his words. Angie was bubbly, loud, and full of laughter. She wore tight cotton dresses and high heels. In Grand Marais,

Minnesota, a town of understated Ojibwe, Fins, and Scandinavians, Angela Gonzalez could not have stood out more if she'd worn a tuba on her head.

Tony grabbed the handle of a shovel and pushed it further into the far back seat. "What's this for, Mama?"

"Es para tu tío Francisco."

Tony looked at BJ and spun his finger in the air next to his head, then pulled out his phone and began playing a game. BJ had forgotten about Francisco. When the Gonzales family arrived from Chicago a few years earlier, they were the first (and still only) Mexican American family in Grand Marais. There were rumors that they were connected to the drug cartels, which would explain the fancy car, the big house, and the gorgeous wife. When Tony's great-uncle Francisco came from Sinaloa to live with them, suspicions really took off. Kids in school said that he had been a hitman for the cartels. They said he still buried the bodies of his enemies in the woods near their home.

They turned off the highway and drove 100 yards down a black asphalt road that ended at a massive earth-tone house with a three-stall garage. BJ hopped out and crossed the weedless lawn to study the bronze statue of a chubby, mustached Mexican cook. He held a frying pan in one hand and a large tortilla in the other. BJ counted twenty-three smile wrinkles around his eyes. The statue was one of those creations that seemed likely to come alive the minute you turned your back on him. BJ pretended to turn away, then jerked back around. Nothing. BJ backed away, keeping his eye on the cook until he stepped in something squishy. "Really?" he said, scraping the dog poop from his sandal. He scanned the rest of the yard for El Chapo, the ankle-biting Corgi. The dog was as quick as he was sneaky, and BJ had rarely left the Gonzales's house without a set of small teeth marks on his leg. The worst part about this wasn't the injuries; it was that neither Tony nor his parents ever believed him because they had never witnessed El Chapo bite anyone. BJ reached the front door and slipped in. Maybe the dog had been plucked away by an eagle or run over by the mail carrier. One could hope.

Tony was on the couch, playing on his iPhone, and Angie was busy behind the kitchen island. The house was no more than fifty yards from the lake, and the view was stunning. BJ walked to the south wall and looked out on the water, still expecting to see a wolf, but there was only water all the way to the horizon. His eyes moved to another statue, this one of a little girl, her hands on her hips, arching her back impishly. She had pigtails and a short, flowy skirt and reminded him of Charley. As BJ was studying her face, the statue stuck her tongue out at him. BJ flinched so hard, he pulled a muscle in his back. Just then the doorbell rang, drawing his attention across the room. David was there, his white grin shining nearly as brightly as his green and orange hair. BJ looked back at the statue, which had resumed her normal posture. Again, he backed towards the boys, milling just outside the door.

"So, did you do it?" Tony asked David.

"Yep."

"What did you do?" asked BJ.

"I hacked the school website and changed the mascot from "Indians" to "White Boys.""

"What would be a good mascot outfit for 'White Boys'?" said Tony.

"I dunno," said David. "Maybe a business guy?"

"My dad's a business guy, but he's not too white," said Tony.

Angie finished loading groceries and closed the refrigerator door. "In Mexico, he was considered white," said Angie. "In Chicago, he was Chicano, then Latino. Now he's Mexican all over again."

"I don't get it," said BJ.

"Me neither," said Angie.

"Anyway," said David, "my mom caught me and made me change it back, but she gave me a fist bump first.

"Guapo!" Angie yelled to David. "You going to stand there all day or come see me?" David came in, set down his bag, and was wrapped up in a big, mushy Angie hug and plenty of kisses. Tony followed, but BJ lingered, staring at the statue of the cook. Did he just see it move? BJ wasn't sure anymore. He didn't feel sure of anything anymore. There was just too much going on. He rubbed his cowlick, turned to walk inside—and felt a hard pinch above his right ankle. "Ow!" He spun around to defend himself, but El Chapo was several strides away. The dog ran to the lilac bushes and disappeared. BJ's calf was decorated with a familiar set of dents. No one in the house had noticed a thing. BJ felt his face grow hot with anger, and he jabbed a finger towards the lilacs. "That's it, Voldemutt! Before this summer is over, you are going to GET IT!" BJ limped inside and closed the door.

Chapter Thirteen

For BJ, one of the great benefits of being at the Gonzales' house was not having to eat burned tofu or pine nuts. It's not that he didn't appreciate his mother's cooking efforts, but every once in a while, a kid just wants a big hamburger. As it happens, that is what they were eating that night, and BJ made every bite count, almost wishing he had a bib to catch the juice from the meat and the crisp sweet corn. He had just finished his second slice of watermelon when Tony's dad came home, wearing his usual business suit and sunglasses. Antonio Sr. had neatly cut jet-black hair and was of light complexion. He set his briefcase on the kitchen counter, kissed Angie on the cheek, and joined the boys at the table. "So," he said, squirting a dollop of ketchup onto his burger, "what's your dad doing about this wolf?"

BJ assumed the question was addressed to him. Mr. Gonzales always had a keen interest in his dad's work. "What wolf?" he said.

"A cow was killed last night up at Johnson's farm, and his dog is gone," said Mr. Gonzales before taking a big bite of his burger.

"Who said it was a wolf?" asked Angie.

"There's just too many wolves around. What else could it be? We gotta do something about them. Soon, they're going to start taking our moose and deer." He took another bite of his burger.

BJ knew perfectly well that Mr. Gonzales's idea of hunting was to go sit in a big, heated deer stand with four walls, a roof, and windows. He would read a magazine or watch the stock market on his phone until he noticed a deer on the other side of the field. If it was a large buck, he would shoot it with his high-powered rifle, then drive back and forth through town to show it off before leaving it with the butcher for processing.

Angie took a seat and served herself. "They're not your deer."

"I've been thinking about getting a wolf tag this year," he continued. "I could play my part in keeping the population in check. Enough of this politically correct, save-the-wolves crap!"

Angie gave him a side-eye. "You shoot a wolf, you sleep with the dog."

"And how about the break-ins up on Reservation Road?" added Mr. Gonzales.

"What about them?" said BJ.

"Is your dad doing anything about that?"

"I don't know," said BJ, which was the truth.

Tony headed for the door, David following close behind.

"Adonde vas, tu?" said Angie.

"To the dock," said Tony.

"Prefiero que me respondas en español, por favor."

"Fine. I mean 'bueno,'" said Tony before heading out.

Tony Sr. wiped his mouth with his napkin, folded it into a neat triangle, set it next to his plate, and stood up. "It would be easier if we stuck to English." He picked up the TV remote and sat on the couch.

"Easier doesn't mean smarter," said Angie. She and BJ visited about summer plans and wildflowers and Mexican food, which she said she missed. They finished eating, then cleared the dishes, and BJ wiped down the table. When BJ came back to the kitchen, Angie seized him by the head and planted a big kiss on his cheek. "You, young man, are a perfect gentleman!" She plucked the cloth from his hands with a wink. BJ swept from the house, feeling his face growing hot.

The boys were sitting at the end of the dock, their feet dangling in the water, playing Minecraft when he arrived. BJ sat behind them on the side of the dock and pulled out his blackberry. He didn't have any games on his device, so he opened the pictures of the cave wall and stared in silence. A loon slipped silently back and forth along the drop-off, diving underwater every few minutes in pursuit of minnows. The sun, low above the hills, illuminated the eastern clouds in blaze orange. A little cloud of insects the size of a beach ball hovered above the smooth water. Bleep, bleep! went the video game.

Mr. Gonzeles' words about the dead cow and missing dog were nagging at BJ. Was there some rogue wolf prowling near homes? If so, it would indeed fall to his father to deal with. And if more animals were killed or lost, Mark would get much of the blame. BJ had seen public meetings where some locals seemed to take great pleasure in yelling at his dad about fishing or hunting regulations. BJ squinted at the photo of the red hand, recalling the warning from his history book. *Your family is in danger.* Where is the threat, wondered BJ? Was it a rogue wolf or maybe the guy breaking into homes? Was this what the red-hand guy was supposed to help out with? BJ glanced at his friends, absorbed in their game. "Hey," he said. "So, I found a cave."

David pointed at his phone. "I made a cave, too," he said. "A super big one."

"Mine is small," said BJ. "But there are Native paintings."

"I didn't know the game could do that," said Tony, not looking up.

"You guys!" BJ spat. "It's not Minecraft! I went back in time and almost got shot by an arrow, and these Ojibwe dudes said my penis looked funny, and they fed me and told a story about Shadow Walker, and there's a cute girl, and I slept in a wigwam!"

Both boys looked up from their phones and turned to look at BJ with blank expressions. David said, "Well, does it look funny?"

"Does what look funny?"

"Your penis."

"THIS ISN'T ABOUT MY PENIS!"

"Well, you brought it up," said Tony. "Can we see?"

"NO!" BJ rubbed his cowlick furiously as the boys resumed their game. Why did nobody believe him? It wasn't like he was someone who made stuff up, for crying out loud. BJ wanted to scream. He wanted to … something was moving through the trees near the shore. Something with two legs. "There's someone over there," he said, pointing.

"Huh?" mumbled Tony, not looking up.

"I said"—BJ shoved Tony's head—" There is someone sneaking around over there."

"That's Tío Francisco." Tony looked back at his phone and added a brick to a castle turret. "Uncle Francis is kinda weird. Mostly keeps to himself. He's usually around his cabin, but Mom says he takes walks up on Reservation Road sometimes."

"Reservation Road?" said BJ more quickly than he meant to. "What does he do way up there?"

"Buries the bodies of his enemies, of course," said Tony.

BJ didn't laugh.

Tony pocketed his phone and stood up. "Yeah, yeah, he's a cartel hitman or whatever. Well, let's go see what he's up to!" He motioned to the others to follow. BJ felt a little shiver run down his spine as the three of them swept from the dock and into the woods. Slowly, they made their way toward a faint outline of a building, trying hard and failing to walk quietly. They came to a small, well-kept garden plot with newly planted rows of vegetables barely protruding from the soil. The cabin was built with dark brown horizontal logs and an old shingle roof covered with a generation of moss and pine needle duff. One large window looked out onto a 4x4 wooden post and a set of bird feeders.

The boys peeked into a small window on the east wall. BJ could make out the edge of a bookcase and a rifle with a scope hanging on the wall. Guns on walls were not that unusual around here, he reminded himself. It did not mean he was an assassin! Inside, he could see a shadow moving around but couldn't directly see Tony's uncle.

Then, all of a sudden, he stepped out from behind the bookcase. BJ moved away from the window and bumped into something big and furry, which swung back and forth, making a tree limb creak. A deer suspended from a rope! BJ lurched backward—and into David, who fell over a wheelbarrow.

"Quien es?" shot a voice from inside. "Pinchi oso! Who's there?" Footsteps marched across the floor, and a door on the other side of the building opened and closed. The boys flew back through the woods like panicked rabbits, tripping over logs, stumbling through brush, and even running into trees until they arrived back at the main house. Tony was giggling with fright. BJ was less amused.

"Time for a safer activity," said Tony. "Xbox!" They settled on the couch with pop, chips, and joysticks. For hours, they played alien games, flying games, monster games, soccer, hockey, baseball games, singing games, dancing games, and, of course, lots and lots of shooting games, only pausing briefly for a trip to the bathroom or a supply trip to the kitchen. BJ could not remember the last time he stayed up this late. By midnight, he could feel the fatigue setting in. By 2:00 a.m., his eyes had trouble focusing. Then, he began to feel nauseated, as if he had drunk a cup of acid. His muscles began to fail. Drunk with exhaustion, BJ's head swiveled wildly, loosely, like a tomato on a toothpick. He tried to speak, but all that came out was "urgphzittt" and some spittle. The last thing he remembered was David and Tony pointing at him and laughing hysterically. Then everything went dark.

BJ dreamed of being chased through the forest by a giant joystick. His mother was calling him. He tried to run faster, but his feet were heavy. The branches of the trees tore at his clothes. The birds laughed at him.

"BJ! BJ!" yelled Molly.

BOOM! The joystick crushed everything in its path, like a steamroller. It was getting closer. BJ was not going to escape. He would be smashed to bits.

"BJ! BJ!" called his mother. "Wake up! What's wrong with him?"
"I dunno. Poke him or something."

The "something" turned out to be a thump on the head with a large book.

"Ow—hey!"

"Whew!" Tony set down the book. "I so did NOT want to tell your mother that you were dead."

BJ groaned. His eyes, swollen and stiff, did not want to open. He felt like someone had poured sand into his skull. For a time, he lay on the bed and tried to rid himself of the dream.

"Gamer hangover," said Tony. "You get used to it."

"Not sure I want to."

Later, at home, BJ was sitting in front of a bowl of arugula salad, trying to stay awake, when Mark drove up and came inside. He had been up and working since 3:00 a.m. "A neighbor saw a big black wolf near Johnson's place," he said, "so I guess that's our prime suspect for the killing of that cow." BJ found himself feeling angry towards the animal. Ten million deer in the woods, and this thing has to kill a cow!

Molly handed Mark the salad bowl. "How is Orton reacting?"

"Not well, and I don't blame him. It's tough to have something kill an animal you've been taking care of. But he's already calling around and getting people riled up. I'm sure we'll see one of his letters to the editor again. The Deer Hunter's Alliance left me a message."

Molly threw her hands into the air. "They already got their wolf-hunting season! What do they want, for you to harvest their deer and wrap them in a red bow?"

"That would be cute," said Charley.

"What are you going to do, Dad?" said BJ.

"I've got trail cameras set up. If it's one animal, maybe we can deal with it."

BJ wasn't so sure. For the first time in his life, he felt like his dad might not be able to deal with something on his own, and this was very unsettling. BJ felt a little twist in his gut. The little voice in his head telling him to find that warrior was getting louder. Maybe it was time to listen.

Chapter Fourteen

The creature stalked the road for several days, feeding on the farm animals. They were stupid and slow but tasty. The forest killers came from their homes, holding guns, too afraid to enter the woods. They did not spend much time looking at the ground or listening to the birds who were trying to inform them of the creature's presence. How could they be so blind and so deaf? What had happened to them since it had last been lurking in these hills? Had the Original People not taught them, or did the forest killers continue to wipe them all out until they were gone from the earth?

One day, while the creature was sitting still and watching, a man arrived in a maroon truck. He talked to the homeowners and then spent much time looking at the ground and scouting the forest. He put little square boxes on some of the trees along well-traveled game trails. Were they traps? It could not tell. While the man's skills were not like The People, the creature was reminded of them. The man returned many times to study the ground and check his little boxes. He did not mind moving in the darkness or being alone. This man had the aura of a predator. The creature would have to begin paying attention to him.

Chapter Fifteen

BJ's dreams were filled with wolves, big men chewing on cigars, and burned-down homes. He awoke in the dark at 3:00 a.m. and rolled around for an hour before giving up and climbing out of bed. He pulled on a pair of shorts and a T-shirt, grabbed *Hatchet* by Gary Paulson, and tip-toed down to the kitchen. An hour later, he was still reading when Mark came in, wearing his uniform and gun. "What on earth are you doing up?" he said to BJ.

"Couldn't sleep."

"Right." Mark checked his watch. "Wanna go for a drive? I need to collect something from the office, then check on one of the houses that got broken into."

BJ closed his book, glad for the chance to spend some time with his dad.

Elmer was standing by the road in his Twins cap, watching the sun rise. "Bouzhoo, boys. You two are up early."

"Gonna check on some stuff," said Mark. "Some cabins got vandalized."

"Reservation Road is a tricky spot. What are you doing about the big bad wolf?" Mark told him about the trail cameras. Elmer adjusted his cap. "How many cameras you got?"

"Just two for now."

"You sure it's a wolf?"

87

"What else would it be?"

Elmer shrugged and walked back into his yard.

They stopped at the Holiday gas station for coffee, then drove to the regional Department of Natural Resources office, a dark-brown split-timber building on the south end of town. Mark parked next to a yellow DNR firefighting truck and climbed out. BJ followed him inside and down the hallway past posters warning about invasive species, photographs of pristine shorelines, and displays of mounted birds and mammals. BJ counted twenty-three floor tiles between the door and his father's office. Mark took two manilla folders from a stack of paperwork on his desk and tucked them under his arm. He made to leave, but BJ pointed to a wall map dotted with different colored pins. "What's this for, Dad?"

"Different colors mean different things." He touched a purple pin. "This is our place."

BJ pointed to a group of red pins to the northeast of their home. "What are these?"

"Those are the places that got broken into or burned," said Mark.

BJ indicated two black pins. "And those?"

"Those are the wolf kills, or whatever Elmer thinks they might be."

BJ thought he heard a note of sarcasm in his dad's voice. "Dad, did you say 'kills'? Is there more than one?"

"The Knutsens lost a sheep as well."

Another one, then. BJ felt a rock land in the pit of his stomach. He remembered Elmer's words about Reservation Road. "Dad, what did Elmer mean by that area being tricky?"

Mark indicated for BJ to follow him to the truck. "One side of Reservation Road belongs to the tribe. The other, the west side, is a mixture of state and federal land. When stuff happens to the rez cabins, we don't usually deal with that. But the ones that got vandalized are on the other side of the road, and most are owned by people from the Twin Cities or Chicago or somewhere else. When those homeowners have problems, the state takes notice. This is why my supervisor has been calling me nonstop." They climbed in the truck and began heading north.

"Are you… I mean, is your boss mad?"

"He's concerned," said Mark, checking his rear and side mirrors.

"Do you have someone posted on the road?"

"We don't have enough people for that, but I've been scouting up there a lot. It's not easy to keep track of everyone who travels in an area, and besides, the forest here is huge, and there are lots of trails. I can't patrol them all. The trail cameras haven't recorded anything of note yet, but you never know. I'll go check them again in a few days."

BJ recalled the map back in the office and asked about the different colored squares near Reservation Road.

"The reservation is checker-boarded," explained Mark. "That means non-Indians were allowed to buy parcels of Indian land."

"Inside the reservation?" This made no sense to BJ. "But how can the tribe keep the reservation if it can be bought up by non-Indians? Is that legal?"

Mark grunted. "The government made it legal. I think that was the point." Mark rubbed his chin in thought. "Say, did you mention anything to Elmer about those break-ins?"

"No. Why?"

"Elmer said something about stuff happening on Reservation Road, but I don't recall actually telling him where the vandalism had occurred in the first place."

They continued northeast along the shore as the morning light worked its way down rocky cliffs in warm reds and yellows. Ravens skipped out into the road to pick at the squirrels, raccoons, or skunks that hadn't managed to cross in one piece, then strutted back to the side in slow contempt of the tires that had provided them their meal. By the time BJ and his dad reached the red, white, black, and yellow sign welcoming them to the Gichigami Indian Reservation, the sun had cleared the horizon. BJ looked at it differently today. From the time of Running Wolf to now was an almost imperceptible blink in the life of the sun. As far as the stars were concerned, BJ and Running Wolf were living on the earth at the same time. So weird!

They turned up Reservation Road and followed the windy gravel through the forest; hungry deer flies bouncing off the windshield. About a half mile past the snowmobile trail, Mark pointed to a small beige house with a pasture and a red outbuilding. "That's where the cow was killed." They continued past a pair of burned-out shacks, around a big curve, then down a stretch with nice-looking cabins with cute signs that said "The Olsons" and "Idle Wild" and "Ted's Place," which had a For Sale sign out in front.

A large moose was standing in the middle of the road. Mark slowed down to let him cross. It stood on gangly legs, its velvety antlers sparkling in the morning light. After a moment, he stepped off the road. "Watch him," said Mark just as the moose tilted his head back, allowing his antlers to slide through the branches with remarkable efficiency. In two seconds, he was gone. "Isn't it cool the way they do that? I never get tired of seeing it." BJ grinned and nodded.

Further on, they slowed down and nosed into the drive of a tarpaper-sided cabin with boarded-up windows and a moss-covered roof. The blue number at the driveway read 24675. Mark studied the cabin and adjacent woodshed. An aluminum rowboat covered with a thick layer of pine needles rested upside down in a patch of overgrown grass. A chipboard-sided outhouse stood nearby, the door hanging on one hinge. A seasonal cabin at most. There were no vehicles other than a four-wheeler parked next to the woodshed.

"My note says that 24675 was broken into and set on fire," said Mark. "This one isn't burned down. I bet they got the number wrong, but I'll look around anyway, just to be sure. Wait here." He climbed out and disappeared behind the cabin.

BJ sat still for a few minutes, then pulled out his Blackberry to check for messages. No service. He turned on the radio and hit scan. The numbers performed one full rotation of the frequencies without stopping and continued. A blue jay cawed. BJ felt drowsy. The radio stopped at 90.5. BJ half listened. *Highway through the danger zone, highway through the danger zone...* BJ recognized the song from an old Tom Cruise movie. His eyes were closing when a voice came across the radio, jolting him awake again: "...a little tune by Kenny Loggins, howah! The time is 5:12 in the morning. Bouzhoo, you're tuned to 90.5, Gichigami, 91.7, Grand Marais. It's the morning show on Indian Country Radio."

BJ glanced at the empty yard. His dad was taking his time.

"This is Coyote One," continued the smooth voice. "Thanks for tuning in! I'll be here bringing you a mix of folk, rock, blues, jazz, and maybe some drumming and flute music for the rest of the morning."

BJ studied the four-wheeler, admiring the shiny chrome and leather seats.

"I hope your day is off to a great start and you got some strong makade-mashkikiwaaboo to get you going—that's 'black medicine water' or 'coffee' for you non-Ojibwe."

A No Trespassing sign lay on the ground at the entrance to the yard. It was in the middle of a rope that was usually tied to two trees. It was only attached to one tree.

"...and now for the traffic report."

BJ twitched. "A traffic report? In Grand Marais? Are you kidding?"

"No kidding," said the radio. "Betty Fairbanks is ten miles south of the rez, doing thirty-five, mostly in her lane, but not always, so anyone driving north, keep your head up! She had an argument with Audrey Giizis last week and wouldn't give her a ride, so Audrey's walking down the road on that bad hip. Someone give her a lift if you can, please. A beauty of a moose was spotted on Reservation Road, howah, and if you happen to be in a green-and-brown F-150, parked in front of blue number 24675, it is time to skedaddle. Yessir, time to scramble. Blow the popsicle stand..."

BJ blinked. "Hey, I'm parked in front of 24675 Reservation Road!"

"Why, yes, you are, BJ Maki, and if I don't say so myself, you're a bit slow on the uptake this morning. Fish net's got a few too many holes in it. Probably a couple arrows short of a full quiver."

BJ's eyes narrowed. "What… are you talking about?"

"Well," said the radio voice, "it sure looks like one of our listeners needs me to be a bit more direct, so how about this: time for BJ and his dad to get their lily-white butts the hell off Reservation Road RIGHT NOW!" A jolt of energy shot through BJ. "Go!" said the radio. "Go, go, GO!"

BJ leaned out the window. "DAD!"

Mark was running towards the truck, his hand resting on the butt of his gun.

"Dad, I think we should go!"

"Yep!" said Mark, jumping into the truck and shifting into reverse in one smooth motion. On the road, he threw it into forward and stepped on it, throwing gravel into the air behind them.

"What's up, Dad?"

"Don't know," said Mark, glancing in the mirror. Suddenly, the rear window shattered. Mark shoved BJ's head to the seat, hard, and stepped on the gas.

"Ow!" yelled BJ.

"Stay down!"

With one hand on the steering wheel and the other on BJ's head, Mark was unable to shift, and the truck roared forward in second gear. BJ felt the vehicle take two big curves, then slow down. Mark took his hand off BJ's head and shifted into third. "You hurt?"

BJ sat up, rubbing his neck. "I, uh, don't think so. What did you do that for?" He didn't see the point of freaking out from a broken window. What had hit it anyway?

Mark grabbed his radio. "Twenty-one fifty, dispatch."

The back seat was covered in dime-sized bits of tempered glass.

What a mess! Maybe they should stop and clean it up.

A voice on the radio crackled. "Go ahead."

BJ faced forward and then noticed that a set of cracks had appeared like a spider web near the top of the windshield. In the center of the little web was a neat, tiny hole.

"I'm four miles up Reservation Road," Mark said to the dispatcher. "Someone just shot at my vehicle."

Chapter Sixteen

The response to Mark's call was impressive. In less than an hour, the area up and down Reservation Road was crawling with law enforcement, in vehicles and on foot, searching in and around abandoned buildings, knocking on doors, questioning homeowners. But without any leads, suspects, or even evidence, there was nothing to do but record the incident as a random event. The truth was that this would not be the first time an errant bullet had hit a home or vehicle in the area. One need only glance at the Swiss cheese road signs as a reminder of the prevalence of flying lead. For BJ, the experience was nerve-wracking enough to make him forget all about the cave and traveling back in time for his second visit.

At home, Mark's supervisor called to express his concern—for the governor's deer opener. In Minnesota, it was tradition for the governor to participate in each fishing and hunting opener, choosing a different part of the state each year. For deer season this year, he will be in Grand Marais, and the DNR commissioner wants everything to go smoothly. The rogue wolf, said Mark's boss, would have to be figured out quickly. Mark hung up, then said, "Why, thanks, boss, my son and I are fine."

Molly was not. "Who in the hell cares about the governor's stupid deer opener?" she said, waving a butcher knife in the air. "Tell these guys to jump in a lake! You got shot at for crying out loud!"

Mark almost put his arms around her, then thought better of it. "This isn't okay!" she shot. BJ had seen a few of these discussions before and always marveled at how his mother got madder when his father got calmer.

"It is possible that someone was shooting, and…" Mark held up his hand to keep Molly from interrupting (or possibly stabbing) him, "that the bullet hit our truck by accident. Sometimes bullets do fly up there, and we don't have anything more than that, so we're stuck. At the moment, all I can do is deal with this wolf. I've got the cameras out and a couple of good informants keeping an eye out for me." Molly dropped the knife into the sink and stomped outside into the garden, where the air was soon filled with flying weeds.

When BJ came into the kitchen the following morning, he discovered a Tupperware container loaded with cookies and a pink sticky note that said "Elmer." He picked it up and headed outside. Charley was under the bird feeder and raised one index finger in greeting. At the base of the driveway, BJ paused to listen to a very loud and very proud robin singing from somewhere high in the canopy. Across the road, a pair of red squirrels spiraled up, then down, then up again in a game of tag on an old poplar snag. The sky was half a dozen shades of blue, and the air was crisp and clear, somewhere in the forties. BJ inhaled a big breath, appreciating the temporary absence of mosquitoes. He tried to picture the village and the locations of the lodges. By his reckoning, he was standing close to where the arrow-maker had been carving shafts. Who would be standing here in another five hundred years, he wondered? BJ decided he would go into the cave today. It was time.

He began to head towards Elmer's and was immediately distracted by a meandering set of deer tracks in the sand and gravel. Back and forth, down the middle of the road, they moved. These tracks left more prints than BJ expected, and this was confusing to him. Normally, a walking deer will register a simple diagonal pattern: front left/rear left, then further up, front right/rear right, and so on. BJ knew just enough about deer tracks to realize that this animal was moving differently, but he didn't know why. The trail made it look like there were two animals, but he was fairly certain it was just one. He followed along, puzzling at this until they ended at a pair of black sneakers. BJ looked up at Elmer, who pursed his lips at the ground. "That's GW." Gichie Waashkesh! It was the nickname Elmer had given a very large and mature buck. This particular buck had been spotted by locals a handful of times, but he always managed to slip around hunters in the fall, melting into the woods like a ghost. GW had become a legend in the area, and here he was, strolling down the middle of Man Gun Road like he owned the place. Maybe he did.

"So, why does he walk that way?" said BJ.

"You gotta watch and learn to figure that out," said Elmer. BJ flinched at the expression, the one used by the strange man. "I was finishing my thanksgiving prayers," continued Elmer, "when he walked by this morning. Hi, Charley."

Charley had arrived without a sound. "Hi!" she chirped.

"Any new freckles this week?"

"Fourteen more!" she beamed.

BJ turned to Charley. "These are GW's tracks!"

"Yeah, he hangs out by the Cannonball Rock sometimes."

BJ felt his face go slack. For all he knew, Charley had been riding on the deer's back and feeding him by hand. He turned back to Elmer. "Did you say 'thanksgiving prayer'?"

"That's what I call it. It's the way I like to pray every morning. Organized religions do similar stuff."

"Do you have turkey every day?" asked Charley.

Elmer chuckled. "No, no, not that kind of thanksgiving. It just means being thankful for everything around you—the earth, the sky, the living things, and my friends. It's one of the prayers I was taught, and it makes me feel good. It's probably what brought GW by this morning." The kids frowned at him. "When you are in a thankful or

97

prayerful mood," Elmer explained, "the birds and the animals and even the plants respond to you differently. Haven't you ever noticed that? When you take a walk in the woods and are in a bad mood or if you are thinking about too many things, all the critters disappear, and the birds get nervous, but when you are happy or calm, they like to be around you, and you see more of them."

BJ rubbed his chin. "I've never thought about it before."

"I'm always happy," offered Charley.

"Sure makes me want to be around you!" said Elmer.

Charley blushed.

BJ jerked his thumb at his sister. "The birds land on her all the time."

"That doesn't surprise me."

Mark's truck drove up the road and stopped to greet them.

"Mauer hit for the cycle," said Elmer.

"Huh?"

"What about his knees?" said Charley, causing everyone to stop and stare at her. She shrugged. "Mom says he wrecked his knees playing catcher."

Elmer rubbed his chin. "He could play first, I suppose. Makademashkikiwaaboo is hot," he said to Mark.

"Is that coffee?"

"Black medicine water, yeah."

"Best word I've ever heard for it." It looked to BJ like his father was about to say no but then changed his mind. "Sure," said Mark, "that's nice of you."

They weaved through a rusted dishwasher, a faded blue car on cinder blocks, then past a fire pit to the back door, which opened directly into a medium-sized kitchen with a yellow vinyl floor and a recently refinished oak table. Elmer poured two cups of coffee from the pot, heated up more water, and made hot chocolate for BJ and Charley. They sat around the table with the Tupperware of cookies in the middle and visited about family and tradition and history.

Elmer had been a high school history teacher before retiring and buying the house from his elderly uncle. He had grown up on the reservation and was one of the few fluent speakers of Ojibwe. "Most of my generation were raised by parents who went to the boarding schools and had their language beaten out of them," he said simply, then reached for a cookie. "Nice and dark! I like whole wheat!" BJ and his father exchanged a worried glance just as they heard a "crunch!" Elmer winced and pulled a small white chip. He curled his lip at the kids. A small corner of his front left incisor was missing. BJ was appalled. His mother's cooking had certainly done a lot of damage over the years, but, to his knowledge, it had never broken any teeth.

"Oh my God," said Mark, putting his hand to his forehead.

Elmer set the white chip on the table. "I won't tell if you don't." He took a sip of coffee. "Any news on that bullet through your window?"

"Accident," said Mark, holding quote fingers in the air. "I don't suppose you've heard anything from folks up on the rez?"

"There's always someone shooting something on ceded lands."

"What seeds did they plant?" Charley.

"Trauma trees and Forgetful flowers," shot Elmer. He winked at her, then said, "C-e-d-e-d means 'forced to give away,' which was what the tribes here had to do when the colonizers came and made them sign treaties." Charley pursed her lips. "Anyway," Elmer continued, "someone's been poaching deer around there as well. Couple of abandoned places got burned, but that's not terribly unusual."

"I'm getting calls from St. Paul."

"You're stuck neatly in the middle, aren't you?"

"The wolf kills are one thing—"

"What makes you think it's a wolf?"

"I've seen signs, and one's been spotted near the kill sites—"

"But no one's seen him do the killing?"

"No, not yet. Maybe the SD cards will show something," said Mark, tapping his shirt pocket. He lifted up the cookie he had been softening in his coffee, but it broke off halfway to his mouth. He caught the piece with his left hand and ate it. "Anyway, the cabin break-ins might end up causing more trouble than the wolf."

"Alleged wolf," Elmer corrected.

"There are some expensive cabins across the road, and if those get vandalized, I'm going to sure hear about it."

"You know how that land got settled by white folks?" asked Elmer.

Mark shook his head.

"Larry Sourmeister's grandfather swindled it from my great-grandfather."

"How?"

"I'll tell you another time." But Charley was full of questions for Elmer, and he was coaxed into sharing more about himself. He had ancestors on both sides of the border, and his childhood was "complicated." He talked about the logging of the late 1800s and early 1900s and how that was a particularly difficult time for the tribe. "They came in and mowed down the forests. Some built dams that flooded ricing areas and burial sites." BJ felt a knot form in his stomach, knowing that the descendants of Running Wolf, Stalking Bear, and the others were the ones who had to live through this time. He couldn't imagine what that must have been like for them.

"But not all the loggers were bad, and not *all* the trees got cut down," said Elmer. "There are a few grandfather pines left if you know where to look."

BJ and Charley exchanged a glance.

"So, although the ancestors moved with the seasons, they spent a lot of time along these shores." Elmer waved a hand, "For all we know, they were right here in this yard!"

"Oh, they were," said Charley, and she proceeded to describe the village, people, trees and animals exactly as BJ had told her.

BJ stood abruptly. "Time to go, Charley!"

"Now?" she said.

"We were going to head up the creek, right, Charley?"

"Don't forget your paddle!" said Elmer.

"What do you mean?" said BJ.

"Never mind," said Mark, catching the joke. "Thanks for the coffee, Elmer."

Back in the Maki yard, BJ asked Charley to wait while he and Mark looked at the images from the trail cameras. Inside, they sat down in front of a little desk in the living room, and Mark pulled a white envelope out of his pocket and opened it. Two SD cards clattered onto the desktop. Mark inserted one of them into the back of the computer and waited for the images to load. There were 133 photos from the previous four days, most of them multiples of the same animal or bird: A pileated woodpecker pounding the base of a dead poplar. A raccoon meandering by. A fox. The rear feet of a deer in midair, running past the camera. Mark pulled the card out. "No wolves there." He inserted the second card and waited.

"Where's that camera located?" asked BJ.

"Same trail, but higher on the tree. Sometimes, I'll place one aimed at the first camera in case someone tries to tamper with it. No one messed with it, so I don't expect we'll see much."

A series of video clips popped up on the screen and, one by one, Mark clicked on them for review. The clips of the raccoon and fox were fun to watch. Each animal weaved back and forth across the trail, sniffing here and, in the case of the fox, peeing there. The deer charged through at full tilt, leaping past the camera. A large doe. Mark double-clicked on the final clip and waited. The first ten seconds were of the pileated woodpecker, working on the base of the poplar tree, sending large white chips down to the forest floor. The bird straightened, then stood still a moment before flying off. Seconds later, the head of a large dark wolf appeared at the bottom of the screen.

"There he is!" pointed BJ. Mark leaned in close to the computer. The rest of the animal appeared, moving towards the camera at a slow trot.

"He's heading down the trail," said Mark in a low voice, "Why don't we have a picture of him? He—" The wolf had stopped and stood stone-still.

"What's he doing?" said BJ.

"He's thinking." Mark had said what BJ was afraid to express. This animal was definitely looking at the first trail camera and trying to make a decision. After a full minute, he did something that left BJ and Mark speechless. The wolf veered off course, looping *behind* the camera through a tangle of heavy and burdensome brush, then hopped back onto the trail and continued on, out of sight. Mark replayed the bit again, then a third time. There was absolutely no doubt as to what they were seeing: the wolf saw the camera and avoided it. It was purposeful. And it was intelligent. Mark pulled out the SD card and sat in silence.

"Dad," said BJ, "do you think that's your wolf?"

Mark dropped the SD cards back into the envelope, folded it, and put it in his shirt pocket. "I don't know, BJ. But if he is, I don't think anyone's going to catch him, including me."

Chapter Seventeen

Charley sat in the moss and pulled from her pink backpack enough supplies for what looked like a three-week trip: a hairbrush, a small doll, two books, an apple, a pear, a box of graham crackers, some crayons, a notebook, and a kit for making beaded necklaces. "Charley," said BJ, "what the heck are you going to do with all that stuff?"

She handed him a beige hemp bag. "Here. It's got a watch, your compass, and a Honeycrisp apple."

"Thanks, Charley," he said, accepting the bag. He climbed up to the cave entrance and slipped through the hole. Inside, he set down the bag and faced the wall. He had made one trip, so there were three left. The last time he was here, he had placed his hand on the red hand mark and wished to see the maker. Nervous, he procrastinated by studying the wall, noting a number of paintings he had not perceived before: a man with a tomahawk facing off against another with a knife. A bird shape… thunderbird-like. Below that, a giant, dark shape with long fingers, pointed toes, and slits for eyes, standing in what looked like a deep hole. BJ felt a shiver run through him. Windigo. BJ returned to the red hand. "Who are you?" he whispered.

Find the warrior.

BJ took a breath and placed his right hand over the image. He closed his eyes and thought of going back in time. Precisely nothing happened. At least nothing that BJ noticed. He cracked open an eye and looked at what seemed to be an unchanged wall. *Better make sure,* he thought, and climbed out of the hole to see a gray sky, buzzing mosquitoes, and his sister lying on her belly, humming and coloring.

BJ climbed back down. Why had nothing happened? The terrible thought that he might have imagined it all struck him, and he felt the knot form in his stomach. Could the whole thing have been a hallucination? Could he have fallen asleep in the cave and dreamed the whole thing? That would explain the short passage of time from Charley's point of view. No. It was real. It had to be. He was sure of it. Mostly, anyway. He returned to the handprint and tried to recall exactly what he had done the first time. He had wished he could meet the maker. That was it. BJ put his hands up again and tried to repeat the thought.

Still nothing.

He tried again, this time closing his eyes. Nothing. BJ stepped away from the wall and put his hands on his hips. What was he doing wrong?

BJ tried singing the words out loud, shouting, dancing, and even rapping with no results. Then, boiling with frustration, he dropped his drawers, put his rear end on the wall, and hollered, "I WANT TO GO BACK!!!"

Charley yelled from outside. He couldn't hear what she'd said, but he assumed it was something like, "What's going on in there?" "Nothing!" he shouted back, then sat down on the floor in a heap, grabbed his hair, and almost started pulling. A clear spot on the wall showed where his naked butt had pressed against the dusty rock. It was a ridiculous image among the others. *Great White Butt,* thought BJ. *There's a name.* BJ allowed a grin at the idiocy of the image. His naked butt. His... wait! BJ looked at his shorts and T-shirt, then at the wall. Naked. He had been naked when he had gone back in time. Could that be it?

BJ undressed and stood before the hand, exposed and bare. "Okay." He put his hands back on the wall. "Birthday suit! One last—" The ground shook before he could finish his sentence. The images on the wall blurred, and some of them disappeared. When the ground was still again, BJ stepped back. The hand was gone, along with half of the drawings. Lying in the corner of the room, where he had just placed the hemp bag and his clothes, was the crumpled form of a breechcloth. BJ put it on in a flash and climbed through the hole. There was the great white pine, its thick, needled branches feathering up and down in the breeze like a giant set of lungs. A solitary raven was calling from near the top. Somewhere on the other side of the river, the sound of kid's voices could be heard.

In a few leaps, BJ was on the ground and running in their direction.

It was fifty paces to the edge of the river, then nine to get across and onto the Tabletop. The red squirrel chattered, and the blue jay screeched as he hurried down the path to where he thought the kids would be. A log was lying across the path. Where had the kids gone? Their voices had disappeared. Did they return to camp? BJ shrugged and stepped over the log.

And that is how he ended up dangling from a rope by one ankle. The forest exploded in laughter. Upside-down faces appeared all around and approached as BJ flailed and squawked like a snared grouse. Stalking Bear put his hands on BJ's cheeks, steadying him, then stood, nearly touching noses. "Didn't you see the log?"

"Aaarrgh!"

A skinny girl with sharp features helped Stalking Bear lower BJ to the ground, one supporting his head while the other worked at the rope with a stone knife. Right side up once more, the blood rushed from BJ's head, and he toppled over onto the ground. The kids gathered around him, still chuckling, and helped him to sit up. After a few moments, the world stopped spinning, and BJ could take stock of the kids around him. In addition to Stalking Bear and the sharp-featured thin girl, there was a round-faced boy with a droop to his left eye, and Shines Bright, who had originally helped BJ with the

105

breechcloth. All seemed to be waiting to see how BJ would react to the prank. This many wide eyes staring at BJ struck him as amusing and he smiled. The others joined him, and soon the whole forest was echoing with their laughter. This went on so long, the kids fell to the ground around BJ, holding their sides. BJ found himself laughing at their laughing, and they became stuck in an endless loop of arms, legs, and tears. They wrestled and crawled over each other, with BJ somewhere in the middle. In the midst of this, the youngest boy with the round face farted violently.

Stalking Bear stood and, with a fake air of ceremony, said, "The spirits have spoken to me in a dream. Your name will now be 'Little Fart'!" The group cracked up, but the round-faced boy fell back, groaning, his hands over his face. BJ suspected it would be a long time before he could rid himself of the nickname.

Out of breath, holding their aching stomachs, they lay on their backs beneath a patchwork of branches, leaves, and sky. Within five minutes, maybe fifteen—BJ couldn't tell—the wild sounds of the forest resumed. Chickadees picked and pecked their way around tree trunks. Ravens rattled. Squirrels leaped from branch to branch. The passage of white marshmallow clouds beyond the canopy made the trees appear to move. BJ closed his eyes and wished his sister could be there to experience it with him. How long would he stay this time?

"Grandfather Running Wolf has not told us your name," said Stalking Bear.

"My name is Bjorn, but most people call me BJ."

"Beejay?" said Shines Bright.

"Buh-jay?" said the girl with the sharp features.

"Ble....ble," said Little Fart.

"BJ. BJ." He repeated it slowly for them. He could still hear himself speaking Ojibwe, or at least he heard Ojibwe overlapping with his words. But this didn't happen when he said his name. BJ was just BJ. There wouldn't be a translation for his name, of course.

They practiced a few times, then Little Fart said, "You smell."

"At least my name's not Little Fart," BJ shot back.

They laughed hard, and BJ felt a twinge of guilt for teasing the boy and made a mental note to call the boy by his proper name.

"What is your clan?" asked Shines Bright.

"The Broken Penis Clan," said the girl, causing another explosion of laughter.

"OH MY GOD!" yelled BJ, falling back into the moss just like Little Fart. Did everyone in the village know he was circumcised? Once everyone recovered, the questions resumed:

"Are you sick?"

"I don't think so."

"You look sick."

"What do you mean?"

"You are too pale above the knees and elbows," said Little Fart, rubbing BJ's arm. "Maybe you have been bleeding?"

BJ laughed. His tan lines must, indeed, look very strange. "I haven't been bleeding. All the people in my, um, tribe are like that."

They told BJ about themselves. Stalking Bear said that he was of the Otter clan. The girl with the sharp features said her name was Runs Swiftly and that she was of the Loon clan. Shines Bright was of the Bear clan. Little Fart's name was really Little Otter of the Otter clan. BJ studied the handsome features of Stalking Bear as he lay relaxed on the ground. Would he be the one to make the red marks? He was young but already a defender of the village, having pursued the two invaders alongside Running Wolf and the others. BJ couldn't imagine doing anything so brave and dangerous at his age.

Stalking Bear motioned into the trees at a small furry red form on a branch. "Morning Flower is coming to join us."

BJ looked up. "Is that Morning Flower?"

Stalking Bear turned his head sideways and eyed BJ. "No," he said slowly. "That is a squirrel. Morning Flower is over there." He indicated behind them.

BJ sat up. The girl with the big brown eyes had arrived, barefoot, her hair in a messy ponytail. She sat cross-legged and batted away Stalking Bear's hand as he reached out to poke her in the ribs. She grinned at BJ, and he completely forgot what he was about to say.

A flake from the pinecone the squirrel was eating landed on BJ's head, and he remembered his question for Stalking Bear. "How did you know she was coming?"

"The squirrel told me."

BJ was reminded of Elmer, who was prone to such answers. Short and not to the point, as far as he could tell. There was always something beneath the explanation as if BJ was presented with a trowel and told to dig under the surface for an answer.

Shines Bright said, "Do you watch the birds and animals where you live?"

"Well, I guess so," said BJ.

"Maybe there are no Sacred Places where he lives?" said Little Fart.

Shines Bright cocked an eyebrow at the youngster. "There are Sacred Places everywhere."

BJ's memory clicked. "A Sacred Place? Like in the story of the boy and Shadow Walker?"

"Yes," said Shines Bright. "A Sacred Place is somewhere to be alone and silent, where you can learn about yourself and about the world."

It sounded like a yoga studio to BJ. "So, do you all have Sacred Places?"

They nodded. "Mine is a ten-minute walk to the east," said Runs Swiftly with a jut of her chin.

"Mine is over that hill," said Shines Bright, pursing his lips.

"I was at mine just now," said Little Fart. "I saw the fox come by with a mouse in his mouth."

"Ha!" said Stalking Bear. "At least you were awake!"

The others laughed, and Runs Swiftly explained to BJ, "He fell asleep at his Sacred Place recently and woke up with a bear next to him. He practically peed on himself!"

"No, I didn't!"

"That was a good medicine sign." Shines Bright nodded.

"A sign he should stay awake!" quipped Stalking Bear.

More laughter.

"You're lucky you didn't get eaten by a Windigo," shot Runs Swiftly.

"DON'T SAY THAT!" yelled every other kid in the group, and suddenly, the atmosphere went from playful to cold and serious. At length, their smiles returned, and they resumed their chatting. BJ enjoyed watching them laugh and tease each other. It was a comfortable group of kids, and they had accepted him with ease, which was surprising considering how different BJ was. Charley would definitely be in her element. The talk of Sacred Places inspired them to share stories, and they told of the things they had seen, everything from moose to caribou, bear, and wolf. They described dozens of smaller animals that BJ barely knew about, like weasels and fishers and shrews. Some of the kids had seen caribou giving birth. Stalking Bear once saw a wolf chase down a rabbit right at his feet. They argued which animal was the hardest to hunt or to stalk.

BJ listened, feeling more ignorant by the minute. Sure, he had hunted, fished, and camped ever since he could remember, and he had spent a fair amount of time in the woods behind his home. But he had never come close to seeing the things that these kids spoke of so casually. Were there just not as many animals around in the modern world? Did the ancient Indians have special abilities that allowed them to see so much?

Little Otter said he was hungry, prompting Morning Flower to motion to the east. "There are some berries on the hill that are ripe." This sounded good, so they headed towards the river. Once across, they walked up a slope covered with yellow lady slippers and large-flowered trillium and wild ginger until they reached a thicket of Juneberry trees whose branches were sagging with plump, dark fruit. Runs Swiftly and Little Otter grabbed handfuls of berries and began stuffing their faces. Stalking Bear circled the area, studying the ground. Shines Bright did not pick berries but instead combed his fingers through the leaves, inspecting, almost caressing them.

"He is giving thanks," Morning Flower explained to BJ. "Shines Bright is the best at ceremony and tradition. I think he will be a shaman when he is older."

Runs Swiftly and Little Fart, their mouths packed with berries, dark juice streaming down their chins, paused, looking sheepish.

Shines Bright put a berry in his mouth but didn't chew right away. Instead, he held it on his tongue, then moved it around in his mouth thoughtfully before swallowing. BJ glanced at a fat, shiny clump of berries and felt his mouth water instantly. He plucked a few and turned to Shines Bright. "Who do you give thanks to?"

"The bush is fulfilling its original instructions by growing strong and giving us fruit, so I thank it directly."

BJ held his hand, cupped, in front of him and studied the berries for a moment, then popped them in his mouth. The back of his mouth watered even more, and it was near torture not to bite down right away. Finally, he allowed himself to do so and moved the mealy contents over his tongue. Tart, but not as much as a blueberry. He had eaten Juneberries before, but this one was… something special. *Thanks!* he thought and reached up for more.

"Why do you walk funny?" Little Fart was staring at him with a purple-and-red streaked chin.

"What do you mean, Little Otter?"

The boy looked pleased at BJ's use of his proper name. "I mean that you are very loud." BJ squirmed. "All the animals will hear you." It felt odd to be lectured to by a little boy. Then again, it wasn't that different from being told off by Charley.

Stalking Bear said, "I noticed that, too. Is that the way people walk in your tribe?"

BJ was perplexed. Didn't everybody walk the same? Did people from different cultures have different ways of moving?

"You see," explained Stalking Bear, "you bang your heels down on the earth when you walk, and that is how you make so much noise. You cannot feel the ground, and you end up breaking branches and pounding Mother Earth in the face like a drum. All the birds can hear you coming. They will tell everybody else in the forest."

BJ's head was positively spinning. The birds will tell everybody? What were they talking about?

Runs Swiftly cut in, "Enough about BJ's clumsiness. Let's go play a game."

"How about the doll-taking game?" suggested Shines Bright.

Runs Swiftly motioned at BJ. "What do we do with Thunder Walker of the Broken Penis clan?" This time BJ joined in with the laughter because what else could he do? Runs Swiftly was straight-up hilarious.

"He'll probably be fine," said Stalking Bear, finally.

BJ didn't like the way this sounded. Probably be fine? What did he mean by "probably"? Stalking Bear explained: "Don't worry. Nobody's been killed playing this game in a long time."

Chapter Eighteen

They walked west. After a while, Morning Flower said to BJ, "No one has died playing this game. Stalking Bear is a jokester, have you noticed?" He had, but he had also noticed that they were not all that far away from the one and only person he had seen die—with an arrow in his back—so her words were not entirely reassuring. They came to a section of the forest with a mixture of pine, mountain maple, birch, spruce, and fir. Bracken and ostrich ferns covered the ground in thick patches of lime green, two or three feet high in places. Elsewhere, the trees and shrubs grew close enough, so there was not a good line of sight for more than fifteen yards, but it was not so tight that it couldn't be navigated. It was, BJ thought, a perfect place to play hide and seek.

Stalking Bear pushed the bangs from his eyes. "What should the teams be?" After some discussion, Runs Swiftly and Shines Bright agreed to be Chiefs and pick players for their teams. Stalking Bear and Morning Flower were quickly chosen. BJ and Little Otter waited expectantly.

Runs Swiftly ran her eyes up and down BJ with what looked like an expression of pity. "He is loud." BJ suddenly felt transported back to fourth grade and waiting to be picked for kickball. He was never the first one to be chosen.

"We will take him," said Morning Flower, defiantly. Technically, it had been Stalking Bear's choice, but nobody objected, and BJ felt a surge of fondness towards her for standing up for him. He had no idea what the game was about, but it felt good to have a defender.

The others were left with Little Otter, so the teams were set. "Go get your dolls," said Shines Bright. "I'll explain the rules to BJ." Runs Swiftly and Morning Flower took off, scanning the ground and stopping every now and then to pick something up. The rules were like this: On either side of the river was a "territory," which belonged to a team. Dolls were to be placed somewhere at the rear of each territory. The goal was for the players of the opposite team to sneak across the river, steal the doll, and return to their own side.

It was a familiar game to BJ. "This is just like Capture the Flag! What happens if you get caught?"

Shines Bright shook his head. "No catching in this game. If you are seen, then you have to go back to your side and start over."

"Seen?" said BJ in disbelief. "Only seen?"

They nodded.

BJ's heart sank. How on earth was he going to play that game? He would get caught right away! Heck, half the time they played Capture the Flag at school, everybody just lined up on the football field and ran back and forth across the fifty-yard line. The team with the fastest players usually won. This was going to be impossible. He could hardly see the point.

Runs Swiftly and Morning Flower returned, each carrying a little figure about ten inches in height made from knotted grass and birch bark. Shines Bright finished explaining the rules of the game to BJ, then pointed out the boundaries: to the north, a small hill with exposed granite on one side and to the south, a large red pine. The river ran past each of these, serving as the natural dividing line. BJ figured that they were about 100 yards apart. The width of the playing area was about twice that. One football field by two. A lot of room.

Shines Bright spoke to Runs Swiftly: "Go to your side and put your doll about this high." He held his hand even with his chest.

"Remember to make it visible. Shout out when you are ready." He turned to BJ and Morning Flower. "Let's go."

They swept from the scene like deer. Shines Bright and Morning Flower ran ahead, twisting, bending, and turning through the trees and brush as easily as water rolls over the ground. But they weren't sprinting. It was more of an easy lope, landing on the balls of their feet, which made them look bow-legged. As they ran, they reached out to move the branches that would bend and ducked around those that wouldn't, and BJ didn't hear a single snap or crack.

They reached a low, wet area full of cattails and speckled alder, where the spring peepers and western chorus frogs had been singing loudly. "I'll get the clay," said Morning Flower, speeding off. Shines Bright dropped an armful of leaves, bark, and branches that he had managed to gather as they moved. He waded into the shallow, muddy water, reached down, pulled up a large clump of mud, and brought it back to BJ. Morning Flower had returned, and her hands were full of thick, gray clay. She and Shines Bright stood face to face and began to paint each other all over, like circus performers preparing for an act. Noses, chins, shoulders, and elbows were covered with mud, while the clay was used on their cheeks, neck, and eyes. Then, dipping a pinecone into the mud, each took turns rolling it over the other's face and neck, creating a mottled and dappled effect. After this, a few large grass blades were held over bare skin and covered with either clay or mud. When removed, an image of grass was left, like a tattoo.

Finally, they took turns tossing dirt and pine needles all over each other, eyes and mouth closed tightly. Morning Flower spat out some dust and flashed a white grin at BJ. "Your turn!"

With four hands working on him, it took no time at all. They stood back and surveyed each other: three mud-and-clay-covered kids, so well camouflaged that they looked positively blurry when standing near any foliage. Morning Flower held the doll up to one of the many oval-shaped woodpecker holes in a nearby snag. "Here?"

Shines Bright nodded.

She placed it into one of the holes as a loud "Whoop!" sounded from near the river. Shines Bright answered it in kind, and the game was on. "You watch the middle and don't let anyone through," he said to BJ. "I'll go north, and Morning Flower, you go south!"

They were off once again, BJ following the other two, full of nerves and excitement, hoping that he would do well for his team, but knowing that Runs Swiftly was right in her criticisms of him: he *was* loud and felt like a fish out of water around the others, who seemed to move so effortlessly through the brush. He was also still not used to running through the woods barefoot and so kept his head down to watch for roots or rocks and—BAM!—BJ's nose crunched as he plowed into the side of a red pine. He staggered, head filling with bright lights and eyes filling with tears. BJ reached for his nose and found some blood on his upper lip but not much. Morning Flower and Shines Bright had already veered to the left and right, respectively, and had likely not noticed. BJ continued on towards the river, more slowly and with his head up.

A whisky jack hopped from branch to branch. A gust of wind blew across the ground, making the ferns bend in a wave, but there was no other movement. The river rushed and gushed, making it hard to hear any soft noises. Above, the sky grew dark, the air was heavy, and a grumble of thunder sounded somewhere in the distance. For a fleeting moment, BJ wondered if they shouldn't go inside to play but then nearly dope-slapped himself. There was no "inside." What do you do when there is no inside? You make do.

BJ stretched his eyes and ears for anything unusual, his heart beating in slow, heavy thumps. A blue jay swooped in, landing near the whisky jack with a loud "CAW!" drawing BJ's attention. BJ scanned the forest again. Nothing. For all he knew, he was the only person for a hundred miles. But he recalled the mistake he had made back in the village while waiting for Running Wolf to exit the council lodge. He had thought himself alone then, too. The other kids had to be here somewhere. If he sat still long enough, BJ figured he would catch someone trying to sneak into his territory sooner or later. That would show everyone—especially Runs Swiftly—that he was not so clumsy. After all, he had played Capture the Flag since he could remember and was very good at it. All he had to do was sit still and wait.

So, he slid down among the ferns and leaned his back against a log. A few dark-eyed juncos twittered from somewhere nearby and then flew up into the overhanging branches. The blue jay flew over his head and disappeared behind him, cawing away. Somewhere in a thicket, a winter wren babbled like a little feathered fountain. As usual, the sound of the river made BJ feel relaxed and drowsy, and he felt like he was sinking into the ground. To stay awake, he counted the red spots clustered like bunches of eggs on the back of a fern, but the scent of warm pine needles in the afternoon made him want to close his eyes, and a few times, he jerked as if he had fallen asleep. He lifted his head and looked around for movement and saw nothing. Had they left? Would they have done that? How long had he been waiting here? BJ was considering giving up and heading back to the village when the voice of Morning Flower cried out from some thirty yards to BJ's left: "I see you Little Otter!" BJ's jaw dropped when, no more than four paces *behind* him, Little Otter stood and walked back towards the river.

"Your head is visible at thirty paces," said Little Otter without looking at BJ. "You are moving too much."

BJ's shoulders sagged. Not only had he let an opposing player get past him, but that player had seen him the whole time. As he had feared, he was the weak link on his team. BJ glanced towards Little Otter, but he had already melted into the surroundings without a trace. Deciding the best course of action was to lie still and try not to screw anything up, BJ slid low to the ground near a smooth outcropping of rock about the length of his body and watched a line of ants moving across the granite. Thunder sounded again in the distance, but the sky above them was filled with big, cottony, cumulous clouds. BJ's mind wandered again, this time to his father and rogue wolves and bears, and he wondered if his dad would be in trouble with his boss if he didn't do something about them. Although, BJ mused, he couldn't imagine what his dad was supposed to do.

"CAW!" yelled the blue jay from somewhere above. A few pinecone scales floated down onto BJ's shoulders. A ruffed grouse drummed his wings, sounding like a tractor trying to start.

BJ fidgeted. He didn't think he'd ever sat still for so long and was tempted to think that this time they really had left him, but he forced himself to remain there and contented himself with watching ants crawl across the granite. One was struggling to drag a much larger, winged insect over a lip in the rock, falling, then catching himself half a dozen times in a row. BJ was mesmerized by the effort. After the ant finally made it up and over the edge, he dragged his supper into a crack near the top of the rock. BJ watched him disappear in admiration, then blinked and remembered to look around. Runs Swiftly was standing tall across the river and holding his team's doll high in the air. She whooped in triumph as their eyes met.

The others had won.

Shines Bright materialized not far from her, holding Runs Swiftly's doll. He had nearly made it back to his territory, but since she had crossed the river first, it was they who had earned the victory. Morning Flower appeared on the far bank, and Little Otter stood not far from BJ, who, once again, was flabbergasted at the number of people that seemed to appear out of nowhere.

"Good game!" smiled Shines Bright.

Stalking Bear strode past BJ. "Yes, very close! Little Fart," he admonished, "you let whisky jack follow you again."

BJ stood and took a step forward to join them, then fell flat on his face. Stalking Bear instantly doubled over in laughter, almost losing his balance.

"Did you do that?" said Shines Bright to Stalking Bear.

BJ tried to stand up and found a tiny piece of cordage wrapped around his left ankle, linking him to a nearby sapling. This is what had tripped him. "Oh My GOD!" shouted BJ to the sky. "I am, like, blind *and* deaf!"

"No," said Stalking Bear, laughing and helping BJ to his feet, "but you are too busy watching ants." Another roll of thunder and a gust of wind shook the leaves and announced the storm's approach. They gathered by the river and took turns trying to make BJ feel better about having another joke played on him.

Shines Bright put his hand on BJ's shoulder and said, "He has done that to all of us."

"I nearly sat on him at my Sacred Place," admitted Runs Swiftly.

Little Otter added, "He took my bow from beside me when I was hunting once."

Morning Flower sat in the water and splashed her arms, then her face. "Do you know how he got his name?" she asked BJ. "He snuck up and touched a bear that was rubbing against a tree."

BJ's eyes widened. "Really?"

They all smiled knowingly, and Stalking Bear nodded proudly. There was a PLOP, PLOP of the first raindrops falling around them. "Here it comes," said Stalking Bear, and not ten seconds later, they were standing in a downpour. But since there was no place to run and since they were all covered with mud and clay, they ignored it. Instead, they sat at the edge of the river and washed off.

Shines Bright splashed himself with creek water and indicated Stalking Bear. "He is one of the best stalkers in the village, even among the adults. He will probably be a scout when he is older."

BJ thought about Stalking Bear's role in defending the village earlier and looked at the boy with a new level of appreciation. Then he thought about the story of Shadow Walker. "What," he shouted over the sound of the rain and river, "is a scout?"

Shines Bright gave BJ a puzzled expression. "You do not have scouts in your tribe? How do you know if there is an enemy nearby?"

Enemies? BJ considered the term. Did he mean foreign invaders? Thieves? Murderers? How about arsonists and poachers?

Stalking Bear finished rubbing the mud from his face. "How do you know where to set up your camp or where the good hunting is? This is what scouts do: they have to go out far into the wilderness and live by themselves and survive. They must read the signs of the earth and know if there are enemies nearby. They must gather information and bring it back to the village to keep the people safe. Sometimes, scouts must fight. They are protectors. It is an honorable position among our people."

The others nodded. It was a succinct definition, and the term "scout" made sense in this context. In the modern world, though, there was no such position. Or was there? There was a Boy Scout troop in Grand Marais. They were supposed to be helpful to people. Policemen? Firemen? Conservation officers. It seemed to BJ that Shadow Walker and possibly the Red Hand Warrior guy must be scouts. "How do you teach someone to become a scout?" he asked.

Shines Bright put his hands on his hips. "What do you mean 'teach'?"

BJ was not sure how to respond. They had to know about teaching. Surely every culture does some teaching. He gave his best explanation of how teachers worked in the modern world. The kids listened, looking confused, but BJ plowed on. "So," he summarized, "when you need to know something, the teacher can explain it to you."

The others were silent for what seemed like a long time. Finally, Shines Bright said, "You have special places to learn?" BJ nodded. "Do you stop learning when you leave those places?"

"Well, yes," said BJ, but then thought better of it. "I mean, no, of course you don't. But that's where most of our learning—" He paused again, suddenly unsure of himself.

"So," said Stalking Bear, "the teachers talk, and you listen?"

BJ nodded.

Runs Swiftly folded her arms and almost glared at BJ. "How do you learn something if they just tell you?"

"Just like that," said BJ. Why didn't they get it? He tried once more. "They explain something to you, and then you have learned it. That's what a teacher does." The obvious confusion on their faces was beginning to frustrate BJ. The storm was passing over them now, and rays of light were shooting beneath the dark clouds. A rainbow began to form out over the lake, and they paused to look at it.

"Beejay," said Shines Bright cautiously, "if somebody has explained something to you, you cannot have learned it. You need to earn the knowledge. You can only do that yourself."

"Well, sometimes an elder can help," cautioned Stalking Bear, "but Shines Bright is correct: our best teachers are the animals, the plants, the wind. The earth, really. You need to pay attention and learn."

That evening around the fire, Running Wolf queried them all about the game, asking about the clouds, the wind direction, the plants, the trees, and even about the tracks and animal signs. The elder grandmother was there, too, a blanket over her shoulders, and so was Bent Nose, the man with the limp, who listened with a quiet intensity. BJ listened to his friends give lengthy answers to most of the questions asked of them. Then Running Wolf asked about the birds, at first wanting to know what they had seen and how many. He asked about their behavior, wondering which direction they were flying and where they were looking. It sounded to BJ like Running Wolf was trying to solve a mystery about the birds himself and that he was interested in finding out what the kids knew. There was much discussion, and, once again, BJ found himself feeling left out. He kind of hoped Running Wolf would ask about ants.

"Why did the juncos go up into the trees just then?" asked Running Wolf. "Have you ever seen that happen before?" The more questions he asked, the slower and less sure the responses were, until the kids began to look at each other for support. Running Wolf smiled at BJ. "I hear that you were a victim of one of Stalking Bear's tricks." There were giggles around the fire.

Little Otter lay with his head in Morning Flower's lap. She caressed his hair with one hand like an older sister or a mother. BJ's eyes wandered up to hers and saw that they were looking back at him. He looked away, embarrassed at being caught staring at her.

"Stalking Bear," prompted Running Wolf, "maybe BJ would like to see your Sacred Place tomorrow." BJ looked towards Stalking Bear for a reaction but saw none. They sat in silence, listening to the fire crackle and the occasional hum of a mosquito. The stars made their evening appearance in twos, threes, and then, it seemed, by the thousands, shining from one end of the sky to the other in a display so magnificent that BJ completely forgot where he was and who he was with. He felt as if he were in the cosmos, floating among the stars and the planets.

"They are a Great Mystery," said Running Wolf, looking skyward. "The stars are beautiful, aren't they? They hold many of our stories and help us to live well. They are fulfilling their original instructions. I am thankful for them."

There were some nods and grunts around the fire. Afterward, BJ followed Running Wolf to his wigwam and asked about his name. Many of the children (and some adults) called him "Grandfather," while others referred to him as "Running Wolf." Morning Flower, he noticed, called him "Uncle."

Running Wolf answered by explaining his relationship with Morning Flower. "I adopted her when she was younger. Her parents were killed during a raid by a tribe from the northwest. My children are grown now, but she is like a new daughter for me and a granddaughter for my mother."

The lodge was a typical-sized birchbark wigwam. The frame was composed of what appeared to be ash saplings lashed together with basswood bark and spruce roots. BJ had seen similar ones on their field trips to the Gichigami Reservation. The inside looked well-maintained and organized, as far as BJ could tell in the dim light. He could make out shelves and hooks along the walls and furs covering the floor. The center was an open area surrounded by bedding and household objects. On the far side of the door, the white head of Running Wolf's mother protruded from one of the fur blankets, which rose and fell in the steady rhythm of a deep sleep. Running Wolf indicated to BJ where he could sleep, and he lay on a bed of dried grass and pulled an animal fur over himself. Running Wolf lay near his mother and soon joined her in sleep. BJ stared at the ceiling and counted little marks on the birch bark.

Morning Flower arrived silently, and BJ watched breathlessly as her shadow slipped the clothing from her body and placed it near the wall. BJ was afraid to move, to even breathe. There was just enough light to see the outline of her figure. Quickly—too quickly—she lay on the floor, pulled a blanket to her chin, and fell asleep.

It was a very long time before BJ managed to do the same.

Chapter Nineteen

BJ ran towards the birch log splashed with multiple shades of lichen. The moss covering the boulder nearby was another green all its own—darker, deeper. The ground was cool and wet. The needles and leaves felt good against the balls of his feet as he leaped over the log and skirted the boulder. BJ inhaled the bitter, waxy scent of the conifers, noting the dawn chorus of the birds ringing loudly around him. Slowly, the entire scene began to dissolve into a crisscross of ash saplings, basswood rope, and birch bark. BJ blinked at the ceiling of the wigwam. The birds still sang with abandon, the tune of each thrush and robin weaving with that of each warbler and vireo, forming a great symphonic tapestry that unfurled, spreading out over every den, cavity, and lodge on the mountain.

"Is he awake?"

"No."

"Why does he sleep so long?"

"He must be like the flying squirrel and sleeps during the day."

"Maybe he is sick."

"No, he's not sick. He just looks like that, remember?"

"He still smells funny."

"And walks loudly."

"Also, the tip of his—"

"Stop that!" said Morning Flower. "He is a kind boy."

BJ rolled over and laughed quietly at the sight greeting him: five faces scrunched together in a jumble, their cheeks pressing against one another, staring eagerly at him.

"Now he's awake!" Little Otter grinned.

"You sleep like a bear in winter!" shot Stalking Bear.

Runs Swiftly pulled back the hide the rest of the way. "Hey, sleepy, you going to lie there all day or come out and play?"

BJ sat up. What time was it? Then he remembered that there were no clocks here, so the answer hardly mattered. It was morning. And he was hungry. He crawled through the door and into the sunlight. The village was a bustle of activity, people carrying baskets laden with food, wood, or bark. Many were busy on projects. Laughter could be heard from all directions. A group of young children were sitting on the Cannonball Rock with their pet raccoon. None of them appeared to pay any attention to BJ.

"What should we do?" said Shines Bright. It was a happy question. The day was wide open. No schedule. No clocks. Absolute freedom.

"How about the doll-taking game?" suggested Little Otter. But the others didn't want to play it two days in a row.

Stalking Bear held up a stone knife. "We could go chip some tools."

Runs Swiftly shook her head, then suggested they go to the shore to explore and play. No one objected to this, so they headed out of camp.

Morning Flower was scrutinizing BJ as they walked. "Are you hungry?" He nodded, feeling embarrassed and not wanting to delay the fun by making them stop for a meal.

"We can eat on the way!" yelled Stalking Bear over his shoulder. "Come on!"

BJ stumbled along, thinking that Juneberries might not be enough to fill his belly this time around. The criticism of his clumsy, loud movements was still ringing in his ears, so he tried to

126

mimic Morning Flower's easy lope, landing on the balls of his feet, keeping his arm swings and bouncing to a minimum. The stride gave BJ a strange sense of déjà vu. There was something familiar and comfortable about this gait, though he couldn't figure out why this was. It felt... animal-like.

They descended through patches of raspberries and blueberries—not yet ripe—and across bare granite. Little clouds of insects hovered on warm thermals at head level, forcing BJ to close his eyes as he ran through them. Morning Flower held out a handful of juicy leaves. "Eat." BJ took them and made to shove the bunch into his mouth, but Morning Flower said, "It is a good idea to try each one by itself so that you see what it tastes like." BJ tried the clover-like petals first. Their sour taste made him scrunch up his face. Morning Flower giggled at him. The second plant had larger leaves with pointy ends. It tasted like lettuce but... with more flavor. He stopped chewing and said, "Should I give thanks?"

"It is always a good idea," said Morning Flower. "Shines Bright is the one who always remembers. But the rest of us sometimes forget." That made BJ feel better. Morning Flower, he decided, was good at that. They continued on for another hundred yards or so until Morning Flower stiffened and slowed down. Ahead of them, clustered together, the kids were watching something beyond a grove of young birch trees. BJ and Morning Flower snuck up behind them and saw that they were watching Stalking Bear. He was on the other side of the birch grove, strolling casually, his long leather case strapped to his back. Every few moments, he bent down to pick something from a branch, then ate it. He looked up at the sky, then down at the ground, and picked something again and placed it in his mouth. In his right hand was a stick, about arm's length and wrist-thick. He held it like a club. "What's he doing?" whispered BJ.

"Grouse," explained Little Otter.

So that was it! BJ knew ruffed grouse well, having hunted them with his father on many occasions. Plump, ground-dwelling birds, masters of camouflage, grouse would often wait until a person nearly stepped on them before bursting into the air in an explosion of wingbeats. At times, they could also be careless, standing still in front of a vehicle or even a person, which often cost them their lives. After a minute, BJ managed to spot the bird, quartering away from Stalking Bear and clucking nervously on the opposite side of a raspberry bush. Now BJ understood Stalking Bear's demeanor. His movements were purposeful and designed to lower the bird's defenses, to look as if he didn't care about the grouse at all.

BJ and the others held their breath. Stalking Bear leaned down to pick at another pretend berry while simultaneously tilting the stick into a horizontal position. BJ wondered if he was going to try to club the bird on the head. That hardly seemed possible. The bird was making its way towards a small opening between the raspberry bush and a pine tree, some ten feet from Stalking Bear. A few more steps and there would be a brief window of opportunity. Unless it flew. It reached the edge of the opening and hesitated for nearly a minute, forcing Stalking Bear to wait in position while still trying to look casual. It took one step. Then another. All at once, Stalking Bear let the stick fly like a helicopter. BJ had not expected that at all! Stalking Bear bounded forward in three leaps, reached down, and held up the flopping grouse.

The kids ran towards him with a cheer. They laid the bird on its back and began poking and prodding at its gray and brown feathers. The throw had been perfect: a drop of blood was behind the left eye where the bird had been struck, but there was no other visible damage. Stalking Bear stretched out the wings, fanning out the long primary feathers and the shorter, downy secondary ones. Until now, BJ had believed grouse to be rather boring brown, black, and beige birds. The more he looked, however, the more beautiful he found them. They held the feet, taking turns bending the toes back and forth, watching the skin fold and wrinkle. They noted how the toes curled in when the legs were pressed up against the body. After they had poked, prodded, twisted, turned, and even smelled the bird, they stood and resumed their trek down to the lake.

On the way, Shines Bright asked Stalking Bear, "Can you see their tracks in summer?"

"Almost. My father is very good at it, but I need more practice."

"It is not easy to see any tracks in the summer," offered Runs Swiftly.

"That's true," said Stalking Bear, "but it is possible."

"How about a wolf?" said BJ. If it was possible to see grouse tracks, then wolf tracks must be easy.

"We passed the trails of five wolves on the way here," said Stalking Bear.

"Howah!" exclaimed Runs Swiftly, "I thought so! I saw them but wasn't sure if they were cat tracks."

Stalking Bear held his hands together in the air. "Wolf, coyote, and fox are more oval shaped. Cat tracks are round."

BJ felt a jolt of excitement. So, it *was* possible to track a wolf through the needles and moss.

They reached the base of the hill and began paralleling the shore, moving southwest. A while later—BJ couldn't tell if it was thirty minutes or two hours—their trail led out onto a rocky point, which gave a view of the inland hills. BJ nearly reeled at the familiarity of this place. He had spent hours upon hours here with Charley and other friends, exploring crag and cracks, sitting on great, open exposures of granite and watching the lake. He knew this place intimately. He found a flat spot where he and Charley would often sit and look back towards town, but of course, there was no town, only trees.

Stalking Bear was next to him, holding out the grouse. "Morning Flower's leaves are good, but this will fill your stomach even better."

BJ held the still-warm bird in his hands. "How do you want to cook it?"

"What 'cook'? You don't cook grouse!" said Stalking Bear. "We eat them like that. We will even let you have the best part." The others nodded solemnly.

BJ was moved. He liked grouse and wondered whether his friends preferred the breast meat or the legs. There was never much meat on the wings. "What is the best part?"

"The head," said Stalking Bear.

BJ flinched. The head? Did they mean the brains? "Are you serious?" They all nodded. "So," said BJ, "how am I supposed to eat the head? I mean, how do you prepare it?"

"You just bite it off," shrugged Stalking Bear.

How would he get through this without puking? They had to be kidding. But none of them were smiling. Indeed, Runs Swiftly, Morning Flower, Shines Bright, and Little Otter all looked like they'd just presented him with a tremendous honor. BJ didn't recall Elmer ever saying anything about Ojibwe eating raw grouse heads. The more they stared at him, stone-faced, the more he felt trapped. BJ really didn't want to insult them or break any traditions, so after a long wait, he held the bird up. How was he supposed to do this? Swallow it whole? No, definitely too big for that. There was no avoiding it—he was going to have to chew up the head. His stomach lurched. Wait until Charley hears about this. A raven whooshed its wings over them with a loud croak! Even the birds were egging him on. "What does it taste like?" he asked, stalling.

"Like duck head!" said Stalking Bear. The others nodded knowingly.

"Duck head is thicker," said Shines Bright. "Harder to bite through."

BJ opened his mouth, closed his eyes, and placed the bird head on his tongue. *Just do it quick!* He took a big breath and then heard a snort of repressed laughter. He opened his eyes. Morning Flower was holding both hands over her mouth, looking suspiciously like Charley when she was trying not to crack up. BJ pulled the head from his mouth. A few feathers remained on his tongue. "Wait a thek! Are you guyth kidding me?" At this, they doubled over in laughter, a few of them toppling to the ground in hysterics. BJ spit feathers. "You thicked me!"

"Well, we didn't trick you entirely," gasped Stalking Bear, "If Morning Flower hadn't snorted, you'd be crunching brains by now! I wonder what they taste like?" They laughed even harder.

BJ looked from one laughing face to another. "You've never eaten grouse head before?"

Shines Bright slapped Stalking Bear on the back. "None of us have! 'Like duck head!' That was a good one!"

Morning Flower said, "Come on, funny people, let's cook it."

BJ felt embarrassed at having another trick played on him, but the fun was good-natured. They were treating BJ as a member of the tribe. They walked away from the lake some thirty yards to a sheltered spot among the spruce and birch. Here, Stalking Bear removed the long leather bag he'd been carrying and shook out what looked like a crude bow and a few blocks of wood. "I need tinder and wood," he said to no one in particular. What happened next was simple but had a powerful and profound effect on BJ.

While Stalking Bear laid out the pieces of his bow drill, the others retrieved dried grass, birchbark, and twigs, which they set at Stalking Bear's side. Morning Flower and Shines Bright got to work building a little tipi-shaped structure while Stalking Bear bundled the dried grass and birchbark into a large ball and set it on the ground. He took a flat board with a row of round burn marks, each with a pie-shaped notch cut into them, and he set this on top of the soft tinder ball. Stalking Bear got up on his knee and stepped on the board with his left foot to stabilize it. Then he took a hotdog-sized wooden spindle and wrapped it once in the string of the bow with one quick movement. He placed the burned end of the spindle into the black hole that rested above the tinder. Then he palmed a little wooden block in his left hand and placed it on top of the spindle to hold it

131

steady. Leaning over the spindle and bracing his left wrist against his left shin, he began to move the bow back and forth with his right hand. The bow spun the wooden spindle into a blur. Stalking Bear leaned forward to pressure the spindle into the flat board. Within seconds, smoke arose from where the spindle and board met. BJ gasped. But Stalking Bear was not done. He kept spinning until the amount of smoke increased to the point where BJ could barely see the spindle.

BJ watched, mesmerized. After maybe ten or fifteen more seconds, Stalking Bear stopped and carefully removed the spindle. A tiny wisp of smoke was rising from the notch in the wood. Stalking Bear grabbed a little twig and used it to push the smoking coal out of the notch and into the tinder bundle. He set the board aside. Then he picked up the smoldering grass, folded the bundle around the little coal, and blew into it. Thick, white smoke arose almost immediately. BJ could see the coal pulsing with each of Stalking Bear's breaths as if he were breathing life into it. Then the ball burst into flame, and in one swift movement, Stalking Bear shoved the bundle into the side of the tipi. The twigs crackled and burned, then the larger sticks above them. Fire! The entire process had taken maybe two minutes. BJ was stunned silent.

Stalking Bear seemed amused by his reaction. "You have a different way of making fire?"

"We sure do," said BJ, feeling stupid.

"Hand drill? Sometimes, I use a hand drill."

BJ looked at him blankly.

"Fire plow?"

BJ shook his head.

"What then?"

"Never mind." BJ felt almost useless. He had just witnessed something ancient and simple but profound. The words of his history book came back to him: *They could build a fire by hand in less than a minute.* So much for the struggles of primitive living, thought BJ. Life seemed to be so… straightforward. Food. Shelter. Fire. There was more, of course. There had to be sickness and war and death. There had to be sorrow and sadness and betrayal. It wasn't utopia. But still, living here, outside, and interacting with the elements every moment of every day was all so… normal. He wished that he had more to contribute.

Watch and learn…

Morning Flower was just starting to pluck the bird, and it was then that BJ saw an opening. "Hey, do you guys know the other way to clean a grouse?" Morning Flower and Stalking Bear exchanged a glance, then shook their heads. "What do you mean?" said Stalking Bear. The others came in close to see what BJ was on about. "Maybe BJ has a teaching for us," said Shines Bright.

"Sure," said Runs Swiftly. "How to make noise in the woods?"

Morning Flower glared at Runs Swiftly, then handed the bird to BJ. He laid it on its back and spread out the wings, feeling a tiny rush of excitement at being able to show off. He stepped on the wings and took hold of the feet.

"What are you doing?" said Little Otter. "You are cra—" A smack in the head from Runs Swiftly silenced him.

BJ gave the group a little grin, hoping he looked as cool as Stalking Bear. Then he pulled hard. The sound of tearing tendons and ripping skin caused all the kids to make faces. The next thing anyone knew, BJ was holding the feet in the air. Attached to them was a bundle of feathers and guts. On the ground lay a perfectly clean, skinned grouse breast with two wings. The old grouse-hunter's trick he had learned from his dad had worked like a charm. "Howah!" said Stalking Bear, grabbing the grouse breast. "That is a very good trick!" Morning Flower beamed. BJ felt his chest swell with pride.

Shines Bright examined the feet, feathers, and guts. "I guess Creator must have meant for us to eat these birds!" BJ laughed at the sentiment, which was almost identical to that expressed by his own dad, whose favorite phrase was "made for consumption!"

Morning Flower took the bundle from Shines Bright. "Don't forget the legs," she said, beginning to pluck feathers. "We shouldn't waste any!" They cut the meat into pieces with a stone knife, then—except for Little Otter, who ate his piece raw—cooked them over the fire like marshmallows. There was just enough to satisfy the little bit of hunger that remained in BJ. His growing confidence nudged him to gather rocks and show them how to skip, and everyone picked it up quickly except for Stalking Bear, who had trouble getting the angle just right. BJ coached him until he could throw a three. Morning Flower was especially persistent and kept at it until she managed a ten. BJ practically swooned.

The sun crept higher, and they lay on the warm rock and watched a mother loon carrying two fluffy chicks on her back as she lounged about on the water. Further up the shore, villagers in canoes were casting nets. BJ recalled how the sports fishermen accused Indians of netting out all the local fish. The claim seemed absurd now. The vastness of Lake Superior and its bounty could hardly be at risk from such a modest population. His thoughts turned to the rogue wolf and vandals.

On a whim, BJ decided to tell his friends about his father's dilemma. They listened intently as BJ tried to relate the situation in terms that would make sense to them. When he finished, Stalking Bear said, "Your father is a protector of the animals, the water, and the forest?" BJ nodded, rather pleased with the description.

Runs Swiftly said, "You will have to protect your animals from that wolf."

"My dad is trying to catch him," said BJ.

"He can trap him," said Little Otter. "He will probably have to kill him."

"That would be serious, killing brother wolf," cautioned Shines Bright. "They have been connected to the Anishinaabe ever since First Man walked the earth."

"Yes," countered Runs Swiftly, "but if this one is dangerous, they might have no choice."

"You will have to track him down," said Stalking Bear.

Morning Flower plucked a yarrow leaf and rubbed it between her thumb and fingers, then smelled it. "Does… the rest of your tribe track like you do?"

BJ knew she was being diplomatic. He wasn't sure anyone in Grand Marais could do more than recognize Nike prints in the sand, although he wondered about Elmer. He wasn't about to try to explain trail cameras to them. "Stalking Bear," he said, "can you tell the difference between individual animals?"

Stalking Bear gave BJ a funny look. "A good tracker can tell sex, age, speed, hunger—even health."

BJ didn't know what to say to this. He wasn't sure if his friend was pulling his leg or not. Were they playing another joke on him?

"Your scouts and elders could show you," suggested Runs Swiftly.

BJ studied the group and decided that they were, indeed, serious. At least, he thought so. How could anybody read that much into a print? He explained to them that, as far as he knew, there was no one in Grand Marais who had these skills anymore. Nobody could identify hard-to-see tracks, much less follow them. In fact, he said, most of the people he knew didn't know more than a handful of plants or birds. The looks on his friends' faces ranged from disbelief to horror.

"Why do your people not know these things?" said Shines Bright.

"They must be stupid," said Runs Swiftly. "How can they survive?"

"Beejay is not stupid," said Morning Flower, "and he does not know how to track."

"Are their eyes bad?" asked Little Otter.

"No," said BJ. "They can see." He thought for a moment. "They just look at different things."

"Like what?" shot Stalking Bear.

TV, thought BJ. Phones. YouTube. There was no point in trying to describe any of it. BJ felt perfectly horrible. For a long while, they all sat in silence. BJ thought about the video of the wolf, of what his father had said about likely not being able to catch him. He felt powerless. But then he remembered his task. "So," he said, "I'm here because, um, I'm supposed to find someone to help. Like a warrior."

"Like Shadow Walker?" said Little Otter.

"Yes! Well, kind of. I don't know his name. He has a red hand." BJ felt stupid saying it that way.

"A red hand?" said Morning Flower. "What does that mean?"

The others looked similarly confused. "I'm supposed to watch and learn, then he will come to me. At least someone told me that."

"Ah," said Little Otter, "that's just like Shadow Walker!"

"Stalking Bear might know him," said Shines Bright. "Right, Stalking Bear?"

Stalking Bear shrugged. "I may have seen him."

"Really?" said BJ.

Shines Bright said, "Stalking Bear, you might show BJ your Sacred Area."

Stalking Bear nodded. "I think I have seen your warrior. But he is shy and may take a long time to come see you. I can show you how to get him to show himself."

BJ was ecstatic. If he could go hang out at some type of Sacred Place, the red-hand guy would show up. Then, he thought ruefully, all he would have to do was talk him into going into a strange cave, traveling to the twenty-first century, learning to ride in cars, drink coffee, and count money. Sure. Before BJ shook his head, contemplating all of this, and was about to speak, Stalking Bear slipped out of his breechcloth, issued a war whoop, and ran headfirst into the icy water. Runs Swiftly followed suit and began splashing like a duck. Shines Bright and Little Otter stripped down and joined her. And then Morning Flower. With another splash and a shriek, BJ was left alone on the rocks amidst a pile of discarded leather outfits. "Come on!" yelled Morning Flower.

"Don't you know how to swim?" said Shines Bright, performing a backward roll.

"Maybe that's what happened to him," said Little Otter. "Maybe a fish bit him on the—"

"Shut up!" said Runs Swiftly and Morning Flower simultaneously.

"You can stay shallow if you can't swim!" yelled Shines Bright.

"If I can't...?" BJ gritted his teeth and glanced around for a place to change, then realized that he had nothing to change into!

"Come ON!" chided Stalking Bear.

"Oh, what the hell!" BJ dropped his breechcloth and sprinted off the end of the rock, yelling "Kowabunga!" as he cannon-balled through the air and into the middle of the group to the sounds of whoops and laughter.

Chapter Twenty

The sun was above the trees, and the birds were taking a break from their morning chorus when BJ and Stalking Bear strode, barefoot, past the Cannonball Rock and out of the village the following morning. Once in the trees, they veered east, crossed the river at a shallow place, and zig-zagged along a route BJ could not make out. BJ tried hard to emulate Stalking Bear's easy gait. "You are moving better now," said Stalking Bear over his shoulder. "You only sound like a small calf instead of a big bull!"

BJ wondered how long it would take for the red-hand guy to show up. If it took the kid in Running Wolf's story years, BJ was sure he could do it in weeks, maybe days. He would apply modern learning methods and get it done in no time! As they worked their way alongside the mountain, the vegetation changed from mature pines to a mixture of younger pines, spruce, and poplar no more than six inches in diameter, interrupted occasionally by rocky openings with spatterings of blueberry and raspberry bushes. At one of these open areas, Stalking Bear walked up to a solitary red pine with a large black scar five feet up the trunk and standing like a lone sentinel. He faced BJ.

"How far to your Sacred Place?" said BJ.

"This is it."

"Oh." BJ turned in a slow circle. It was… he tried not to look disappointed. After all the stories about the kids' Sacred Places and the adventures of Shadow Walker, BJ thought maybe there would be something more. As soon as he had this thought, he became annoyed with himself. After all, what did he expect? Rainbows? "Well, it's a nice tree," he said finally.

Stalking Bear was watching a warbler hopping from branch to branch down the hill below them.

BJ rubbed his fingers across the black scar, picking up coal dust as he did so. "So, do you have a warrior guy like Shadow Walker or the red-hand guy?"

"Yes," said Stalking Bear.

"You do? Really?"

"We all do, but each person's warrior or protector is very shy and hard to see," said Stalking Bear. "It took me a very long time to notice him. Now I see him nearly every day."

"That's great!" said BJ, suddenly hopeful. "What do you do when you are here?"

"Everything!" said Stalking Bear. "I sit. I sleep. I play." He removed the leather pouch from his back and emptied the contents. "Sometimes, I work on projects. I come when I am happy, when I am sad, when I am angry, or even bored. I often sit against the tree. And…" He grinned. "I even fall asleep!" Stalking Bear spread his arms in a wide circle. "This is my family. All of the plants and trees, the four-legged animals, the winged creatures, are my relations. I have gotten to know them all, and they know me. I have watched every single thing here for years." Stalking Bear walked to a lichen-covered rock. "Here is an ant colony. They like to travel along this tiny path down the hill, gathering food along the way. I once spent an entire day just following them back and forth! Over here"—he leaped to the end of a partially rotted log—" is the home of a mother deer mouse. She had five babies a few days ago, and she comes and goes many times a day to find food for them. She will have to be careful of the weasel that likes to hunt along the hill." Stalking Bear pointed at a bird on the side of an old snag. "There is the female downy woodpecker that has a nest near the creek. Her eggs should hatch soon. And over here"—he indicated the ground—" is a trail that raccoon and deer like to use at night. A deer had twin fawns a month ago, and she likes to bed down on the slope this time of day to catch the warmth of the morning sun. She has come to visit me many times. The raccoon is friendly as well, and I knew him when he was a baby."

Stalking Bear continued for over an hour, describing in detail every plant, insect, bird, and animal that lived or passed within 100 paces of the red pine. BJ burst out, "How did you learn all that?"

Stalking Bear crossed his arms and said, "Do you mean did a teacher teach it to me? No schools for this, my friend. Just the teachers you see here. Sometimes," he said, "my father or Grandfather Running Wolf will ask me questions of this place, and I will come back later to think about them."

BJ walked to an old stump and sat. "How long have you been coming here?"

"Seven years."

"But… what about Shadow Walker or the Red Hand Warrior? When do they come help?" BJ didn't have seven years. He had until the end of the summer. That's what his book said. And the man had said he only had four visits.

Stalking Bear studied BJ for a moment. "For everyone, it is different, Beejay. I don't know about you. Maybe Red Hand will come to you soon." He thought for a moment. "You should have your own Sacred Place, Beejay."

BJ sighed. By the time the warrior guy showed up, his dad's job would be long gone, the wolf would have killed someone, and for all he knew, they would be relocated to Bemidji! Besides, what good would a Sacred Place here do for him when he would eventually have to return home to Grand Marais? He didn't have seven years to spend here! "Isn't there a way to get him to come faster?" BJ was feeling desperate. "Maybe we can ask Running Wolf."

"You can ask him," said Stalking Bear. "But he will probably not give you an answer like your teachers. In the meantime, so that you don't get into trouble, you should pay attention to the things around you—like deer trails, birds, and especially," he said, "ant hills."

BJ squirmed as Stalking Bear's words sank in. For the last few minutes, he'd been scratching his legs without realizing it, but as BJ looked down, he saw that his legs were almost entirely covered with little red ants. And they were biting him. "Aaargh!" BJ shot from the ground and began to leap around in a circle, swiping at his legs.

"Is that called 'the ant dance'?" teased Stalking Bear. "I like it!" He jumped around, imitating BJ.

BJ flailed wildly, rubbed his backside against a drooping balsam branch, then tore off his breechcloth, bolted through the woods, and flopped into the river. The cold water rushed past, pulling away the remaining ants and soothing the bites. He must have looked like a beaten wet dog when Stalking Bear caught up, holding BJ's breechcloth. "You are funny, Beejay. Don't feel bad. I might have sat there, too, but I saw the deer mouse get chased away from that spot last fall, so I knew about the nest."

BJ felt like an idiot, but at least the stinging was gone.

Stalking Bear brushed the hair from his eyes. "I cannot help you find a Sacred Place. That is your own decision. But I can give you some advice on its general location."

BJ nodded. What choice did he have? He stood, shivering, not bothering to cover his privates. Stalking Bear handed BJ the breechcloth. "It doesn't really matter if your Sacred Place is near the village or not. There are some kids who sit within sight of the camp. If you want to be farther away from activity, you might consider going to the northwest—in the direction from which you come. If you find an area that feels right, then that is probably a good choice. You will see more animals where there are mixtures of openings and trees." Stalking Bear plucked a few leaves from a plant with round, juicy-looking stems.

"What are those for?"

"For your butt," said Stalking Bear. "When you dry off, mush the stems and leaves together and rub them on your skin. This plant is good for bites and rashes." They headed inland. BJ recognized the spot where they had played the doll-taking game. "I know this place."

Stalking Bear nodded, then left him without another word.

BJ stood in place for a long time, his head filled with a jumble of thoughts, images, and emotions. So, he was going to find his own Sacred Place. But how? And why? Wasn't he going to go back home soon? This didn't make any sense. "What's the point of having a Sacred Place here," he wondered aloud, "if I'm just going home again?"

"Yeah, Pale Butt," said a voice, "but when you go home, you'll be right back here again."

BJ nearly leaped out of his breechcloth. There, sitting against a birch trunk, looking sleepy, was the strange man. His hair was pulled back neatly, as before, his braid crisp and tight. "You!" blurted BJ.

"Me." He cleared his throat and spat a large glob onto the ground. He spread out his arms. "So, having a good time?"

The question struck BJ as thoroughly bizarre as if the man had just led BJ on a tour of the pyramids of Egypt. "Are you the Red Hand Warrior?"

"Definitely not." A few crow's feet stretched from the corners of his eyes, but there was no gray hair or wrinkles. BJ could not tell at all how old he was. He looked younger than Running Wolf. At the same time, he seemed like someone who had seen it all and would be difficult to surprise, someone who had managed to avoid growing up, like an Ojibwe Peter Pan. A large black fly buzzed between them, then tried to land on the man's nose.

"Are you sure?" said BJ. "I mean, that's twice you've kind of appeared when I was still in the woods. That sounds like what Shadow Walker and the red-hand guy would do."

"Shadow Walker!" said the man. "Isn't that, like, the coolest name ever?" He swatted at the fly.

"And," persisted BJ, "you're not him?"

"Nope." He readied his open hand to strike at the fly, which had landed on his nose. *You are not going to hit yourself on the nose*, thought BJ. But that is exactly what the man did. So hard, in fact, that his head bounced off the tree behind him, and he fell to the ground in a heap. BJ's stared at him, dumbfounded. He had never met anyone remotely as strange as this person.

The man stared at his palm while the fly buzzed away. "You're here for your family and community. You're here because you care about them. You need to find Red Foot."

"Red Hand."

The man stood on shaky legs. "What?"

"You said 'Red Foot.' It's Red Hand, right?"

"Oh, right. Red Hand. Find your Sacred Place, then hang out. He's already watching you. The more you watch and learn, the quicker he'll show up. Then bring him home, and he can help out."

"With the wolf?"

"The wolf is the least of your problems," shot the man, and BJ felt a little chill run down his spine. "I gotta go help my grandma get a fire started. Hey," he said, pointing, "watch out behind you!"

But BJ crossed his arms. "No way. Last time I took my eyes off you, you disappeared. I want to know what you're talking about. What do you mean 'least' of my problems? And how do you know about Grand Marais or my family—"

"I'm serious," said the man. "Watch out behind you!"

BJ began to shake his head but suddenly realized that there *was* a sound behind him. He turned and gasped. A large porcupine was no more than an arm's length away, munching on a clover stem. At the sound of BJ's gasp, the animal went into a defensive posture, hunching its shoulders and bristling its tail, full of thick brown and white quills.

"Okay, you were right," said BJ, "I…" But the man had disappeared. "Oh, come ON!" said BJ, throwing his arms into the air. This was getting ridiculous! BJ rubbed his cowlick and considered the porcupine, which had returned to browsing. "Sorry I scared you. But you scared me first!" BJ decided to let him eat his lunch in peace and walked away, then stopped to think. What had the man said to him just now about finding a Sacred Place? "I'll be right back here again… oh yeah!" Of course, he would be right back here again—he could find a spot here, and it would still be here when he returned to Grand Marais! Duh!

This was a happy realization. BJ followed the river south, picking his way through speckled alder and willow brush while humming like his sister. The river would be a perfect landmark for relocating a Sacred Place once he had returned home. At the bend, a hundred yards down, he waded into the middle of the cold water and surveyed the area. A tree would be nice, but would it still be here centuries later? The tip of a red pine protruding from the surrounding canopy caught his attention, so he headed that way and was soon standing at the base of a very old and large tree. The ground was a thick bed of rust-colored needles, which smelled warm. Again, BJ turned in a circle. Was this all there was to it? Find a comfortable place and sit down? *Well, now is the time to find out*, he thought. He wiggled his butt into the needles, arching his back to find a comfortable position. BJ crossed his legs and gave a sigh of contentment, feeling a bit like a yogi atop a mountain.

A minute later, his back started to ache, so he stretched out his legs and dug in his heels. That hardly helped. He lay on his side with one arm under his head, but his arm fell asleep. He tried to scratch his nose but ended up slapping his face with his rubbery appendage. With a grunt of frustration, BJ spun onto his knees and dug into the needles to make a hollow spot for his rear end. After some work, it was comfortable enough. Now what? Watch. Learn. Wait. Again, he sighed and assumed the learned yogi posture. What to watch? Well, there were trees. Plants. Some birds, somewhere…

For what felt like a long time, BJ sat and waited for something to happen. But the more he waited, the more nothing happened.

BJ grew bored and fidgety. A shower of tiny cinnamon-colored flakes sprinkled down onto BJ's lap, and he looked up to see the nuthatch, which had been scratching, pecking, and rrr-rrr ing without BJ paying attention. Now that he was, he began to notice all the different sounds the little bird made with each movement. Peck, peck. Scratch, scratch. Hop, hop. Rrr-rrr… BJ flinched. Had he slept? Maybe. He checked the sun's position. It didn't seem like too much time had passed. Maybe he had closed his eyes for a few minutes. A prickly sensation of being watched came to him. BJ scanned in all directions but saw no one. Once more, he was quite alone.

Later, while sitting around the fire with the other kids, he answered the questions posed to him by Running Wolf as best he could. "I think," said BJ, batting Wood Tick's hand away from his breechcloth for the fourth time, "I was facing east."

"Very good to greet Brother Sun when he awakes in the morning." Running Wolf asked about the surrounding vegetation, the birds he'd seen, and the sounds he'd heard, and BJ pointed out the nuthatch. The weird man had appeared, but he thought it best not to bring this up.

Running Wolf added a stick to the fire. "I can't remember if the wind changed direction this afternoon. Did anyone notice?"

Morning Flower and Shines Bright both said that a western wind blew until about mid-day, then changed to the southeast.

Running Wolf frowned. "I wonder what these winds will bring tomorrow?"

"Rain!" Stalking Bear had arrived. He sat down next to Morning Flower and got his hand slapped when he reached for a piece of fish on her plate. She let him take it anyway, and he popped it into his mouth, then winked at BJ.

They talked more about Sacred Places and what they liked to do there, and then Running Wolf said, "Did you see any animal signs?" BJ hadn't thought about that and shook his head.

Running Wolf looked at Morning Flower. "Niece, would you please get me a cup of water?" She strode to a clay pot, filled his cup, and returned. Running Wolf took a drink, then stood and pointed to the ground. "Beejay, can you see the tracks Morning Flower just made?"

BJ saw nothing but dirt and grass.

Running Wolf nodded. "Do not feel bad. Now I know how much you have to learn."

Runs Swiftly dropped to her belly and began studying the earth. Stalking Bear put his cheek to the ground and closed one eye. "There is the left foot."

Running Wolf looked at them approvingly and then turned back to BJ. "Tracking is an art that takes much practice, but anybody can do it. The best way for you to start is to watch an animal at your Sacred Place and then look at the ground after it has gone. It is easier to start on soft ground or snow."

The fire danced and crackled, and BJ stared into the flame and thought of roast grouse and Sacred Places and skinny dipping and his family. The hands of Runs Swiftly caught him before he slumped to the ground. Shines Bright said, "I think BJ has had a long day!"

Morning Flower pulled him to his feet. "I will put Beejay to bed."

"Hey!" squeaked Little Otter, "Why is Morning Flower—" Another smack on the back of the head from Runs Swiftly, and he shut his mouth.

Morning Flower led BJ to the lodge and put a heavy caribou hide over him, and he felt like he was being pressed into the earth like a figurine into a clay mold. The scent of balsam boughs, birch bark, earth, and smoke carried him into a deep sleep, and by the time he awoke the next morning, he remembered none of it—including the kiss that Morning Flower gave him on the forehead before she left.

Chapter Twenty-One

It had been five days since the creature had slipped into the yard of the burned and broken home and taken the deer that the three men had killed in the dark. Four days earlier, it had followed them and watched as they broke into buildings. Like the owners of the animals, their awareness was dull. The creature had left a sign that, in another time, would have been seen in an instant. But these men were too busy arguing and hiding and watching the road. Were they looking out for the man in the uniform who seemed to be getting closer and closer to them? He had come very close to them on one occasion, narrowly avoiding their clumsy attempt at killing him. Somehow, he had sensed the danger, and so had the boy in the vehicle.

If the awareness of that father and son is like that of The People, then they are a threat. The creature pondered this while lurking among the trees behind a home where the three men had been sleeping, drinking, and smoking. They had taken another deer and left it hanging from a branch near the edge of the yard. Fools. They might as well send an invitation to come and feed! It stepped into the yard and reached up for the deer when suddenly a bright light shone in its face and a voice said, "I've got you now, you deer-stealing son-of-a..."

The man had a metal weapon in his hand, the same one they had used to kill the deer. But his face had gone white, and his mouth hung open like a loose hinge. Until now, the creature had planned on waiting, on biding its time, but the man's appearance forced a change of plan. No matter. Now was as good a moment as any. Besides, it had grown tired of deer.

Chapter Twenty-Two

BJ sat cross-legged in the moss and recounted every detail he could remember from the past few days. Or was it weeks? He had completely lost track of time. The notion of days of the week was downright laughable. "How long," he asked, "was I gone?"

Charley was tracing a big puffy cloud with her right index finger. "Maybe an hour?" It seemed there was no real relation between the time BJ was gone and the time that went by in the present, except that it was always short for Charley. In a sense, this was lucky because it allowed him to disappear for an extended period without freaking out his parents. "I heard wolves again, but they were far away," she added. Her blue eyes, set among a thick cluster of ever-darkening summer freckles, remained focused on the sky. BJ was struck by how different she looked from Runs Swiftly and Morning Flower but how similar their spirits were. Without warning, he lay on top of his sister and squeezed the air out of her in a playful hug.

"Ooof!" she grunted. "Get off me, big butt!"

BJ rolled off and leaned on one elbow. "So, I think I was gone for… hold on. Did you just call me 'Big Butt'?" BJ thought of Little Otter and how a nickname could stick if you weren't careful

Charley giggled. "You also smell funny," she said, standing and gathering her things. They walked back together along the river, Charley peppering with questions about his second trip.

What did they eat? (All sorts of stuff). Did they have underwear? (Definitely not). Was the girl with the big brown eyes pretty? (Shut up!)

At the bend in the river, BJ strode out into the water and stood as he had when searching for his Sacred Place. Some of the large rocks and boulders were the same, but the sand washes and gravel were not. The change in vegetation was disorienting, but he picked a course and headed into the woods, using his intuition more than anything else. Charley followed along. After a minute or two, he stopped and began surveying the area. Other than the typical forest debris and mixture of spruce and maple, the only thing that stood out to him was a mound about the size and height of a card table. Next to this was a hummock—a small, dish-shaped depression roughly the same size. Together, it looked as if a giant ice cream scoop had carved a lump of earth from the ground and plopped it nearby. BJ stared at this for a long time, without thought, until a realization crept into his mind. "Charley," he said," I think this is it. I think this was where my big red pine stood."

"Why was it yours?"

"Well, okay, it wasn't mine, but I sat here once."

"Oh. What else did you do?"

BJ laughed, making Charley jump. He had, indeed, learned a hard lesson when he had sat against the tree. He told her of arriving early in the morning and sitting against the trunk, not noticing that the debris at its base had been disturbed. Before BJ knew it, two hands had reached out of the duff, like a graveyard scene in a horror movie, and grabbed BJ by the legs. BJ had launched himself forward, screaming and scrambling to get away, but the voice of Stalking Bear laughing hysterically stopped him, and he turned around to see a mud- and leaf-covered figure rising from the needles. BJ had sat on top of him without knowing it.

"He got you good," said Charley. "I like him."

"I'm sure he'd like you, too."

"So, the red-hand guy will come to your Sacred Place?" said Charley.

"I guess. I don't know how long it will take."

"When you bring him back, can he do my chores for me?"

"I doubt it." BJ stepped into the hummock, his hands on his hips. "I think the root base was here, and when the tree finally fell, it tipped over this way, and the root ball disintegrated into this mound."

Charley pointed beyond the mound. "You can see the outline of the trunk on the ground." Sure enough, the faint outline of a tree trunk, long since fallen, was visible along the forest floor.

Charley hopped onto the mound. "There are lots of these holes and hills in the woods."

"Yeah." BJ grinned. "And now we know why!" A robin chirped sharply then flew past them and landed somewhere high in a birch. BJ listened to it "tut-tut!" for a few seconds, then said, "Charley, do you know that, in the old days, people used to be able to follow tracks across leaves and grass, and they could read the sex of the animals they were tracking?"

"Seriously? Why would they read about sex? That's gross! What is wrong with them?"

"No, I mean... I... never mind." BJ grinned all the way home.

Over the following week, BJ spent as much time as he could at his new (or was it old?) Sacred Place while Charley hung out in the yard or took walks, and Molly spent her time on long runs, working at the co-op, and weeding the garden. Mark was almost completely absent, busy patrolling lakes and campsites and fielding calls from farmers or cabin owners, worried about the wolf.

BJ's sit time was mostly uneventful. A blue jay squawking here. A robin tut-tutting there. Once, he thought he saw a deer moving in the distance but couldn't be sure. More than once, a red squirrel made a point of harassing BJ with a loud and annoying trill. After seven days of this, BJ started losing his patience. How long was he going to have to keep this up? A few twittering birds and a deranged squirrel were not going to bring any warriors to help out. On day eight, tired and sore, he trudged back into the yard, shoulders slumped.

Charley was at her bird feeder. "What's wrong with you?" she said.

"Nothing, why?"

"You're annoyed. Kinda obvious."

"I'm… I don't know. I'm getting bored. I cannot imagine doing this for weeks, months, or years!"

"Hmmm," she said, standing up and watching a chickadee fly off the feeder. "What birds did you see?" said Charley.

"Um, a robin, I think. Bluejay."

"What trees?"

"The usual. I don't know, some birch. Spruce. Maybe a white pine."

Charley made a face that BJ couldn't read. He waved at his mother in the garden, then wandered down to pet Max, who was lying in the sand and gravel at the base of their driveway. As he stroked the dog's belly, BJ noticed the dog's prints, which he supposed led down to Elmer's and then back again. He decided to follow them. The tracks left the driveway and then meandered down the middle of the road before entering the woods. BJ walked along the edge of the trees until he found the trail resume, where Max came out of the woods and walked into Elmer's driveway.

BJ thought about the tracking discussion he had with Stalking Bear and returned to where Max had left the road and entered the woods, then found where they exited again, some ten yards further down, and thought back to Stalking Bear's comment on trackers reading age, gender, speed of travel. How could anybody see tracks in the leafy, grassy environment? BJ knew it was possible because he had seen Stalking Bear and Running Wolf do it. He backed up and stared at the spot where the dog had entered the woods.

After a while, he noticed a few grains of sand in a depressed poplar leaf, some twelve inches from the road. Max's track? Further on, there was more sand in some bent grass. A second track? BJ eyeballed the distance from the track in the road to the first bits of sand, then from that spot to the next clumps of sand. The distance was nearly the same. Two tracks! They didn't look like tracks, but that's what they had to be. BJ headed back to his yard, walking upright. This was the first time he had really identified a track in leafy debris. It seemed easy, really. Maybe, he thought, they didn't need the red-hand guy after all. Maybe BJ could help his dad track down the wolf on his own. "Hey, Mom," he said, getting an idea. "I might head up the snowmobile trail on my bike in a bit." The trail crossed Reservation Road about five miles up. The wolf had recently been spotted near there.

"Can I come with?" said Charley.

"Sure."

"Bring a snack and a water bottle," said Molly.

After lunch, BJ and Charley gathered their gear, hopped on their bikes, and headed down the road. Elmer waved at them from his yard as they rode past. At the base of their road, they met Tony and David, each on their own bikes and out of breath. David's hair was a uniform canary yellow. "Mom kicked us out of the house," explained Tony. "I texted you, but you didn't answer, so we just came up to see what you were doing."

"We're heading to Reservation Road," said Charley.

Tony and David decided to come along. The four of them pedaled up the trail, which paralleled the highway for a while, then curved to the left, then right, crossing a rust-colored iron bridge over the Manitou River. From there, the trail angled further inland through groves of young aspen and birch. About twenty minutes in, they stopped to watch a rainbow that had appeared in front of a storm system directly to their north. Then, the mosquitoes chased them back onto their bikes and up the trail. About a mile further, they came to another bridge, built high over the Taconite River, which rushed by in a tea-colored torrent. Halfway across, they parked, leaned against the thick iron railing on the upstream side, and spit into the fast-moving water thirty feet below. BJ wondered if Stalking Bear, Morning Flower, and the others had good places to spit into the river.

About fifty yards upstream, where a little waterfall poured into a small pool, they decided to take a dip, splashing and laughing and playing in their underwear. Refreshed, they climbed back to the bridge and continued their ride. When they arrived at Reservation Road, they found fresh puddles dotting the ground, indicating the passage of a small rainstorm. An old wooden sign nailed to a pair of sunken posts read Welcome to the Gichigami Indian Reservation in faded red letters. The woods sparkled, and the branches dripped.

"There's our rez," said David.

"Where did you live?" asked BJ. David and his family had only come down into Grand Marais two years earlier.

"Between the casino and the school."

"What's it like there?" said Charley.

David shrugged.

Tony swatted at a mosquito. "Okay, we're here. Now what?"

BJ didn't really have a plan other than to head up the road and look for tracks. They were still a mile or so from the spot where the bullet had hit his dad's truck two weeks earlier. They pedaled north, past a few dirt driveways with closed gates, until they reached an old and dilapidated cabin with a thick layer of moss and needles covering the roof. The log siding and wood deck were cracked and gray. Two windows facing the road were smashed. The corner of the building had been burned, and the flames had caused the nearest branches of a pine to turn brown from the heat. A rotten pile of wood beneath a shredded blue tarp sat next to a doorless outhouse.

They laid their bikes on the ground and investigated the yard. "There's a lot of old buildings like this around here," said David. "Places that aren't lived in end up getting burned or torn apart."

156

Charley picked up a pinecone and sniffed it. "On purpose?"

"Don't know. Maybe drug users or something. Maybe a Windigo."

"What's a Windigo?" said Tony, holding out his phone, trying to get a signal.

"A giant that eats people," said BJ and Charley simultaneously.

"My uncle said he saw one once," said David, "but Dad says he was drinking, so who knows?"

Tony waved his phone in a large circle. "There's, like, no reception here at all!"

Charley walked around the yard, looking up into the pine branches. Somewhere, a blue jay and a raven traded insults. Far away, a low rumble of thunder sounded as the storm cell traveled east across the lake toward Michigan's Upper Peninsula. BJ squinted at the house and then at the ground and began to question the wisdom of coming all the way up here. What did he expect to find, really? The ground looked like ground. There were ATV tracks in the yard, but that didn't mean anything. ATVs were common on the back roads.

"A wolf!" David was pointing down the road towards an animal running in their direction. BJ felt his stomach clench and the hair stand up on his neck. The animal was running towards them.

"That's Max," said Charley. Sure enough, a moment later, their Labrador came trotting into the yard, tongue lolling, panting. He had followed them all the way up the trail.

BJ wiped at his cowlick and studied the house. The building was dark and moist, like an old mushroom. It was also eerily inviting. He decided to go inside. The screen door protested like an old dog being forced to get up from a nap. BJ nudged aside an empty whisky bottle with his toe and stepped into a kitchen with yellow cupboards and a green Formica counter The beige linoleum floor had peeled and buckled as if an earthquake had come through. It cracked loudly with each step. An overturned chair, torn books, and empty beer cans littered the floor. Five empty whisky bottles lay in the sink. Mouse droppings and dead flies dotted the countertop like grains of pepper. Between the kitchen and the hole in the corner of the cabin, the remains of a wooden table lay black and burned where the fire had been lit. Around it, charred pieces of paper—probably used to start the fire—were strewn, some edges chewed on by rodents. The scents of smoke, mold, and urine permeated the building.

Outside, Max began to bark. "Let's go!" yelled Charley.

"Just a minute!" shouted BJ. He walked through the kitchen towards a hallway with three doors, one open and two closed. The open door was a small closet with a wavy particleboard shelf and a dowel holding a dozen wire clothes hangers. On the floor, an old oilcloth jacket lay draped over something. BJ lifted the jacket, then jumped back with a shriek when a mouse leaped onto his left leg, then onto the floor, before scampering down the hallway. Beneath the jacket was a cardboard box full of thick manila folders and a mouse nest the size of a softball. "Yuk!" BJ set the jacket back down. He walked to the second door and made a face as an acrid smell struck his nose. He grasped the handle and turned. Flies and putrid air greeted him. BJ peered in. A bathroom. A yellow claw-foot tub with brown stains around the edges sat on one side, and a sink basin and toilet with no seat were on the other. In the center of the floor lay a dead raccoon. BJ grimaced and closed the door.

BJ's nose was still burning when he reached the third door. He grabbed the handle and tried to turn it but was locked. Locked? BJ dropped to his knees to peer beneath the door—and found himself staring into someone's eye. BJ lurched back against the wall.

"BJ!" yelled Charley. "Come on!"

BJ scrambled into the kitchen. He was heading out the door when something on the counter caught his eye, something he had not noticed when he'd come in: a spent .22 shell casing. He picked it up. It was shiny and yellow. It was the only shiny thing in the entire building. He pocketed it and hustled out into the yard. "BJ, come here!" shouted Charley from the edge of the woods. Tony and David each stood by their bikes, not moving. BJ hustled to Charley, who pointed at the ground. Lying a few feet into the woods, near a poplar sapling, was a basketball-size pile of scat. "What on earth?" said BJ, marveling at the giant turd.

"But look," said Charley.

BJ looked at the pile. There were little pieces of bone and hair. It was typical of a bear or wolf to poop out... but then he saw the glint of a shiny object. It couldn't be. BJ grabbed a stick from the ground and prodded at the object. It was a watch. BJ stepped back, stunned. Charley grabbed his arm and pulled him back to the bikes. BJ needed no convincing. They all pedaled home without stopping. When they came out on Man Gun Road, Tony and David continued on towards town while Charley and BJ climbed the gravel road back to their house. It was only when they got to their yard that BJ realized something.

Max had not returned with them.

Chapter Twenty-Three

Mark came home that night quieter than usual and admitting, after intense interrogation from Molly, that he had spent an hour listening to his boss yell about wolves and the upcoming governor's deer hunting opener. "I don't know what he wants me to do," said Mark, sniffing a bowl of mystery food and then handing it to BJ. "It's too late to change the deer harvest numbers, and their population is down after last winter. He thinks we should issue more permits to hunt wolves, but that wouldn't help with this particular animal." He glanced at BJ when he said this.

"That is so random," said Charley.

Molly put down her fork, and BJ knew a grammar lesson was imminent. "Do you know what 'random' means?"

"Doesn't it mean 'weird'?" said Charley.

"No," said Molly. "Random is 'accidental' or 'unorchestrated'." She pointed at the salad and then at BJ's plate, indicating that he should take some. "Your boss," she said to Mark, "doesn't have a conservation background, does he?"

Mark snorted. "He's a friend of the governor's. And of Larry Sourmeister, for what it's worth. It's an appointed position, remember? You know how these things work. And since the governor will be hunting here this fall, the boss wants to make darn sure he bags one. Pass the salt, please, Charley." He shook it vigorously over his plate.

BJ cleared his throat. "Anything from the trail cameras, Dad?"

"I have a couple of SD cards," he said, patting his shirt pocket. "We can look at them after supper. I also have an informant who walks that road, and he's keeping an eye out for me, too."

"Who's that?" asked Molly.

"Can't say. Oh, another cabin got broken into, by the way, but nothing was taken."

"Weird," said BJ.

"Random," said Charley.

"Definitely," said Molly to BJ. She shot a glance at Charley. "And probably not."

After supper, Molly headed for the garden, Charley sat beneath the bird feeder, and BJ joined his dad at the computer. Mark was looking at a dark image with a few wavy lines on one side. "What is that?"

"Don't know," said Mark. "I just got to this image. This camera is set up on a dead calf—no, not a wolf kill," he said before BJ could ask. "It died overnight from an illness. I asked Roland if we could use it for bait in a live trap. Look." Mark clicked the left arrow on the screen and rolled back through the last few photos, all of which were nearly identical photos of a large cage with one end propped open. Inside was the dead animal. Mark scrolled forward to the dark image and shook his head. Something was covering the camera lens. Something dark, maybe brown. But it was not uniform. A faint, straight line ran from the top right of the screen towards the bottom left. To the right of the line were what looked like two small pitchforks with horizontal lines on the handle. Or bird's feet.

"Did a leaf or something get stuck to the lens?" said BJ.

Mark grunted. "Those little pitchfork things look drawn to me. It looks man-made." Mark clicked the right arrow, and both he and BJ gasped: The dead calf was gone, and the door to the trap was closed. "What the…" He clicked forward a few more times, and the same image of an empty trap repeated. "Somebody covered the camera while the trap was emptied," said Mark.

"Do you have a secondary camera, Dad?"

"Not this time. We only have the budget for a few of them." Mark rubbed his jaw in thought.

"I don't get it," said BJ. "Who would do that?"

"Maybe someone who's not happy about trapping or killing wolves. There are plenty of people like that in the area."

"But none who know you have a trap set out."

"Almost none," said Mark.

Max had not returned by the time BJ went to bed, and he tossed and turned in his sleep, dreaming that he was at his Sacred Place, surrounded by a hundred phones, TVs, Xboxes, and speakers. They were all playing "Born in the USA" by Bruce Springsteen. BJ was singing along loudly, enjoying himself. Then, suddenly, someone was standing in front of him. BJ couldn't identify the person, but he saw that the person's right hand was bright red—just before it slapped BJ hard across the face.

BJ sat upright in bed and rubbed his left cheek. "Ow!" Far off in the woods, a wolf was howling.

"I want Max," said a voice from the lower bunk.

"Charley, what are you doing awake?"

"Kinda hard to sleep with you singing 'Born in the USA,' you know."

"Oh, sorry." BJ thought for a moment, then came to a decision. He climbed down and began to get dressed.

"Where you going?"

"To get Max. You stay here, all right?"

Charley agreed, but barely. BJ knew his folks would not be happy with him riding up the trail in the dark. If Charley came, he would really get it. He slipped downstairs, grabbed a headlamp from a hook near the door, and went outside. No dog came to greet him. Why had Max not returned with them? BJ shuddered to think what might happen if Max ran into the wolf. He grabbed his bike and coasted down their driveway and past Elmer's place. A light was on in the kitchen. He pulled out his Blackberry and checked the time. It was 2:30 in the morning.

Half an hour later, BJ popped out onto Reservation Road, legs burning and breathing hard. The waxing gibbous moon was high in the sky and cast enough light to see by. "Max!" BJ whistled. BJ stood astride his bike, not wanting to go up the road to the creepy house. But what choice did he have? That was where they had left the dog, so that was where he would have to go.

BJ turned off his headlamp and pedaled quickly, more to calm his nerves than to get there fast. At each driveway, he slowed down and gave a low whistle, but he got no response. He felt the creepy old cabin before he saw it and slowed down to a crawl. Just before the yard, he swung his leg over the seat and stopped. "Max," he whispered. BJ laid his bike on the edge of the road and walked into the yard, heart racing. "Max!" BJ stuck to the shadows, circling the inside of the yard. "Max, are you here?" Just then, he saw something that made him freeze: a faint light flickering through the back window of the cabin. Someone was inside. By BJ's reckoning, it was the same room where he had seen the eye earlier in the day. The hair was standing up on the back of BJ's neck, and little prickly sensations all over his body seemed to be telling him to leave. This was how he felt just before he and his dad got shot at. BJ was just heading back to the road when his ears picked up a faint sound. Whining. Whimpering.

BJ spun and scanned the darkness. "Max. Come here, boy!" The whining was coming from near the window. BJ crept to the shadow of the white pine in the yard, then to the window. The whining was coming from beneath the cabin. BJ dropped to his knees and waved towards the darkness. "Max, come here." Another whimper. What was wrong with him? Was he stuck? BJ shoved his head under the cabin. He saw the outline of Max's head some ten feet away.

BJ squirmed forward, forcing his skinny frame under the building. "Come on, boy."

Just then, the floor above him creaked. A trickle of dust landed on BJ's neck. A deep, gravelly voice spoke. "What time is it?"

A higher-pitched but equally raspy voice of a second man answered. "Time to go shoot that dog if he doesn't shut up." BJ's heart nearly stopped. They knew about Max.

"Leave him alone," said the first voice. "I don't need you shooting at anything other than deer no more. We're leavin' anyway."

"What if he follows us?"

"Fine, shoot him then." BJ's mind raced. The men were leaving. What if they found his bike? They would know he was here..."

"What the hell happened to...?"

BJ couldn't hear the rest.

"Stop asking me about Clyde. I told you I don't know. He went out to check on the deer and didn't come back. Maybe he chickened out and ran."

"He dropped the rifle in the yard."

"Okay, so maybe the wolf got him."

"Wolves don't mess with people, Niichi. I'm telling you, we got something else out here."

"Like one of your spirit monsters? Whatever, bro. We got enough trouble with law enforcement after Clyde took a shot at Maki. There's just too much going on. We've done what he asked us to do, and it's time to get out of here. Come on."

BJ was shaking. These were the men who shot at the truck. One was clearly Native. He had used "Niichi," which David often used for "dude." They were the poachers and, likely, the vandals as well. The floor groaned as the men crossed the room. BJ heard a door creak open, then more steps. The broken screen door squeaked open, then shut. It was then that BJ remembered that his legs were protruding out from under the building. As quietly as he could, he slipped all the way under the cabin and tried to rotate so that he could face forward. As he completed his turn, he kicked something metal, which made a clanging noise, and he froze. Suddenly, a face appeared where BJ's legs had been only moments before. "Don't try to follow us, dog. Got a bullet with your name on it if you do!"

"Holy shit, Niichi, come here!" said the other man. BJ heard the sound of vomiting.

"What is it? What's wrong with you?" said the other.

"Look there."

"Is that… a hand? Jesus."

"Now we know what happened to Clyde. I'm getting out of here." The sound of an ATV engine broke the silence of the night. From beneath the cabin, BJ watched it drive into the yard from where it had been parked, hidden, in the woods. The man who had threatened Max climbed on. They drove out onto the road, and instead of turning left and driving by BJ's bike, they turned right and disappeared with a lot of noise.

BJ waited for a long time before he dared move. Finally, he peeked out and scanned the yard, then crawled from under the building. "Come on, Max, they're gone." BJ heard sounds of movement and more whining. What was wrong with him? BJ looked under the cabin and saw Max struggling to move towards him. Eventually, he made it, crying and licking BJ on the face. There was a sudden explosion of snarls and barks just out of sight as if a huge fight had erupted. Something shrieked, and the sound made goosebumps pop up over BJ's body. "Let's go!" he yelled to Max, leaping on his bike and pedaling hard down the road. The snarling, barking, and shrieking faded into the distance. Max followed along behind, but slowly. BJ had to stop multiple times on the way back to let him catch up. When they finally got home, BJ leaned his bike against the garage and turned to greet Max, who had collapsed in the yard. BJ went to pet him and saw the blood covering his entire backside. BJ gasped.

Max was missing a leg.

Chapter Twenty-Four

News of the attack on the Maki dog spread around town and seemed to confirm suspicions about the rogue wolf. Even though Max had made it to the vet in time and survived the attack, the incident was fuel for the fire of those who wanted an all-out war against wolves. Anti-wolf and anti-DNR bumper stickers began to pop up around town. "Deer, not wolves," "Shoot, shovel, and shut up," and (BJ's least favorite) "DNR: Does Nothing Right," which was on a wooden plate attached to the back of Eddie Sourmeister's bike. A few pro-wolf signs began to appear as well—among liberals and local Ojibwe— and the tension in town increased.

Charley barely left Max's side while he recovered, mostly in the living room. Molly kept herself busy by going on longer runs, tending to the garden, and working at the co-op. Mark seemed to work every hour of the day, checking licenses, patrolling trails, and monitoring boat launches. BJ barely laid eyes on him. The close call at the cabin and Max's near death left him feeling vulnerable and scared, and he wanted more than anything to head into the cave and… what? Play? Stare at Morning Flower? But the words in BJ's history book came back into his mind.

Your family is in danger. Your community is in danger. Find the warrior!

So, against all instinct, BJ forced himself to head to his Sacred Area and watch and listen and explore. At first, it felt unproductive.

His mind was busy with images of wolves and blood and broken homes. But on the fourth day after Max's surgery, BJ felt like he had established a bit of a routine and was starting to feel like less of a stranger in the wilderness.

On the fifth day, while he was sitting still and feeling drousy, he fell asleep and dreamed of running around the mossy boulder and leaping over the birch log. Max was with him, his partial rear leg still bandaged. They sat on the ground, and BJ stroked the dog's head. Max's fur felt strangely soft. And he smelled funny. BJ awoke to find he was petting a skunk curled up in his lap. It was nothing short of a miracle that he did not scream, jump, or shake. The little black-and-white ball of fur, eyes closed, breathed steadily, peacefully, in the rhythm of a deep sleep. From time to time, he actually squeaked! Slowly, BJ's heart slowed down and he wondered if the skunk realized he was sitting on someone. He must. No creature was that clueless. He had probably been watching BJ come and go for weeks and finally decided that the two-legged visitor was harmless. He had climbed onto BJ's lap while he was asleep. BJ watched his little eyes dart back and forth behind closed lids as he dreamed. What did skunks dream about? Maybe of spraying Labradors. After maybe half an hour, the skunk stood and stretched in one motion, its rear terrifyingly close to BJ's face. It stepped off BJ's lap and waddled into the brush.

When BJ returned home, a green notebook and pencil lay on the table of the back deck. He did not see these on his way out. He opened the notebook. Inside the cover was written *BJ's Nature Journal*. On the opposite page, one of his parents had written *July 13. Here's what I saw and heard and smelled today.* BJ picked up the pencil and wrote: "One nuthatch, two chickadees. Heard a raven. Got yelled at by a red squirrel. No Red Hand Warrior. Fell asleep in Sacred Area again. Woke up with skunk in lap." He put the pencil down, then picked it back up and scribbled. "Maybe random. Maybe not."

BJ continued to spend time in his Sacred Area for nearly another two weeks. When he returned to the house, he wrote what he'd seen, heard, felt, or smelled. Each entry started the same way: Date, time, weather, then "Still no Warrior." Sometimes, he wrote about his moods ("Got out of bed grumpy this morning), his feelings ("I miss Morning Flower"), or his fears ("I'm worried about dad's job"). Beyond making him feel better, the simple act of journaling began to have a curious effect on his awareness. The more BJ wrote, the more he noticed, and the more he noticed, the more he wrote. Even in town, he became aware of things that, previously, he had ignored entirely, like the color of a roof or the seagull droppings at the base of each lamppost. He wrote this down, too, feeling silly, but it couldn't hurt, so he kept it up. If the red-hand guy was watching him and would show up after BJ did plenty of watching and learning, then, by God, that's what he would do.

After a while, BJ's journal began to show patterns in animal behavior. They were most active early in the morning and late in the evening. Light rain didn't seem to affect them. Nor did the sun or clouds. But wind did. On windy days, the birds could be silent and the animals invisible. He noticed that the river was lower and warmer than a month earlier, and the juicy green plants growing along its edges attracted small animals, which, in turn, attracted larger ones. BJ was now more aware of the eyes on him while he sat at his Sacred Area.

On one occasion, he sensed something was watching him from behind a cluster of Juneberry bushes, so he stood up and walked over to investigate. Nothing was there, but he found a hollow log nearby. It was the skunk's den. BJ began to train his attention on that log, and by forcing himself to get up very early for several days in a row, he began to learn the animal's routine: Each morning, between six and seven, he returned to his log to den up. So, BJ started bringing organic, gluten-free crackers, which he set on the ground and the little animal gobbled up. After a week of this, when BJ had no more crackers to bring, the skunk waddled up and put its front paws on BJ's outstretched legs with a look that clearly meant, "Hey, where's the food?" That day, when he told Charley about this, she came up with the name "Ref," short for "Referee," after the black-and-white stripes in his fur. BJ agreed it was a good name.

The next day, when returning from his sit time, BJ decided to take a different route back to his yard, looping to the north where the slope down to the lake was rocky and open. The sun was a third of the way across the sky, warming up the hillside and sending scents of dry pine needles and old granite into the air. BJ stopped near a cluster of blueberry bushes and squatted to look at a deer track in a bed of semi-dry moss. The print showed a northeast direction of travel. The tips of the toes were slightly open, leaving the moss unbroken and unbent between them. BJ looked for the next track, but some woody debris and moist ground made it impossible. Maybe the deer had turned around or jumped? He looked for a long time without success.

How, he wondered, could Stalking Bear and Runs Swiftly have tracked on this hillside? The more BJ looked, the more frustrated he became. If he couldn't see a simple deer track, then there was little chance he could find a wolf. BJ shook his head and stood, then gasped. In the spot where he had been staring for five minutes and seeing nothing was the second track. By backing up and looking at the whole of the scene, it was revealed. In fact, looking in this way, eyes relaxed and focused on nothing, BJ was able to perceive an entire set of marks where the animal had traveled—even across an exposed slab of granite.

He dropped to his knees to study the tracks, but they disappeared the minute he did so. He rubbed his cowlick with his right palm, straightened up—and there they were once more. What was going on? BJ was suddenly reminded of the hidden pictures at the science center in Bemidji. He had stubbornly stared at them for almost an hour until something clicked in his brain, and the Statue of Liberty was revealed. Once he saw her, he had to be careful not to change his focus or shift his position, or the image would disappear in a blur of random pixels. BJ regained the image of the deer marks and squatted slowly towards them—all while keeping his focus relaxed. In this manner, he managed to get his face close to what he knew was a track, and it was then that he could see the tiny bits of broken moss and lichen on the ground where the animal had placed its foot. His chest filled with joy. He wished Stalking Bear and Running Wolf were there to experience it with him. Just then, a voice spoke out from close by: "Morneau went three for four last night." Elmer was leaning against a birch, his hands in his jeans pockets.

"Holy cow, Elmer, you scared me! Who did what?"

"Justin Morneau. First base."

"Oh."

"Whatcha lookin' at?"

"Deer tracks."

"You've been out a lot. See anything interesting?"

"Not really. Well, yes, I suppose. Quite a bit, actually."

Elmer plucked a three-leaved plant that resembled a clover, popped it into his mouth, then made a face. BJ recognized it as one of the bunch that Morning Flower had given him on their walk to the lake. Elmer offered one to BJ. "Wood sorrel?"

BJ took it, said a quick note of thanks in his mind, and popped it into his mouth.

"I'd forgotten how sour they were," said Elmer, pursing his lips. "Been a while since I've eaten them."

"Same," said BJ. "Like, six hundred years."

The following morning, after feeding Ref his daily ration of crackers, he watched the skunk waddle away, then sat in the little depression and closed his eyes. Soon, he sensed a presence nearby and sat up to look around. A figure, some fifty yards to the south, was looking in his direction. It was not Charley. BJ held his breath. Had the warrior come?

"BJ?"

"Yes, I'm here!" BJ was nearly trembling with excitement. The figure moved through the brush towards BJ's sit spot. He did so with ease and grace, parting the branches with care as he stepped. When he moved into the light, however, BJ's anticipation turned to surprise.

Mark stepped around a young cedar, strode up to BJ, and sat across from him. "You blended in well here. I couldn't see you. Charley gave me rough directions." He took a minute to study the surroundings. "Nice place!" Mark pointed to BJ's hummock. "There must have been a big tree there a long time ago."

BJ's mouth parted. "Dad, how did you know that?"

"Well, I did study forestry, you know," said Mark. "I've been around long enough to see the trees fall over and begin to decompose. There's a lot to read in the forest if you know the language."

BJ felt a bit embarrassed at his own surprise at his father's forest knowledge. "Did you play in the woods a lot when you were a kid?" he asked.

"Actually," said Mark, "I had a spot kind of like this when I was growing up in Hibbing.

"Really?"

"It was right on the edge of a creek—kind of like here, but with more deer and fewer moose."

"That sounds awesome."

"It was. I saw all sorts of stuff. Watched birds and animals for hours there."

"I'd like to go there sometime."

"You could," said Mark, "but it's an outlet mall now."

BJ felt like he'd been punched in the gut. A freaking outlet mall?

"My uncle wanted more retirement money, so he sold the land to a developer from Minneapolis." Mark was quiet, his face reliving memories.

BJ opened his mouth to say something, but at that moment, a man in buckskins with a long dark braid appeared some thirty yards behind Mark. He was snapping his fingers and bobbing his head up and down as if he were listening to music. Two steps, then a snap. Two more steps, a pause, then a little hop in the air. BJ recognized him immediately as the man from back in time, and he gasped.

"Yeah," said Mark, misinterpreting BJ's reaction. "Say, speaking of my job, you're aware of the pressure I'm getting on this wolf issue?"

"Yeah," said BJ, suddenly nervous. The man bent over, grabbed his ankles, and shook his rear end back and forth like some pop star.

"Anyway," continued Mark, "There are rumors that my position may be eliminated."

"WHAT? Dad, how can they eliminate a position? Isn't the DNR short, like, twenty-six officers right now? How can they do that?" The man finished shaking his butt, then shuffle-stepped to a hollow log and began to drum on it with his hands. BJ forced himself to continue looking at his father. "They need to be adding positions, not eliminating them!"

"Tell me about it," said Mark. "This governor's a real…"

"Dickhead!" yelled the man as he drummed on the log.

BJ, thinking quickly, piggybacked on the word. "Dickhead! Because he's a dickhead, Dad!"

Mark cracked up. "Don't let your mother hear you talk like that!"

BJ nearly lost his composure when he saw what happened next. Ref, the skunk, upset at having his nap interrupted by the pounding, came charging out the end of the log and began chasing the man back and forth through the woods.

"Say," remembered Mark, "Did I hear that Charley screamed at Larry Sourmeister's son the other day?"

"Yep," said BJ, whose eyes were flitting from his dad to the scene behind him. "And punched him in the nuts."

"Uffda!" Mark stood up. "She gets that from her mother."

Ref had cornered the man between a small boulder and an alder patch. His hands were up in the air as if he were trying to negotiate with the skunk. Mark began to turn, but BJ shot out a quick question to keep him from doing so. "Hey, Dad!" Mark turned back to BJ, who confessed that he'd gone looking for Max, relating the story about the two men.

Mark seemed to grow pale as BJ spoke. Finally, he said, "BJ, that was dangerous and a very close call." He was silent in thought for a while. "Those are definitely our guys," said Mark. "But did you say two? My informant said there were three of them." BJ told his dad what he had heard about the disappearance of the third man. Mark looked like he wanted to say something, but he stayed silent for a while. "Things are strange right now, BJ."

Tell me about it.

Mark stood and stretched. Just then, the man in buckskin who had backed away from the skunk toppled backward over the boulder and disappeared—just as Mark turned and faced that direction. "Oh my!" Mark pointed. "That's a big skunk!"

"Dad, what are we going to do?"

"Sisu."

"Huh?"

"Sisu is the Finnish word for resilience, strength, and power," said Mark. "My grandparents and their generation used Sisu during the war when the Russians invaded. There are times to tap into it. He turned back to face BJ. "Now is one of them." Mark left without another word.

Sisu thought BJ. Cool! He wondered what the Ojibwe equivalent was. BJ decided to take a new route back to the house. This brought him along a ridge with a partial view of Lake Superior. Looking back down into the forest, he thought he could make out his sit area, some seventy-five yards away. He wondered, when he sat in his little spot, if he was visible from here. Yes, he thought, he probably was. The odds of someone standing here and spotting BJ were tiny, almost impossible, right? It was then that he noticed a shiny object embedded in a pile of dirt. BJ reached down, then stopped cold. It was a watch, yes. The dirt, however, was not only shiny but steaming. It was, BJ knew, a very large and very fresh pile of scat.

Chapter Twenty-Five

August arrived as if someone had opened a giant oven door. Temperatures along the shore soared into the upper 70s. Inland, it was fifteen degrees hotter. People flocked to the frigid waters of Superior to wade and even swim. The still air allowed mosquitoes to swarm like clouds of mini vampires, attacking everything that breathed. BJ was positively spooked about going to his Sacred Area, so he avoided the little hummock and opted to sit against a nearby birch tree, which was more hidden. Two days in a row, he walked very slowly and carefully to his sit area along the ridge to make sure nothing was sitting up there staring at him. The scat and watch were still there.

In addition to the mosquitoes, the warm weather brought the season's first ripe tomato. Molly cut it into five slices, which she spread onto a plate and topped with equally thick slices of fresh mozzarella cheese, a basil leaf, and a drizzle of olive oil. BJ and Charley joined her to eat on the deck while Max lay in the shade, farting at them. BJ chewed his food slowly, thinking of Shines Bright and Morning Flower. Hummingbirds zipped back and forth from the trees to the sugar water feeder and back again. BJ felt eager to go back to the cave and was beginning to wonder if the Red Hand Warrior would only show up in the past. Maybe he needed to do sit time there, against the great tree?

Saturday was the Walleye Daze Festival. Grand Marais was a cornucopia of vehicles from all around the country and even Canada. Closed-off streets and heavy traffic forced Molly and the kids to park along the highway, three blocks from the co-op, and walk to town. Carnival rides and bouncy castles were set up in parking lots, and the streets were packed with food trucks and various booths selling everything from T-shirts to pottery and jewelry. George was singing "Celebration" when BJ and Charley arrived at the bait shop.

For a few minutes, BJ stood beneath the walleye to compose himself, wrinkling his nose at the powerful scents of fry bread, corn dogs, and mini donuts. Artist booths lined up shoulder-to-shoulder and filled with jewelry, paintings, scarves, dresses, and woodwork gave Kalevala Street the look of a Middle Eastern bazaar. Normally, all the fun and commotion would have been exhilarating for BJ, but this time, he felt the sting of culture shock of being back in the loud and chaotic modern world, and he missed a time where the loudest noises were thunderclaps and the strongest smells were of drying fish and hides.

Russ was there in flannel, suspenders, and blue wool bonnet. "Morning, kids!" he said around his thin Paul Bunyan pipe. "Everything's all set inside. Coffee's hot, serve yourself. If you have a question or if any cheeseheads give you trouble, I'll be at log rolling. I appreciate you minding the store."

"I thought you weren't going to log roll anymore," said BJ. Log rolling involved balancing or running on a spinning log, lumberjack-style, for as long as possible before falling into the water. Russ had won ten years in a row before the Walleye Daze organizers suggested he take a few years off and let someone else have a shot at winning.

"Just helping." Russ winked, then he looked up sharply at George, who had begun singing some high-pitched pop tune. "That's still not Lenny Kravitz."

"Miley Cyrus," said Charley.

"Who?"

"You don't want to know," said BJ.

BJ and Charley went inside and jostled for space behind the counter, each trying to look important. Their work began quickly as a steady stream of people wandered in over the next two hours, giving them little time to rest. Customers spent their money freely on lures, line, reels, rods, and T-shirts. Almost all the men, BJ noted, had their faces painted with a rainbow or heart from one of the artist booths. BJ's counting skills were put to the test as cashier. Charley split her time between bagging and keeping an eye on the merchandise. At 11:30, with only two customers in the store, she slipped outside to participate in the minnow race, returning minutes later carrying a giant multi-colored sucker.

A lanky young man with a ball cap and neck tattoos came to the counter and placed down a lure. BJ made change for him just when Charley said, "You put a lure in your pocket." The man, appearing not to hear, accepted the change from BJ and headed for the door, but Charley followed and repeated the charge. "You took a lure! I saw you!"

At this, the young man turned around at the doorway and scanned the store as if he were making sure no one was around. "I didn't steal nothin'!" he spat, then stepped towards Charley.

The next thing anyone knew, he was hoisted high into the air, swung around, and slammed hard against the wall, feet dangling. Russ had come out of nowhere and was holding him fast by the scruff of the neck. Russ' face was calm. His eyes were not. "You do *not* want to be the one to touch my goddaughter." Outside, George began to sing "From the Frying Pan into the Fire." "Where is it, Charley?" said Russ.

"Front left pocket."

Russ grinned. "And I thought you were just happy to see me." The man gurgled a response. "Apologize to Charley, and thank me for coming in and saving your nuts."

The young man glanced from Russ to Charley.

"Hurry up," said Russ.

"S-s-so-sorry, and (cough), tha-tha-tha…"

"Good enough," said Russ, dropping him to the ground and turning to face the kids. The thief staggered out the door and disappeared. "I can watch the store for a while now. Why don't you guys walk around?"

"What about the lure?" said Charley.

Russ glanced out the door. "That's the fifth one he's taken this summer. No big loss for me. First time I've talked with him, so maybe now he'll straighten himself out. All right," Russ announced, "get out of here. See you in a couple hours."

BJ wanted to see log rolling, but Charley insisted on visiting the donkey rides first, so they walked back towards the co-op, where she took a ride on a brown donkey with a white blaze on his chest. After this, they meandered through the corn hole toss, the Tilt-A-Whirl, and down to the Paul and Babe statues where a loon-calling contest was taking place. Most of the contestants were young and made sounds that BJ reckoned were more like a mourning dove than a loon, but the audience was appropriately appreciative.

A dunk tank, sponsored by the Chamber of Commerce, was raising money for cancer, and Larry Sourmeister himself sat on the seat, hurling well-practiced insults at the beanbag throwers. He was very good at this. A picture of a wolf had been taped to the target. Ryan Olafson, the school principal, waited on deck in a swimsuit, looking sweaty and nervous. A large number of middle and high school kids were lined up, waiting for a crack at him. But they had to wait for Bud Davis, the crew-cut gym teacher, to finish with Larry first. Jaw set, determined, and looking as serious as any man with a green-and-red hummingbird on his cheek could, he wound up like a major league pitcher at the bottom of the ninth inning and threw. "What kind of hair…" said Larry before the target was struck, dropping him into the tank to applause and laughter. Bud tossed the remaining beanbag to one of the dunk tank helpers and spat a stream of brown juice near BJ's feet. "Eyes open, Maki," he said, then disappeared into the crowd.

The log-rolling contest had finished by the time BJ and Charley arrived. A few people were paying to see how long they could stay up, but no one was very good at it, so they continued towards the Northern Surplus Store, passing by a steady stream of men walking away from a small red tent with blue stars, flowers, and kittens on their faces. Eddie Sourmeister rode by on a bike, flanked by two friends, his anti-DNR sign displayed prominently at the rear. BJ watched them ride into the alley and past Larry Sourmeister, who was handing Elmer a large yellow envelope and patting him on the back. "Hey..." said BJ, but Charley had grabbed him by the hand and dragged him towards the red tent where they found Angie Gonzales sitting on a stool in a very short sleeveless summer dress, her auburn hair draped down one bare shoulder, doing face painting. "All right, sweetheart," she said to a balding middle-aged man, "what can I put on your cheek?"

"Whatever takes the longest," he breathed.

"A rainbow it is!" laughed Angie, lifting the paintbrush.

BJ and Charlie were still giggling when they got back to the bait store. Russ was posing for a photo, his two-bladed axe over one shoulder. After the picture was taken and the tourists had departed, he motioned for the kids to have a seat, then brought the axe inside and returned with two ice cream sandwiches. BJ accepted his treat and settled into the Adirondack chair. "Hey Russ, the other day, you said you'd tell us about Dad and Troy Gustafson."

Russ appeared not to hear BJ for a while and stared silently out towards the lake. After a few minutes, he said, "Your dad had been running surveillance on Troy and a couple other guys, and he knew they had about ten times their limit in crappies. He waited for them to put their boat on the trailer and drive away, then pulled them over further down the road. He asked to check the coolers, which were still in the boat. When Mark came back to the driver's window, he told them they were way over their possession limit. At that point, Troy tried to hand him a huge handful of cash.

"He tried to bribe Dad?" said Charley.

"Yep. That didn't go well. Mark ordered everyone out of the vehicle, but Troy hit the gas. And your dad," said Russ, "jumped back into their boat.

"Holy shit!" said BJ.

A tiny grin showed under Russ's beard. "They swerved back and forth down the road, trying to throw him out, but Mark shot out the tires of the jeep, then leaped out when it went into the ditch." BJ felt his face go slack. His dad was practically some dude from *Mission Impossible*. "It gets better," said Russ. "The other two guys ran off into the woods, but Troy came running at your dad with a baseball bat."

BJ gasped. Charley covered her mouth.

"Mark would have been within his rights to shoot him, but he waited until Troy was within arm's reach, stepped forward fast, and punched him so hard, he popped out his front teeth, knocking him cold."

"Sisu!" said BJ.

"That," said Russ, "is exactly right."

BJ had never seen his father hit anyone. He couldn't imagine his father hitting anyone. "What happened to the other guys?"

"They were picked up by tribal police and given slaps on the wrist. Troy went to prison."

BJ sat quietly for a while, then said, "When does he get out?"

"Three months ago," said Russ.

They sat silent for a while, then BJ mumbled, "I figured Charley got her temper from *Mom*!"

"Oh, she did," said Russ. "Mark wasn't mad at all—just doing his job. That's the amazing thing about your dad. I've never seen someone who could keep his cool like that. If either your mom or sister had been in his place, Troy would have been in pieces. Guaranteed."

Molly, Keanu, and Elmer arrived. "Nice track," said Russ, and Elmer touched his cheek where a bright blue wolf print had been painted. He shrugged. Mark's work truck pulled up, and the passenger window slid down. "Wanna have a bite with us?" said Russ. "Plenty of fish sandwiches left over."

Mark shook his head. "Thanks, Russ. Just got a call to head up to Reservation Road."

"Another cow?" said Molly.

"A dog?" asked Charley.

Mark sighed. "I'm afraid it was a man." BJ caught a little glance in his direction. "At least, we think so. They only found blood and some torn clothing. I won't know for sure until I check it out. I'll check back in later." He rolled up the window and took off, leaving a ringing silence in his wake. For the first time in Minnesota—and maybe the whole country—a wolf had killed a person. And if things had been bad for his father before, BJ was dead certain that they were about to get a lot worse.

Chapter Twenty-Six

The creature had followed the two remaining men for another week, allowing them to steal food and clothing from a handful of homes. They reeked of smoke, sweat, and now, fear. They were unsure of the fate of their comrade and whispered obsessively about the man in uniform. Their worry and distraction began to cause them to make mistakes. They broke branches and left tracks that anyone could see. It would, the creature knew, be a matter of time before the man in uniform caught them. This would mean the loss of two potential allies. Yes, it would have to alter their plans. So that night, it followed them to a dilapidated and broken-down barn where they lay down in moldy and pungent straw. It let them sleep without interruption. After all, this would be the last night they would spend in a building of any sort. By the time they awoke the following morning, it was there, ready and waiting.

Chapter Twenty-Seven

Everyone was still at the bait shop, drinking tea and coffee and worrying, when Mark called with an update. Molly put him on the speaker phone, and he described a bloody and torn scene in the yard of an abandoned cabin. It was, he said, all they could find. Molly was aghast. "They didn't even find a body? Just like with the cow. It's got to be the same wolf."

"It's not a wolf," said Elmer.

For the first time since BJ could remember, his father's voice sounded impatient: "Elmer, I appreciate your love of wolves and the Ojibwe connection to them, but I'm not in the mood to debate the species in question now. We've got multiple dead animals, pets, and now a person. Please let me do my job. Gotta go." The call ended.

Keanu stood. "You good for that ride, Molly?"

Molly brushed a strand of hair from her eyes and rubbed her temples for a moment. "I need to unpack some stuff at the co-op but will be ready in about twenty minutes." She and Keanu headed out, followed shortly by Elmer, looking serious.

BJ felt like things were beginning to unravel. Minutes earlier, he had been having an awesome day. The sky was bright. His belly was full. And now he was seething with anger at the wolf, at whoever messed with his father's trap, at his dad's boss, at Larry Sourmeister, and this stupid Red Hand Warrior who was not showing up if he even existed. How much longer was he going to have to get eaten alive by mosquitos for this guy to show up?

Russ said, "Do you know that a number of those homes that were broken into have just been bought?"

"No," said BJ. "So what?" People sold houses all the time in the area.

Russ shrugged and headed into the back of the store as he spoke. "Just seems convenient. I mean, if a guy wanted to buy up an area, it would be pretty sneaky to scare the owners by breaking into homes and killing animals."

"Who would do something like that?" said Charley.

Russ returned from the rear of the store, drying his hands on a dirty rag. "We could use some scouts around here to find out."

BJ looked at Russ so quickly that he nearly pulled a muscle. "What did you say?"

Russ gazed at the old photos on the wall as he spoke. "Scouts were the eyes and ears of the tribe. They were protectors. Sometimes fighters. Like your dad."

"Do you think daddy needs help?" asked Charley.

"Might. There's a lot going on. Know anyone who has a serious interest in real estate who might have a business interest in all this stuff?"

BJ exchanged a glance with his sister. *Yes,* he thought. Yes, they did.

At 7:30 Monday morning, Molly parked the car at the co-op, got out, and ran around to the passenger side, where she gave the rear passenger door a hard kick with the flat of her right foot. BJ climbed out, Charley following close behind. Molly went inside to work while they headed down the sidewalk towards the bait shop. Russ was in the big Adirondack chair, talking to a man in the doorway, wearing a beige Mexican sombrero and looking very confused. "Of course, he's in there!" said Russ. "Keep going, he'll hear you. And don't forget the dance!" He winked at the kids, who waved and continued in the direction of Larry Sourmeister's office.

"I don't know if Larry's involved in any of this," said BJ, "but I think it's worth checking out. I just have a feeling that it's all connected. Anyway," he said, "it doesn't hurt to go see what he's up to." Charley had agreed to the plan, suggesting that they hide out in the bushes and try to spy on Larry when he arrived at work. But Keanu was there in a colorful reggae cap, setting up a card table and food display directly in front of the office. "Hey, little dudes!" He unfurled a banner that read "Celebrate Organic!" and then plucked two red berries from a dish. "Here," he said, holding out his hand. "Try these."

BJ raised an eyebrow.

"Organic sea buckthorns! It's a superfood!"

BJ and Charley each took one and tasted it. It was very strong and sour. "Thanks," said BJ, grimacing. They walked past the building to the end of the block.

Charley smacked her lips. "Not bad for a butt-thorn."

"*Buck*thorn," said BJ.

"What's a superfood?"

"Stuff for people who don't know how to pick blueberries. We're going to have to approach from behind, I think." They turned right, walked past the building, then took another right into the alley, quickly arriving at the back of Larry's office. They waited a few minutes until Keanu was busy talking to someone, then slipped up the side of the building and into the arborvitae bushes beneath the front window.

For the next hour, they waited and watched. Both kids were seasoned sitters. Every few minutes, they stretched their legs. At 9:02 a.m., a black Lexus SUV parked in front of the building. Larry got out and strode past Keanu towards the office door, jabbering on his cell phone. "Didn't we just get him a PlayStation?" He used his left hand to pull a set of keys from his pocket and began fumbling with them. "What do you mean out of date? When's his birthday, again?" Larry set down his briefcase. More keys jingling. "Okay, whatever. I gotta go."

Keanu was just behind him. "Heeeey, mister?"

Larry flinched and spun, dropping his keys, which bounced off the cement steps and landed in the bushes, resting against BJ's left leg. "Son-of-a... DON'T DO THAT!"

"It's national Organic..."

"Sure," said Larry, absentmindedly "I'll buy one. Say, Quinoa..."

"Keanu."

"Right, Keanu, do you have to set up right in front of my place? It's going to get in the way of my customers."

"Sure, man, no worries. I'll slide down the walk aways. Peace!" Keanu strolled back to the display and began moving it down the sidewalk.

Before BJ knew it, Larry had dropped to all fours and was groping in the bushes for his keys. BJ held his breath as a pair of ruddy cheeks grunted and strained not two feet away from him. A sudden odor of coffee, cigar, and aftershave seeped into the bushes. Larry's hand swept back and forth, brushed BJ's leg, then found the keys and seized them with a grunt. He stood, unlocked the door, and went in. BJ exchanged a glance with his sister. Larry had looked at both of them but only perceived the bushes and his keys. Why on earth would there be anything else?

Inside, a chair moved. A belch. Some rustling of papers. For the next forty-five minutes, Larry was on the phone with various clients and business associates, discussing interest rates, house prices, and other things BJ didn't understand. A pop can fizzed. Larry paced. "Where are they?" He was trying to reach someone on the phone. More pacing. Then, "Hey, I'm at the office. I need you to take down some signs. Ready? 22510, 22703 and 24675."

BJ's ears perked up at the last number. Where had he heard that before?

"There's one more at the entrance point. I'm sure he'll sell. He'll have to." Larry hung up, then began to rustle some papers and type on a keyboard. This went on for a while until BJ finally motioned to Charley that it was time to go.

Keanu had moved his table down to the corner but was still close. BJ didn't want to take any chances, so they waited again for him to be distracted and were rewarded magnificently when Angie Gonzalez, in big brown sunglasses, decided to stop and visit. "Come on," said BJ, standing and walking directly to the sidewalk. Charley followed closely. BJ giggled at their luck. With Angie in front of Keanu, they could have walked by naked, and Keanu wouldn't have noticed a thing. But Angie *did* see them. She waved them over. "Que pasa, you two? BJ, how about a sleepover in a couple of weeks? Tony hasn't seen much of you this summer, and David's off at coding camp in DC."

BJ wondered if Uncle Francisco was still around. He and Charley followed Angie across the street and discussed possible dates, then waved goodbye and headed north along the sidewalk. BJ felt like his mind was overflowing with information that needed to be organized. He took a deep breath to clear it as they passed Ida's Bakery (two chocolate raised donuts, four strudels). Not a dozen yards further, something inside BJ told him to stop. *Go back*, said a voice in his head.

"What's up?" said Charley, but her voice sounded distant.

BJ returned, dreamlike, to the bakery window and counted the donuts again. A dozen glazed, eleven cinnamon, two chocolate raised, four strudels. BJ rubbed his cowlick. What was wrong with him? Feeling stupid, he walked back to where his sister was staring at him from the curb. But the feeling hit him again—so hard that he nearly stumbled: *GO BACK!* BJ held up his index finger. "Hold on a sec," he said, then returned for a third time to the bakery window.

"Hungry, BJ?" said a voice from the doorway. There was Mrs. Richardson, gray hair curling from the edge of her baking cap. Her shoulders were broad. She smelled of flour, oil, and perfume.

BJ tried to work out the message forming in his head. "I was just looking... at... at..." Four apple strudels. Four... suddenly, it hit him. "Hey, is Mr. Kern on vacation?"

"Vacation?" Mrs. Richardson rubbed a thick, wrinkled hand on her chin. "Why, no, I don't think so. He doesn't really travel, so he hasn't gone anywhere. Now that I think of it"—she glanced at her watch—" he should have been here a while ago. You know, he's always..."

BJ was already across the street, running up the sidewalk as fast as he could. Mr. Kern lived just a block up and around the corner from Rusty's. BJ was knocking on the front door when Charley caught up with him. "Something's wrong!" said BJ, bolting around Charley to the rear of the house. At the back door, he knocked again with no response. A small window was set in the middle of the door with an NRA sticker in one corner. A bumper sticker below the window read, "We don't call 911." BJ put his nose to the glass. Everything looked normal: four chairs, a kitchen table with an overcoat. On the floor, a pair of boots and... BJ flinched. A bare foot was poking around the corner, toes pointed upwards. "There he is!" BJ knocked hard on the window. "Mr. Kern! MR. KERN! Charley, he's not moving!" BJ looked around desperately for a way in. He had forgotten his phone, and there was no one in sight.

"I'll get Uncle Russ!" said Charley, sprinting back to the corner. BJ heard her scream, "Uncle Russ! HELP!" BJ turned back towards the kitchen, but in an instant—an almost impossibly small instant—all 350 pounds of Russ was there with him. BJ explained quickly.

"The door's locked?" said Russ.

"Yes!"

Russ held out a frisbee-sized hand, palm open, and smacked the door near the lock. It flew open like it was made of cardboard, splintering the frame. In one move, he was in, sweeping aside the kitchen table and kneeling, his ear turned towards Mr. Kern's mouth.

The old man's lips quivered. "Chest pain."

Russ pointed at the phone on the wall. "BJ, call 911!" He did so.

Russ swept into the bathroom, returning with a bottle of aspirin. "You on any medications?"

Mr. Kern shook his head.

"Allergies?"

"No," he gasped.

Russ held out a white pill above Mr. Kern's mouth. "Chew this up." Mr. Kern made a face as he chewed. Russ scooped him up and strode out the door, BJ and Charley following behind. They walked south, down the middle of the street. Soon, a police car, lights flashing, pulled up alongside the four of them. The officer leaned his head out the window. "Ambulance is on the way, Russ."

"We'll meet them halfway," said Russ, not breaking stride. "Hold on now, Alfred." BJ thought he could hear "How to Save a Life" being sung from the direction of the bait shop, but he wasn't sure. A few onlookers began to gather along the edges of the street. "A parade!" yelled a little girl, clapping, but there was no candy for her today. They arrived at the end of the block, where another police car was stopped to prevent traffic from slowing the little march. By the time they reached the second intersection, a small crowd had joined in. It did look like a parade. At the head of the procession strolled a giant of a man, a frail figure in his arms. Hustling alongside him were two kids. Behind them, one police car with flashing lights and a growing number of onlookers. The ambulance met them, lights flashing. Russ carried Mr. Kern to the rear of the vehicle and waited.

A young Ojibwe woman with a dark ponytail hopped out of the driver's side, strode briskly around the vehicle, and opened the back doors.

"One aspirin at 0930 hours," said Russ, leaning in to place Mr. Kern on the cot.

"Great!" she said. "Allergies or medications?"

"Neither," said Russ.

The other EMT, a fit-looking bald man, climbed in the back with his partner, and they began preparing the equipment. After a minute, the young woman grabbed hold of the doors and said, "Thanks, Russ!"

Russ tilted his head towards the kids. "Thank them! *They're* the ones that found him."

"Howah, good job, guys!" She gave a thumbs-up and closed the door with a snap.

After the ambulance left and the crowd thinned out, Russ turned to BJ and Charley. "How did you do that?"

"Do what?" said BJ.

"I saw you run up the sidewalk from the bakery. How did you know he was sick?"

"Well, er, there were still four strudels," said BJ.

Russ narrowed his eyes.

"He was late today! I don't know. He always has his strudel at 8:05 sharp. It just felt like something was wrong." BJ didn't know what else to say.

Russ grunted. "So you knew something was up?" BJ shrugged. "Wow!" boomed Russ, scooping both of them up in a bear hug. "You guys are something else! SOMETHING ELSE!" He threw his head back and let loose a thunderous laugh. "Just like *scouts*!"

Chapter Twenty-Eight

News of BJ's and Charley's role in Mr. Kern's rescue spread faster than blackflies in June, and their newfound celebrity gave a welcome—if brief—reprieve from thoughts of man-eating wolves and violent criminals. For days, it was impossible to appear in town without somebody wanting to hear the story or to congratulate them.

The following Monday, BJ and Charley staked out Larry's office for the second time, but the only person they saw was Keanu, who was still on the corner, doggedly offering samples of freeze-dried veggie sticks to passersby. After two and a half hours, they returned to the co-op, where Molly was waiting to take them to visit Mr. Kern.

"He came home from the hospital yesterday, and his two sisters are here from Williston. They would like to meet you. I imagine Alfred is still tired, so we'll just drop off the flowers and leave him alone." Molly handed the kids a bouquet of lilies. Together, they headed down the sidewalk toward Mr. Kern's house. A shiny white Cadillac with North Dakota plates was parked in front. Before they reached the door, it flew open with a bang, and two heavy-set, ruddy-faced women wearing flowery summer dresses lunged forward, nearly getting stuck in the doorway, and descended upon the kids like colorful blimps.

"Oh, de little heroes!" exclaimed the one in the pink dress and seized BJ. "Oh, de little darlins!" exclaimed the one in the yellow dress and grabbed Charley. BJ and Charley's heads disappeared between sets of flabby arms and enormous breasts.

A voice from inside the house pierced the women's exclamations. "Olga! Eva! Would you leave dos kids alone and let 'em come in here!" The women released the nearly purple captives. "Okay, okay," said the one in the pink dress. She straightened out her hair and motioned to her sister. "Come on, Eva, bring 'em inside. Don't get yourself worked up now, Alfred!" She opened the door and waddled in. "It's bad for your blood pressure!"

Eva herded the kids in behind Olga. The living room was packed with flowers, cards, and balloons. Mr. Kern was sitting up in bed, wearing a white-and-red-striped pajama top and a smile. He looked older and paler than before the heart attack. His thin, gray hair was brushed neatly to one side of his head. He held out his arms. Both BJ and Charley hugged him. "Thanks for saving me," he said and held them for a long time. They spent a few minutes going over the whole event. Molly waited at the door.

"I was feeling awful all morning," he explained. "My arm was sore, and I figured I'd pulled something while chopping wood. Next thing I knew, I was on the floor." He heaped more praise on the kids, making BJ feel embarrassed. Finally, Molly intervened. "We'll get out of your hair now, Alfred."

Eva clasped her meaty hands together. "I'm so glad Alfred has friends like you around!"

"So are we," said Molly. "I hope we can stick around for a long time!"

Olga jabbed a finger in Molly's direction. "What do you mean, you hope? You're not planning on leaving, are you?"

Molly cleared her throat. "We're not planning to, but we need to make sure that Mark's position as conservation officer is funded. There's been some talk that it might not be." BJ felt his stomach turn over. Why did his mother have to bring that up? Why now?

"Why on earth wouldn't it be?" said Mr. Kern.

"Oh, you know. Politics. Budget cuts, I suppose."

"The state has a budget surplus!" said Mr. Kern, growing red-faced.

Eva forced him back onto the pillow. "We'll talk public policy later, Alfred."

Molly put her hand on BJ's shoulder and steered him towards the door.

"See you, Mr. Kern," said BJ.

"Come back and visit again!"

Charley reached the door, then remembered something. She unzipped her backpack and pulled out an object wrapped in baking tissue. She returned to the bed and handed it to Mr. Kern. It was an apple strudel. Mr. Kern's eyes became shiny. He nodded and gave her little hand a squeeze.

BJ paid scant attention during the drive home but sat up straight when they turned onto Man Gun Road, and Molly stopped the car with a jerk. "You have got to be kidding me!" she said. In the grass next to the snowmobile trail was a newly planted sign. It read:

CHIPPEWA ESTATES

CUSTOM HOMES–AVAILABLE SOON!

LBS DEVELOPMENT, INC.

"What's that about?" said BJ.

"There's no land they can build on up here! It's all federal, state, and tribal!" Molly shifted the car into first so hard, BJ thought she was going to rip the stick from the floor. Larry's Lexus was parked by Elmer's mailbox. Mukwa and Pukawiss were circling the car, snarling. Inside, Larry was yelling, red-faced, into his phone. Eddie sat next to him in the passenger seat, looking very uncomfortable. Molly jumped out, ran to Larry's door, and smacked the window hard with her hand. "What the hell, Larry, you don't own any of this land!"

Larry finished his call and rolled down the window. "Hi, Molly, nice to see you, too. Well, actually, I just bought my sixth piece of property along Reservation Road. Can't blame them for wanting to sell with a man-eating wolf around and all the vandalism."

"You…"

"Also," said Larry, "if the Feds agree to a land swap—twenty of my waterfront acres for two hundred of National Forest—we can extend the development for a few miles in this direction and create an entirely new community! Swimming pools, nice big lawns, cul-de-sacs, the whole nine yards!" He gestured towards Elmer's house. "This is where the main road is going to go. Say," he said, "Would you mind getting something from Elmer for me? His dogs don't look too friendly, and I'm not sure I should go into his yard."

If the look on Molly's face could kill, there would have been a death zone for fifty square miles. Larry turned and said something to Eddie, who shook his head. At length, Larry opened his door a crack, waited a few seconds, then put a foot out and onto the ground. In a flash, Mukwa was there, seizing the foot and growling ferociously. Larry was yelling. Eddie was screaming. Molly and Charley were smiling. Finally, the dog yanked the shoe from Larry's foot, shook it back and forth, then let it fall to the ground, where Pukawiss urinated on it. Larry's face went sunset red. He rolled up the windows and drove away.

Mark's work truck arrived and nosed into Elmer's driveway. Keanu was in the passenger seat, twisting the peg in his earlobe.

"Did you pass Larry?" snapped Molly.

"Yep. Saw the sign, too."

Keanu held a bag of brown objects out the window. "Hey, dudes, wanna try—"

"Will you knock that off!" snapped Mark. "Anyone seen Elmer?" They all shook their heads.

"How can I help?" said Molly.

"You can find me an extra twelve hours in a day." Mark put the truck into gear. "What we need," he said, "is more time."

Chapter Twenty-Nine

BJ dreamed of chasing a dark wolf through the woods, leaping over the birch log, and skirting around the mossy boulder. He awoke in the middle of the night to the sound of Max barking in the yard. Maybe a bear trying to get near the bird feeder. BJ didn't remember falling back to sleep, but the next thing he knew, it was morning. Charley was sitting across the room, reading *Pippi Longstocking,* puffy-yellow lion slippers on her feet.

BJ sat up and let the dreams fade from his mind, and he thought about what his dad had said. More time. BJ didn't have a holy clue how he could squeeze more time in at his Sacred Area and get the Red Hand Warrior to show up. How many more sticks did he have to carve, or crackers to feed to Ref, or trees to climb? Maybe it was all some kind of joke? Or maybe the warrior was really Stalking Bear or Morning Flower or... BJ slapped his forehead as the realization hit him. More time! If it was more likely for the warrior to come after BJ had spent more time at his Sacred Area, then he could almost "cheat" by going back through the cave and spending those days sitting at the red pine. That way, days or even weeks could go by for him there while time stood nearly still here. This would be the third trip into the past. He would have to make it really count. "Charley, I'm going back in the cave. Will you come be a lookout?"

Charley held her finger in the air, signaling for him to wait while she finished reading. A minute later, she closed the book with a snap. "Okay."

When they arrived twenty-one minutes later, the boulders on the hill glistened from the morning dew and felt cool to the touch. Charley hopped down to the mossy floor, opened her backpack, and pulled out a handful of books.

"Thanks for keeping a lookout," said BJ.

"You're never gone that long anyway," said Charley. "Besides, I feel kind of catastrophic in there."

"Claustrophobic," you mean.

"Yeah, that."

BJ climbed in. He stared a long time at the print. "Where are you?" BJ half expected to hear a response, but none came. BJ placed his clothes in the corner of the cave. He pressed his hands on the rock. "Let's go," he started to say, but the elevator sensation began before the words had left his lips. Some of the images on the wall blurred and then disappeared. There was the breechcloth where he had left it. BJ slipped it on in a flash and climbed out. *Make your time count*, he thought. He wondered what the boy who waited for Shadow Walker must have felt, waiting for years in his Sacred Area. Years! BJ scrambled over the lip of the hill, feeling a twinge of guilt at escaping just when his father needed his help, but he reminded himself that he had a job to do here. Watch and learn. In the meantime, he could hang out with Morning Flower and the others, and it wouldn't harm anyone back home. At least, he hoped not.

A red squirrel with a patch of fur missing halfway down his tail scampered up a fir tree, disappearing in the canopy. BJ breathed in deeply and listened to the sounds around him., Technically, though he was in the same location, the forest *was* different, just as a person is not the same after a lifetime of experiences have altered his look and his personality. Familiar, yes, but not exactly the same.

BJ advanced with precision, his head up and his ears open and noticed wet human footprints on the Tabletop. He put his face close to the rock and saw the little puddles still flowing towards lower pockmarks in the granite. Someone had *just* been there. Something about this made BJ decide on a change of course. Instead of taking the well-worn path, he headed along a parallel route, sticking to cover and pausing often.

During one stop, he noted, somewhere ahead of him, a robin tut-tutting. Another red squirrel, tail arched over his back, sat motionless on the branch of a red pine. BJ waited. For twenty full minutes, he stood almost perfectly still before he saw something moving among the ferns. A raccoon? A fisher? He studied it. A head! Someone's head! A minute later, he recognized Wood Tick, the younger brother of Little Otter. Was he hunting? He had not seen BJ.

Just like the stakeout at Larry's office, BJ's patience served him well now. By standing stone-still and watching and listening, he managed not only to observe Wood Tick, but to pick out the forms of Runs Swiftly and Shines Bright as well. A jolt of excitement shot through BJ as he realized that he'd stumbled into the middle of the doll-taking game. BJ eased to the ground to grab a handful of dirt. He had not been picked. He did not know what the teams were. But he was going to play.

For the next three hours, the only sounds in the forest were the occasional squirrel chase around the trunk of a tree, the birds overhead, and a light breeze through the pines. Muddy, camouflaged forms moved silently through the leaves and across the ground like shadows. BJ let his feelings tell him where to move and when to stop. Keeping his head up and his vision scattered, he was able to monitor the movements of his friends. It was not easy, and many times he thought he saw (or sensed) something else, but he wasn't sure. He took nothing for granted. One tiny mistake, and he would be caught. Even though he had made much progress since he had been caught counting ants by Little Otter, his only advantage today was that nobody knew he was there. The others were still years beyond him in skill.

Sometime later, when the birds and bugs and animals were sleepy and still, Morning Flower marched to the river, looking frustrated and tired. As she stepped into the water, a "whoop!" sounded behind her. There was Stalking Bear, holding her team's doll, triumphant. The other players materialized and gathered around. Shines Bright, apparently on the same team as Morning Flower, stood and addressed Stalking Bear, "Why could we not find your doll. Did you bury it?"

"We hung it up from a branch, like always," said Stalking Bear.

Shines Bright was there. "You couldn't have!" he said. "We have been in your territory for a long time. We looked everywhere!"

"It was visible!" insisted Little Otter. "As plain as the nose of a moose, like always!"

Morning Flower crossed her arms stubbornly. "Then why couldn't we see it?"

"Because," announced BJ, holding the doll high in the air, "it is HERE!"

The reaction from the group was tremendous. With a roar, they rushed through the water towards him. Runs Swiftly was first and knocked BJ off his feet and onto the ground. "Where did you come from? How did you do that? We didn't know you were here! You cheated!"

BAM! She was swept off BJ, and Morning Flower was in her place. "That was great, Beejay! I thought they had buried their doll and that we had lost, but you had it the whole time! You helped us win, ha-ha!"

POW! Morning Flower was knocked off BJ and into a general scrum of arms, legs, and laughter on the forest floor. Eventually, Shines Bright helped BJ to his feet. "Very good job, Beejay, howah! Another good trick—I am glad to see you again!" They headed to the village, each taking turns imitating Stalking Bear's stunned expression when he saw BJ appear and each asking BJ to tell the story from his point of view again and again.

"How did you know we were there?" asked Stalking Bear.

BJ winked at him. "A squirrel told me."

They all laughed.

During the time BJ had been gone, the village turned completely blue. "It has been a good blueberry year," explained Shines Bright, indicating the mats of berries spread out, drying in the sun. Everywhere BJ looked were berries on mats, in clay jars, in birchbark makuks, and wooden bowls. Families were returning with baskets filled to the top, carried by the old and the young. Everyone was working. Everyone was busy. "We did not sleep much this season," laughed Morning Flower. "I picked with Grandfather, his mother, and Bent Nose. We got enough for us, plus a few elders who were not able to go out. We were lucky to have a little time to play the doll-taking game." BJ followed her in between two large woven mats laden with berries. The smell made BJ's mouth water.

"We will dry and store the berries before the ricing moon," said Shines Bright. "It is almost time to go to the inland lakes and rivers for the harvest. Scouts are reporting that the rice is nearly ripe. When that is done, we will return here and prepare to move to our winter camps until the sugar moon."

BJ motioned towards the remains of a birchbark canoe, broken and battered, lying on the ground like a fish skeleton. "What happened here?" he asked.

"This is what happens when you do not respect the harvest," explained Shines Bright. "Two brothers went out to harvest rice before it was ripe. It damages the rice stalks to beat them so hard."

BJ was stunned. "So you wrecked their canoe?"

Stalking Bear nudged one of the broken ribs with a toe. "Grandfather Running Wolf had their canoe destroyed in front of the entire village. This is what happens when people do not respect resources. No one can be allowed to harm the earth, Beejay."

"What if they do it again?" asked BJ. Stalking Bear and Shines Bright exchanged a dark glance. BJ decided to change the subject. "Where will you go after ricing?"

Morning Flower explained, "When the snow falls, the village breaks up into smaller camps. Those places are better suited for supporting a small number of families. It is the way. We will all meet up again when the crust forms on the snow in the sugar moon." BJ had heard about the Ojibwe moving with the seasons, but until now, it had been hard to imagine living in so many locations throughout the year. It made perfect sense. If possible, you went where the resources were plentiful, and the challenges were few. Disrespecting the resources meant you lost your canoe or worse.

They caught up to Wood Tick, who was limping. "I cut my foot during the game," he explained. BJ bent down and gave him a piggyback ride. The boy weighed about as much as Charley. Runs Swiftly peeled off to her own camp, leaving the others to accompany BJ. "Our scouts have found some signs of unknown people to the west, about two days travel," said Stalking Bear. "They're not sure who they are or what they are doing, but we are concerned that they may be a war party. They have put us on emergency status."

"Emergency status?"

"We need to be able to move the whole village quickly if danger comes our way," said Morning Flower. "We can't get caught by surprise. Our scouts are out again, trying to find out what is going on. We may have to go to ricing lakes that are further to the south to avoid trouble." She put her hand on his shoulder. "Will you come with us?"

BJ's stomach did a backflip. Morning Flower wanted him to come along. What would that mean? Could he travel to the ricing lakes and still return to the cave? Should he? What if he got lost? What if they ran into the war party? What then? Maybe he could stay for months or even years and then return home with no time having passed at all? But would he have aged? Wouldn't he be ignoring or abandoning his family? BJ swallowed. He had no answer for her.

Shines Bright could see BJ struggling to respond and gave him a comforting pat on the shoulder before heading to his family's fire.

"We might only have a few days left before we leave," said Stalking Bear shrewdly. "Use them well!" He also left.

Morning Flower stood before BJ, and he wanted to say something smart or brave or interesting, but Wood Tick sneezed in his ear, which made her laugh. BJ had forgotten that he was holding the little boy. "We are close to our camp, Beejay. You can put me down now." BJ set the boy down, and he hobbled off with Little Otter.

Running Wolf was working on a pair of moccasins, setting porcupine quills into the toe area. They were dyed red, yellow, and black. His white-haired mother was with him, her large, looped earrings dangling and dancing as she twisted and wrung a small animal fur in her lap, turning it into leather. A clay pot perched between three stones over a small fire, cooking a stew that smelled salty and rich.

Running Wolf set down his project and put his hands on BJ's shoulders. "Welcome! I am happy to see you!" BJ felt warm and content. "You are still waiting for your warrior?" he asked. BJ nodded. He had begun to suspect that he was doing something wrong. But Running Wolf smiled. "I saw your warrior earlier today."

A burst of hope shot through BJ. "You did? Really? Where?"

"I saw him briefly in the forest. You have been spending time in your Sacred Area?"

"Yes!" BJ didn't mention that most of the time he was just sitting there, or sleeping, or farting around. He couldn't wait to meet the guy, bring him home, and watch him open up a can of whoop-ass on the wolf, the vandals, and maybe Larry Sourmeister himself.

Running Wolf glanced at Morning Flower, who was sniffing the stew with care. "It is almost ready. Why don't you two go scout the hill? I will watch the food. Come back at four hands from the horizon."

BJ checked the sun. They had about an hour. But Morning Flower had already left camp and was nearing the south end of the village. "Wait!" he shouted as she disappeared into the trees. BJ took off after her like a rabbit.

Chapter Thirty

Morning Flower flowed in and out of sight like a stream rolling down the hill. Within a minute, BJ lost sight of her. No matter, he thought, and began scanning the ground for her tracks. The mid-afternoon sun baked the hillside in August heat, and BJ began to sweat. Still, he was comfortable and happy. The heat was real. The sweat was real. Morning Flower was real. He paused to pick a blueberry, thanked the bush, and popped it into his mouth. A young phoebe flew past in pursuit of a dragonfly, about as likely to catch her prey as a puppy running after a snowshoe hare.

Bent grass and depressions in the moss about every twenty inches showed where Morning Flower had passed through a cluster of five birch trees. Was that shiny mark on the granite from her feet? On the other side of the rock was a similar mark, so yes, it must have been her track. BJ followed, head down, for another 150 paces until he lost her trail. He circled the area twice, then retraced his steps up the hill towards her last known sign. Now BJ had his own tracks to contend with. He was reminded of Running Wolf's advice to be able to identify his own trail; otherwise, he would end up tracking himself all over the place.

With some luck, BJ found one of her tracks (at least, he thought it was hers) near a large white pine with many thick branches. He squatted to study the ground, then circled this area. Nothing. Back to the last known sign. BJ stared hard at the twisted and turned moss, the needles standing on end. An idea or, rather, a message began to form in BJ's mind. At first, it was unclear, like a voice in the distance. BJ cocked his head and strained to hear, to understand the thought. A gust of wind swirled its way up the hill, whistling through the leaves. A small shower of last year's brown needles and bits of bark fell to the ground around BJ. The message in the back of BJ's mind became louder, closer until finally… he could hear it.

Look up.

He did, but too late. Morning Flower landed with a war cry, knocking him to the ground. With a strength that belied her slender physique, she leaned down hard with both hands on his shoulders and pinned him, her black hair brushing his face. Fire was in her eyes. "Don't forget to look up, *scout!*"

BJ gave a mighty thrust with his hips, throwing her over his head. She landed face-first in a rotten tree stump but sprang up instantly and spun around, a ferocious expression on her face—a look that would have made BJ turn and flee were it not for the chunk of green moss lodged in one of her nostrils. BJ laughed. Morning Flower threw a handful of rotten wood at him, stood, and sprinted the rest of the way down the hill.

BJ didn't bother tracking her. He knew where she was going. When he reached the rocky beach, Morning Flower was lying on her back, her chest still rising and falling rapidly beneath her dark leather shirt. Together, they watched the sky and listened to the swoosh of tiny waves through the rocks and sand. The white-and-gray ripples of thin cirrus clouds looked like great walleye fillets swimming through the air. A pair of hawks rode a thermal in lazy circles, gliding down, then back up again, working their way south. More hawks followed. Migration time.

For a long while, they lay without a word and, at least for BJ, without a thought. Then they skipped in silence, watching their rocks bounce across the surface of the water. Morning Flower eventually landed a ten. "That's good!" said BJ. "Think you can get eleven?"

"Watch me." She twisted her mouth and let fly... a perfect twelve.

BJ shook his head. "You are so much like my sister, it's scary." He threw his stone, but the rock was too thin, and it curved over on its side in midair and cut straight into the water with a "thup!"

The next few days were spent exploring, playing, hunting, skipping, telling stories, or just lying around and watching the world go by. There was no set schedule or mealtime. When they were tired, they rested. When they were hungry, they ate. The adults, busy preparing for departure to the ricing lakes, largely ignored the young, or at least BJ's group of friends. They were free to wander and explore. Stalking Bear was still mindful of the "emergency status," however, and kept a sharp lookout for signs of strangers. In the middle of it all, BJ made a point to go sit with the big red pine. Running Wolf asked him if he'd seen his warrior. When BJ said no, he asked about the birds and animals there, saying he himself was unfamiliar with that part of the forest. BJ remembered earlier in the summer when Running Wolf had asked this of the other kids after their first doll-taking game. They had given long and detailed responses. BJ did his best to explain what things lived and moved in his Sacred Area to Running Wolf, but he still did not feel like his own answers were adequate.

One sunny afternoon, BJ and Morning Flower were meandering up the spine of the mountain, pausing occasionally to eat a lonely blueberry or rosehip. Gichigami shimmered down below. Chickadees followed, "dee-deeing" from branch to branch. White-throated sparrows sang their "peabody" song. Juncos rose from the ground in little clouds, flashing white bars on the edges of their tail feathers, then settling back down further on. This was a new part of the mountain for BJ, an area he had not yet explored with his Ojibwe friends or with Charley. It was becoming hard to remember which experiences were from which time. Same mountain. Same lake. Different world.

Morning Flower skirted a boulder, then picked up her pace. BJ followed at a distance. Where the ground leveled out, he stopped near a dark tangle of cedar and hazel, some fifteen paces to his left. A cold feeling crept into him. What was over there? Morning Flower was far ahead, but something pulled at BJ, drawing him into the cedars. Goose bumps stood on his arms as he pushed through the dark tangle. After a few steps, he became disoriented and unsure of his direction. Which way had he come in? He turned in a circle, but the low light was uniform in all directions. BJ had broken one of the cardinal rules of the wilderness: if you don't know where you are going, know where you have been.

"Hey!" he shouted and charged randomly into the branches, which tore and scraped at his skin. *Something has to be this way*, he reasoned. Was that a voice? BJ held still and listened. Morning Flower? It sounded far away, but he swiveled his head like a deer and zeroed in on the sound. Yes, further to the right. He pivoted, hunched down, and pushed his way through the tangle of branches, and then he was out, almost bumping into Morning Flower. "There you are!" he panted. "That was freaky! What is that place—hey, what's wrong?" Morning Flower had seized BJ by the hand and was leading him up the hill along the ridge. He could feel her trembling.

When they reached an overlook, Morning Flower turned to face him and held both his hands in hers. Those brown eyes... "That is a bad place, Beejay. A dark place. I tried to call you, but you were already inside. There are bad spirits. Windigos. Our elders have always warned us away from it. Please don't go in there again."

BJ felt a twist in his throat as if he'd eaten something of the wrong shape. He had never liked a girl before, never even had his hand held. But he had never known anyone like Morning Flower. BJ wanted this moment to last forever, to stand still on the edge of the mountain and stare into those eyes. He leaned into her...

POW! Something hard bounced off his head. "Ow!" A jack-pine cone spun to a stop at their feet. BJ looked up. But there were no jack-pine trees near here. Then, a shower of pinecones struck them, and a chorus of war cries rang out. It was an ambush! Stalking Bear, his broad shoulders gleaming, was in the lead not ten yards away, followed by Runs Swiftly, Shines Bright, and Little Otter. Each was hurling handfuls of objects at BJ and Morning Flower. Morning Flower reacted swiftly, grabbing a pile of debris and charging towards Stalking Bear with a banshee scream. The others took defensive positions behind trees and boulders, and the battle was on.

For the rest of the afternoon, BJ and Morning Flower staged a tactical retreat, looping wide through the hills, occasionally stopping to fight a pitched battle during which every imaginable object was hurled through the air—pinecones, sticks, moss, owl pellets, and a dried moose turd. By the time the sun dropped below the horizon, casting a deep red glow against the few clouds in the western sky, they were staggering back into the village, covered with scratches, bruises, leaves, and dirt.

The battle was told and retold around Running Wolf's fire. Stalking Bear was particularly good at imitating the others getting hit by missiles or tripping over tree roots, and they laughed hard at his acrobatic antics. Runs Swiftly had been struck in the head with a handful of rather fresh moose turds, which were still stuck in her hair. Shines Bright had several scratches and bruises, as did both BJ and Morning Flower.

Wolves howled from the forest, and loons called from the lake. BJ thought of his mother, who loved loons. How many days had he been gone? Charley would be waiting by the cave. His father would be working himself to a frazzle while fat fishermen and deer hunters moaned and groaned about the DNR. Once more, BJ felt a pang of guilt. His history book and the weird guy had said to come here and find the warrior and bring him home, but all he had done was run around and throw poop and skinny-dip and fall for a girl with big brown eyes. He was no longer sure he was doing this for his family. He almost felt like he had abandoned them.

Running Wolf held up the moccasin he was working on and studied it. "Beejay, I have spoken with your warrior. Tomorrow we will all leave for the ricing lakes. Afterward, we will return to camp. You should come back then. I think your warrior will be here."

BJ felt his heart skip a beat. Running Wolf had met him? Was that the way it was supposed to work? How big was he? Would he have to return through the cave with BJ? Where would he stay? In the woods behind their home? On an extra mattress in their bedroom? BJ imagined the conversation with his parents: "Mom and Dad, this is Red Hand Warrior. He's here to help." BJ had no clue how he was going to make that work out. But it didn't matter. If Running Wolf and the others managed to meet BJ back at the village after the ricing harvest, then BJ would finally get to meet him. The fire died down, and the conversation faded into a deep and dark silence. BJ counted the stars until they began to blur. One billion. One billion and one. One billion and two… Morning Flower was curled up under a blanket. BJ slept, dreaming of a red hand, birch logs, and a moss-covered boulder.

A soft but determined bustle was the baseline sound in camp when BJ awoke the next morning, stiff and sore. He sat up and arched his back. Families were leaving the village—parents, children, even dogs, carrying baskets on their backs or bags over their shoulders. Morning Flower stirred, then sat up. BJ's eyes widened when he realized he'd slept snuggled up against Morning Flower. She, however, didn't seem to give it a second thought. They stood and took one step; then, both fell hard on the ground.

Laughter erupted from behind a pile of firewood. Stalking Bear was there, a stone knife in his hand. "Gotcha!" He cut the little cord he had used to tie their ankles together. "Come on, time to go ricing!" BJ brushed himself off, still feeling embarrassed, then met the others at the Cannonball Rock, knowing that he would not accompany them to the ricing lakes but instead head to the cave and home.

Shines Bright had a wistful look on his face as he surveyed the nearly empty village. He glanced at BJ, then loped up the trail, closely followed by Morning Flower and Stalking Bear, each carrying packs. BJ brought up the rear. They had not gotten far when a commotion up ahead stopped them in their tracks. Shines Bright, Stalking Bear, and Morning Flower dropped their packs and sprang forward. Stalking Bear pulled a handful of arrows from his quiver as he ran. BJ ran after them, his heart pounding, and was quickly greeted with a terrifying sight: Running Wolf was locked in hand-to-hand combat with a black and red-painted stranger. Two other men, similarly painted, were swinging tomahawks wildly in the middle of a group of adults.

An ambush. A real one.

It took a long time for BJ to process what Stalking Bear did next. It was so incredible that BJ did not realize it entirely as it happened. With stunning speed, he sent two arrows into the man fighting with Running Wolf and a third arrow into one of the tomahawk-wielding attackers. Shines Bright hurled himself into the melee, but BJ stood transfixed, feet glued to the ground. The two injured attackers had little chance against Running Wolf and Bent Nose, who fought with absolute fury. They were quickly put down.

"Watch out!" yelled Stalking Bear, aiming his bow. The third attacker had freed himself from Shines Bright and his father and was charging through the woods, whooping. He was heading toward Morning Flower. Stalking Bear sent his final arrow towards him, but it was deflected by a branch. Morning Flower drew a knife and steadied herself. The next thing BJ knew, he was running towards the attacker like an intercepting rocket. The man focused on Morning Flower did not see the white streak coming. BJ hurled himself hard into the man's legs and saw a burst of light in his head as they crashed and rolled on the ground. There was screaming and yelling. When BJ was able to clear his head and sit up, the warrior lay dead nearby, Morning Flower's knife buried in the center of his chest. The battle was over. The three attackers were dead, and aside from some cuts and bumps, there appeared to be no serious injuries among Running Wolf or the others.

Stalking Bear wore a grim expression as he helped BJ to his feet. "They were waiting in ambush. Grandfather Running Wolf sensed them before they could attack, so they were not able to surprise us." BJ could feel blood running from his nose down past his chin. Blood also covered Running Wolf's left shoulder, where he had been cut by a tomahawk. It ran in a glistening streak down his chest, nearly to his breechcloth. He stood breathing hard, but defiant.

"These braves are young," he said, indicating the bodies. "They must have come to avenge the deaths of their comrades earlier in the summer. I doubt they had the blessing of their elders." He shook his head. "Foolish. There is no glory in this! Now they will never return home!" Then his expression went from anger to sadness to determination. "We need to get to the ricing lakes. There is much to be done before the first snow." He put his arms around Morning Flower, who was still shaking. "You did well, Granddaughter." Then he looked at BJ. "And so did you." BJ didn't feel like he'd done much of anything. At least he hadn't run away.

Stalking Bear explained, "After you tripped him, he got up and was going to cut your head open with that tomahawk, but Morning Flower knocked him back down and finished him." BJ looked at her with awe. Morning Flower had just saved his life. Her hand was covered with blood.

Running Wolf hoisted his pack, as did the remainder of the group. "I hope to see you after the ricing moon, Beejay." He led the group through the trees, single file. Before they were out of sight, Morning Flower stopped and turned back to look at BJ. Stalking Bear waved at him with one hand, then put his arm around Morning Flower and led her into the forest.

Chapter Thirty-One

"How was it?" Charley was looking at BJ out of the corner of her eyes while two chickadees plucked seeds from a pile on her belly. BJ stared at her, the image of his sister and the birds overlapping with that of three bloody and dead attackers. It felt like he had been gone for ages. Had it been weeks? Months? So much had happened. "Hello, BJ?" said Charley.

BJ blinked and considered her question. To be honest, the answer would take five hours or nothing. He turned without a word and began heading home. His nose hurt. Charley caught up in short order and walked along with him, honoring his need for silence. They crossed the Tabletop, waded through the water, and headed towards the cattails. There, they ran into two men carrying signs. One, a man in his thirties, wore jeans, a black T-shirt, and a camouflage baseball cap. The other, in shorts, flip-flops, and a Minnesota Wild T-shirt, was Eddie Sourmeister himself. "Hey!" shouted BJ, making them both jump. "What are you doing here?"

"Who the hell is that?" said the older man.

"BJ and Charley Maki," said Eddie, then jerking a thumb at the man and addressing BJ. "This is my Uncle Todd."

"You two are trespassing," said Todd.

"Bullshit!" shouted Charley, making Eddie take a step backward. "This is national forest!"

"Not after Friday," said Eddie, and BJ felt like an anvil landed on him. "My dad and the Feds are going to do a land swap."

"Yep," said Todd, "and the cutting and clearing begin next week. By spring, there will be a road right next to this creek." He held up a No Trespassing sign to a tree, facing towards the Maki house. "I'll be patrolling this line." He motioned east-west. "If I catch anyone north of it, we'll prosecute for trespass."

BJ clenched his jaw. "Not until Friday, you won't."

"Okay," said Todd. "Friday. Enjoy your last few days here!"

Eddie touched his uncle on the arm. "Come on. I gotta meet Dad at his office in an hour."

BJ felt like he was going to throw up by the time he reached the Cannonball Rock. He leaned against the boulder and looked down at their yard and home, seeing with his mind's eye an entire village covered with blueberries. The images overlapped like two transparencies. Molly was in the yard. BJ judged by her expression that she had already seen Eddie and his uncle. "I'm so sorry!" she said. "I just can't believe it! I called your father, but he's not answering." She leaned back. "What happened to your nose, BJ?"

"Tripped. Mom, can they really keep us from going back there?"

"If they own the land, then yes." She looked carefully at BJ. "You should respect trespass laws, BJ. Don't get any funny ideas! But you have four more days to be out there. Molly began to choke up, and said, "It looks like the DNR is considering reassigning your dad to Bemidji." The kids flinched. Molly continued, "I know we've been bracing for this possibility. But listen. Reassignment is one thing, but a trespass case against a conservation officer could mean losing his job entirely. Do not cross that line. There is nothing on the other side worth that risk." Charley began to sob silently. Molly dropped to her knees and embraced her.

BJ felt like his world was imploding. Everything across that line was worth the risk! If he couldn't cross that line, he could no longer go to his Sacred Area. Worse, he couldn't get back to the cave and bring back the warrior. One more trip was all he needed to get him. Running Wolf had said so. He suddenly felt weak in the knees.

Molly leaned back and wiped a strand of hair behind her ear. "BJ, do you remember that you're sleeping over at the Gonzales's tonight?" BJ shook his head. He was in no mood for Voldemutt the biting dog or Minecraft. "Maybe ask Mr. Gonzalez to donate money to the DNR tonight when you're there," she said darkly before heading inside to answer the phone, which had begun to ring.

Max got up from near the garage and leaned heavily onto BJ's right leg. "Is Larry gonna build stuff back there?" said Charley.

"I don't know."

"Are you gonna go back to the cave?"

"Hell, yes."

"Can I come with?"

"You bet," said BJ, trying to think of something—anything—to do that might be productive. He remembered that Eddie had said he was going to meet his father at his office in an hour. BJ strode to the deck where he'd left his Blackberry and checked the time: 9:05. "Charley, what day is it?"

"Tuesday."

"We have three more days," he said. "Something is telling me to go to Larry's office and see what he's up to."

"Sounds good." In less than five minutes, BJ had an overnight backpack ready and his helmet on. He rode out of the garage and didn't even stop beside Charley, who was waiting at the base of their driveway. She caught up by the time they reached the base of Man Gun Road and turned onto the highway. The snowmobile trail would be too soft and slow. BJ didn't like riding down the highway, and technically, they weren't supposed to. Molly would assume they were on the trail. No time to think about it now, though. BJ wanted to get to Sourmeister's office before ten.

They pedaled as fast as they could reasonably go, passing the green "Grand Marais, pop 1285" sign with seven minutes to go.

They turned left, rode down a sloping street, then pulled into the co-op parking lot and parked their bikes in the racks. "Come on!" said BJ, loping out of the lot with Charley on his heels. Through the alley, then around the office building they went, slipping into the bushes at 11:59. Eddie was across the street, sitting on a bench, reading his phone, presumably waiting for his father to arrive.

Keanu was on the sidewalk again with his food display. At 12:01, the black Lexus arrived and honked. Eddie put away his phone and crossed the street. Larry stepped out and motioned for Eddie to follow him into the office, but Keanu intercepted them, offering samples and holding out a clipboard. BJ couldn't hear what was said. Larry signed the clipboard, then headed into the office, Eddie following in his wake. Inside, their voices were clear, thanks to an already open window. "Did you get the signs up?" said Larry.

"Yeah," answered Eddie. "It's all good. Uncle Todd will be watching the property line for you."

"He'd better. Easiest money he's ever earned. Well, nearly."

"Dad, don't you still need the Delacroix place?"

"I'll get it, don't worry."

"How?"

"Never you mind." The phone rang. "See who that is," said Larry in between rings.

"It says 'Private.' Long number afterward… 414-458-93256—"

"Give me that," interrupted Larry.

"Who is it?" said Eddie.

"Private!" snapped Larry. "Wait outside." Eddie came out the door and sat on the front stoop, an arm's length from BJ.

"Hey, dude!" Keanu was there. "You forgot to write down your phone number in case you win that raffle."

Eddie stood up and took the clipboard from Keanu. "I only have a cell."

"That's fine."

Eddie began to write. "What am I going to win?"

"A free vacation to St. Cloud."

"You ever been to St. Cloud?" BJ almost laughed. Eddie could be a goon, but that was funny.

"Um, no," said Keanu. "I hear they have some nice family farms in the area." He accepted the clipboard and then strolled to his food stand. BJ heard Larry say goodbye to the person on the phone, and a minute later, he came back out the front door. He and Eddie returned to the car, and they drove away.

BJ and Charley waited until Keanu was distracted, then crept out to the alley. "What was that telephone call about?" said Charley.

BJ recited the number: "414-458-932-56?"

"What's 414?" asked Charley.

"An area code, I guess. I don't think it's in Minnesota."

Charley repeated the number again and again, turning it into a song as they rounded the corner and began walking down the sidewalk in front of the office. "Hey, little dudes!" said Keanu. "What's that you're singing, Charley?"

"414-458-932-56," she repeated.

"What number is that?" he inquired.

"Someone who called Larry," said Charley before BJ could stop her.

"Sourmeister?" Keanu looked thoughtful, "It's got one digit too many, so there's a mistake somewhere."

"Where's 414 anyway?" said BJ.

"Milwaukee. My sister lives there. She's got the coolest restaurant. All local ingredients and stuff." Keanu's expression went blank for a while, then he said, "Anyway, one too many digits to be a phone number."

They still had an hour before Angie was to pick BJ up for the sleepover, so they crossed the street to the beach and began looking for rocks to skip behind the Paul and Babe statues. The air was still and heavy and smelled of rain. BJ picked up a nice orange-and-white rock. A bit thick. He threw an eleven. He proudly pointed at the result, but Charley hadn't seen it. She straightened up, studying a pair of rocks she'd found. "When are you going to the cave again?"

"Tomorrow." BJ threw an eight. "Charley, do you remember that old cabin I went into?"

Charley threw a five. "Uh-huh."

BJ threw an odd-shaped rock, which skipped twice. "Remember when Max barked at the woods and the growling and stuff?"

"Yeah."

"What do you think was in there?"

Charley held up a jet-black rock. "Well, there was barking and snarling, like a wolf."

A flock of seagulls circled loudly overhead, then jostled for a place on Paul Bunyan's shoulders. BJ paused in mid-throw to watch them. Above the hills, north of town, hawks spiraled upwards, gliding south, then spiraling upwards again on the next thermal. BJ was trying to work something out in his mind. "So, do you think that was the wolf that ate the cow and killed that guy?"

"Allegedly," said Charley.

BJ narrowed his eyes at his sister. "Do you know what that word means?"

She threw a nine. "It means 'not proven.' It's an accusation." BJ's mouth opened a little. "I asked Mom," she said simply.

"So, you agree with Elmer?"

"I like Elmer."

So did BJ, but he also felt like their neighbor was hiding something.

"I think you should ask Uncle Russ," said Charley.

"About what?"

"About everything. I think he knows lots of stuff. I bet he knows something about the wolf."

BJ thought about that. What would a bait shop owner know about all of this? Then again, Russ had spent plenty of time on the rez and with the locals. He did know about scouts and had hinted that Larry Sourmeister needed to be watched. Now that BJ thought about it, Russ seemed to know an awful lot about things that were happening in and around Grand Marais. Something shiny among the beach stones caught BJ's eye, and he leaned down. "Hey!" he said. "A Kennedy!"

"Cool!" said Charley, throwing. "You might get a twenty with that one!"

"No," said BJ, showing it to his sister. "It's a real Kennedy! Look." BJ had found a half-dollar. It was scratched and worn, but the face of John F Kennedy was as clear as anything. What were the odds?

"If that's not good luck," said Charley, "then nothing is."

Keanu was loading Angie's groceries into the Suburban when BJ and Charley arrived. Co-op employees didn't normally carry out groceries, but Angie had that effect on people. Charley had to physically grab Keanu to turn him around and get him back into the co-op so that Angie could get in the car and leave. BJ sat in the passenger seat, his nose burning from the Drakar Noir. Aside from the old ladies on Sunday mornings, BJ rarely caught a whiff of perfume. The car pulled into the road and then turned towards the highway. "How's your summer been, BJ?"

"Not boring," said BJ. "You?"

"It seems like yesterday you were at our house, but that was more than two months ago! Crazy how fast the summer can go! Antonio had swimming lessons and three different camps. We went to Chicago to visit family for a couple of weeks."

BJ asked about Chicago. He'd never been there.

"Chicago is amazing! The Bean, Millennial Park, Buckingham Fountain. You'd love it! Lights and people everywhere. Great food and music. Theaters. Museums. The place is never quiet. It's awesome. But we're glad to be back," she added. "I can bring Francisco to Reservation Road for his walks again. I don't know if he was able to get a ride there while we were gone. That's one of his favorite areas along the shore. He says it reminds him of northern Mexico."

This was the second time BJ had heard that Uncle Francisco liked to walk up and down Reservation Road. And it sure sounded like he did this alone. He decided to pay another visit to Uncle Francisco's cabin tonight. He sent a text to his mother to let her know he was sleeping over. "Sounds good!" came the response.

The Gonzalez home was as clean and pristine as always, every blade of grass cut to perfection, and every statue and flower in the yard tended with care. Tony and David were on the couch, cracking up at *Queer Eye for the Straight Guy*, when Angie and BJ came inside with the groceries. BJ placed the groceries on the counter and went back outside to get the rest, but there were none. He closed the Suburban, wandered over to the statue of the Mexican cook, and deeply inhaled the scent of the roses at its base. Robins and white-throated sparrows took turns singing from the surrounding trees. BJ closed his eyes and let the sounds and smells massage his spirit like a warm bath. Tomorrow, he would head to the cave and bring back the Red Hand Warrior.

A deep rumble sounded in the distance. Rain was coming. BJ pointed to his own eyes with two fingers, then at the statue, as if to say, "I'm watching you." The statue didn't move. BJ turned and headed back to the door, wondering if a tongue was sticking out at him from behind. He had just reached the threshold when a feeling struck him hard: *Turn around!* BJ spun, catching El Chapo, teeth bared, only inches away. The suddenness of BJ's turn caught the dog completely off guard, and he tried to abort the attack. His momentum, however, didn't allow for a quick stop. El Chapo's claws scratched as he slid and spun on the tile until his furry rear end was placed like a bullseye directly in front of BJ's ready—and very willing—foot. The kick sent the dog into the air, flipping him one full turn before he landed in a heap on the walkway with a sharp "Yelp!" El Chapo scrambled to his feet and fled into the bushes.

Angie's red head popped out of the doorway. "Did you say something?"

"Nope." BJ grinned. "All quiet out here!"

Angie disappeared. BJ raised a middle finger at the bushes. "We're not finished yet."

The sky grew darker throughout supper, and rumblings of the approaching storm made the table and chairs vibrate like the strings of a guitar. They were just finishing their ice cream when a handful of very large drops smacked hard against the picture window. Then, all at once, the sky seemed to open up. Rain came down in sheets, pummeling the window and obscuring everything beyond it. It was an exciting storm.

"All right!" said Tony. "Now we don't have to go outside!"

Angie rolled her eyes. "Oye, muchacho, la lluvia no le molesta a tu tío Francisco."

"Rain doesn't bother him 'coz he's crazy," said Tony.

"Mind your manners about my uncle," said Mr. Gonzales. "He's old school and isn't really adapting to American ways."

"Nothing wrong with that," said Angie.

By the time the dishes were cleared and the table wiped, it was late, and Angie and Antonio Sr. retired to their bedroom. Tony and David whipped out their phones and resumed their game of Minecraft. BJ slipped out the kitchen door unnoticed. The rain was still steady but light. For a few minutes, he stood under the overhang, letting his eyes adjust to the darkness.

The sound of the rain—not to mention the wet ground— would have concealed even the clumsiest of footsteps. BJ stole across the yard and into the woods. Soon, he was next to the cabin and peering inside. Near the main window of the cabin, there was a table with an oil lamp. Two wooden chairs. A bookcase in front of a tiny kitchen area. The corner of a bed. The rifle with the scope leaned against the bookcase. It was no longer on the wall. Where was Uncle Francisco? BJ's heart pounded in his chest. He stood on his tiptoes and twisted to get a better view. Mud-encrusted shovels and tools of all sorts were lined up against the outside wall. Nearby, plastic bags and a flattened stack of cardboard boxes. There was no sign of the deer that had been there earlier in the summer. BJ began to sense that he shouldn't linger. Something wasn't right. It was time to go. He turned away from the cabin and found himself nearly nose-to-nose with a scowling old man wearing a hood over his head.

He held a pickaxe in his hands.

Chapter Thirty-Two

The confidence had been swept from the men like October leaves from a sugar maple. How quickly their world had unraveled! It had always been so. Men will always trade freedom for security. Well, they were secure now. The creature kept them deep in the dark place, far from the light of the sun and the eyes of the law. The pale man with greasy blonde hair and sunken eyes sat unmoving on a tree stump while his partner, a man with darker skin and long black hair, fussed with a lantern hanging from a branch above. They had been brought deep into a tangle of dead cedar and spruce so thick that they could neither hear nor see the outside world. The area of their confinement was a small opening within the tangle, scarcely the size of a living room, big enough to hold the two men, their gear, and some food. On the far end of the little room—the side that the two men avoided—sat a black hole, hollow and gaping like a great mouth whose breath smelled of rotting meat. It was here that the creature waited and watched. At length, the man with long hair got the lantern to produce some light, then took two steps to a makeshift bed he'd put together with an armful of blankets. He sat down gingerly and said, "How long are you going to keep us here."

The question lingered in the air for a long time before an answer came from the dark hole: "I have work for you."

The greasy-haired man looked up from his tree stump. "But we have work. We're earning good money for these jobs."

"Moneeeee," hissed the voice. "Always money. I will bring you where there is money. But first, you must show me that you are worthy of this. I want you to find where someone lives. I want to know if he has a family."

"That's it?" said Long Hair.

"Doesn't sound hard," added Greasy Hair.

The creature hissed at their ignorance. "He is dangerous."

"We've dealt with dangerous people before," shot Long Hair.

"You have already failed to deal with this one."

"Hold on," said Greasy Hair. "You don't mean…"

"Yes. The officer."

"I don't like the sound of this," said Long Hair. "Can you at least give us a general direction?"

"One mile southwest of here is a landmark. Beyond that is a small river. If you follow that, you may come near to where he lives."

Greasy Hair picked up a revolver and loaded six bullets. "So, what's the landmark?"

"A circle of large pine trees on a little hill. You will not miss it."

"No," said Greasy Hair, tossing the loaded gun onto his blanket, "we won't."

Chapter Thirty-Three

The cold, gray eyes glaring at BJ from beneath the dripping hood of the rain slicker were mere inches from BJ's face. A frown. "Pero," said the voice, "You not Tony! Who are you?" A waft of cilantro and onion struck BJ as the old man spoke. *What a stupid way to die,* thought BJ, closing his eyes and waiting for the pickaxe to fall.

"Güero! Come inside! You cold and wet!"

BJ squinted at him with one eye. Inside? What did he want with him inside? Uncle Francisco leaned the pickaxe against the cabin, turned BJ by the shoulders, and marched him around to the door. In the cabin, the old man kicked his boots off and slid them across the tile entryway to the wall, then removed his coat and hung it on a nail. He snatched a towel and shoved it into BJ's hands. A towel? Why was a cartel assassin giving him a towel? "Dry the head, güero! Your brain freezing!"

BJ dried his head. Uncle Francisco disappeared behind a bookcase, muttering in Spanish. BJ hung the towel on another nail and began to take in the cabin. A cast-iron potbelly stove crackled and glowed near a bed in the far corner. In front of the bookcase sat a rocking chair and a little end table with a notebook and the same field guide to Minnesota birds that his folks had left on the back deck for him weeks before. On the lakeside wall, a small, rectangular table stood beneath a large window, lit up like a big screen every few seconds by a lightning flash, revealing a grove of birch trees and the lake. The only sounds, other than the clinking of dishes behind the bookcase were the crackling and snapping of the fire in the potbelly stove on the far wall.

Uncle Francisco reappeared, holding two mugs of steaming liquid. He pointed at BJ's messy shoes. "Quítate los zapatos!" BJ sat on a bench next to a nest of flowerpots with string and rubber gloves inside and took off his shoes. Uncle Francisco shoved one of the mugs into his hands and said, "Drink, güero! Your brain still cold!"

"What's 'weh-do,'" said BJ.

"It's like 'blondie,'" said Uncle Francis. "It's what we call white people. Not a mean word. Drink!"

BJ wrapped both hands around the mug and sipped the smoky, bitter liquid. He was immediately and viscerally brought back to the moment when he had done just this at Running Wolf's fire for the first time. In each instance, he was scared and confused, and each time, a pair of wrinkled and caring hands handed him warm tea. After a few sips and a few minutes, his brain had completely cleared. What a fool he had been! After all the rumors about this old man, after all the disparaging words from Tony and the other kids at school, here he was, like a kindly grandfather, warming him up and giving him something to drink. A sheet of rain slapped the window, making BJ smile.

"HA!" Francisco pointed at him. "I knew you were not like my nephew's lazy son. You are outside boy, no?" BJ considered the question. He hadn't ever thought of himself as "outside" or "inside." Just a boy. "Sit here! Sit here!" Francisco directed BJ to a chair at the table and then sat opposite him. "Dandelion and chicory root coffee. Good for your immunes. Lots of antiox… antiox… anti—"

"Antioxidants." BJ nodded. "My mother's crazy about those."

"Sí, sí—that's it. Drink!"

BJ drank and wondered if Tony truly believed the stories about his uncle Francisco. Had he even spent time with him? The tea tasted good, slightly bitter. "Did you make this?"

"Of course! Who you think going to make it for me? Those guys?" Francisco gestured at the big house. "They don't know a dandelion from a donut!" Francisco set down his own mug and threw his hands in the air. "They busy on their phones or sitting on couch all the time. Well, not Angie. She take walks with me. She good woman. How my nephew get a mamacita like that, I never know!"

Uncle Francisco was the first actual Mexican BJ had ever met, and he could not help but like him. They drank dandelion coffee and talked about flowers, trees, gardening, and the north shore of Lake Superior. BJ asked if it was like the area where Uncle Francisco had grown up. Francisco put his mug down just like Russ when he was about to make a point.

"I come from the mountains of Sinaloa. Tarahumara and Apache country. Beautiful place—hills, flowers, streams. Beautiful! My mother take long walks with me when I was niño—we gather mushrooms, plants, everything. We sing while we do this. I learn about plant food, plant medicine, everything. This is the way!" He looked wistfully out the window and was silent for a while. "When my brother move north to Chicago," he continued, "they do it for 'American dream.' Bah! Life was fine up in the mountains. We not have everything, but we have what we need. Some people have to go north to America because they are in real danger down south, but we had good life. Not rich. Not fancy. Not shiny. But good! My brother wanted big American life. So that's what they got, living big dream in Chicago. Lots of money. Lots of things. Now my nephew and his family live same way—big car, big house. Fancy, fancy. Que pena!" His hands went into the air but with little enthusiasm.

"Why did you come to live with them?"

Francisco smiled wryly. "I had to. I tell you that story another time. I join my nephew in Chicago and see that he going to turn little Antonio into an idiot, so I decide to help out. That's why I follow them up here. But they still busy with big American life— even up here." He put his hand on BJ's arm. "Even here! This place is Heaven, you know that? They always on their machines. No pay attention to sounds and smells and colors. Angie try to teach little Antonio, but not easy."

BJ had been counting the books on the case as Francisco spoke. Some titles and authors he knew. Others, he didn't. Gabriel Garcia Lorca, Cervantes, Aldo Leopold, Sigurd Olson, Vine Deloria Jr., Tom Brown Jr., Dee Brown, many field guides on plants, animals, trees, flowers, and birds.

"You take them when you want," said Francisco, watching him. "I happy to share with another nature boy."

"What are those?" BJ tilted his chin at a set of Ball jars filled with various colors of liquid sitting on the bookcase.

"Medicine. I make oils and other things."

BJ wondered how they compared to his mother's essential oils. "Mr. Francisco?"

"You call me 'Tío.'"

"Tío, would you teach me to make those sometime?"

"I tell you what." He cupped his hands around the mug and leaned forward. "I teach you to make these medicines, and you teach Antonio to get his lazy nalgas into the woods, eh?"

BJ laughed. "Deal."

"GOOD! After all, we gotta look out for our people!"

BJ didn't remember falling asleep or even lying on Tio Francisco's bed, but he jerked awake to the sound of liquid being poured into a mug the following morning. A thin ray of blue on the eastern horizon signaled the arrival of dawn. He had slept dreamlessly, and his mind was clear. It occurred to him that he should probably get back to the main house before Tony's parents worried about his whereabouts, but he didn't want to leave yet. He stood and stretched. Tio Francisco handed him a mug of dandelion root coffee. BJ sipped it, then decided to ask something that had been bothering him. "Tío, where did you get the deer that was hanging outside?"

Francisco thought for a moment. "In June? That was from your dad."

Dandelion coffee shot out of BJ's nose. "My dad?" he sputtered. "You know my dad?"

"Of course, I do! Who do you think telling him about things that happen up on the mountain? I see people during my walks, but they never see me because Tío knows how to be quiet. That deer was roadkill. Your dad sometimes brings me good roadkill. I tan the hides with Elmer."

"You know Elmer, too?"

"What is wrong with you, güero?" Uncle Francisco threw his hands back into the air, making BJ flinch. "You think I some kind of hermit? Por supuesto, Elmer is good friend. We trading medicine recipes and books all the time. He likes to walk same areas I do. Sometimes we go together."

"So, um, have you seen people on ATVs up on Reservation Road?"

"All the time."

"Have you seen the wolf?"

The dark eyes stared at BJ for a moment, making him feel as if his thoughts were being read. "The 'man-killer'? I don't know. I see wolves sometimes. Tell you what, you want to know about wolves, ask Elmer. Or maybe Russ. They know things."

It was then that BJ remembered he had planned on visiting Russ that very morning. How strange that Tío had repeated Charley's suggestion. It was Wednesday. In two days, Larry Sourmeister was going to close the deal on the land behind their home. BJ gulped down his coffee, set the empty mug on the kitchen counter, and held out his hand. Tío Francisco ignored it and grabbed BJ by the head and kissed him on the cheek. "I see you again, güero?"

"Yes."

"Muy bien! You are a beautiful boy. You go out and have some adventure now. Don't forget to bring my nephew's fool of a boy with you some time!"

"I won't."

"Oh, one thing." Francis pointed a crooked finger towards the big house. "Watch out for their dog. The little pendejo likes to bite."

"Oh yeah!" BJ thought for a moment, then pursed his lips at a bundle of twine hanging on a nail. "Can I borrow some of that?"

An hour later, Angie opened the front door, carrying a bag of trash in one arm. "BJ's already gone," she said over her shoulder. "He left a nice, polite note saying he had to get home and that you should come to his house next time and go on a hike." Angie looked across the yard, then dropped her bag of trash with a shriek. Next to the statue of the Mexican cook, El Chapo was dangling by his heels from the branch of an apple tree, thrashing and yelping wildly. He was unhurt but very upset and certainly uncomfortable. "El Chapo! Que te pasó, mi querido?" she cried, running to the hysterical writhing ball of fur.

In the end, no harm was done except maybe to the dog's ego, and none of the Gonzales ever realized that the trap was anything other than a freak accident. Nor did they know that BJ was nearby, standing in the shadows, observing the whole scene with vengeful delight. There was another witness to the event on the opposite side of the yard. Even from where BJ stood, he could see the old figure among the alder and birch, trembling—convulsing almost—as he wiped the tears of laughter from his wrinkled cheeks.

Chapter Thirty-Four

BJ jogged down the shoulder of the highway at a steady pace, with soft, even strides. The cool morning air relieved some of the nervous pressure trying to build up in his lungs as he thought about the man-eating wolf and Larry Sourmeister's big housing development. A loud black Dodge pickup passed him in the far left lane, giving him a wide berth. It was not the same birch, spruce, and hazel trail that he had once run with Stalking Bear, but at least the drivers were good at moving over.

Like his mother, BJ preferred cross-country skiing, but he was a good runner. So was Stalking Bear. They had run for no other reason than to feel the wind in their faces. Today, the wind was there, but it carried the smell of diesel and tar. After about twenty minutes, the harbor and the tips of sailing masts came into view. Three kayakers were visible out in the main part of the lake. Too windy for paddleboarding. BJ picked up his pace, jogging past a slope of purple-and-white asters and browning ferns. Fall was on the horizon.

In town, BJ ran right past his mother's red Civic and on to Rusty's. He wanted to check in with Russ before his mother or Keanu saw him. At the bait shop, he swept under George, who was singing "Little Red Corvette," and went straight inside. "Owner's not here!" yelled Russ from the back.

"It's me, Russ," said BJ. "Want to ask you something." He wasn't sure Russ would have any suggestions about catching the wolf, but it was worth a try.

"Oh, then I'm here. Be there in a sec. Have some coffee."

BJ wondered if it would be easier if he just started drinking coffee. He leaned on the counter and stared at the old black-and-white photographs of early Grand Marais. They had been there since BJ could remember, and he knew each picture by heart. Today, though, he found himself studying the faces of the people more than he had before. Many of the loggers holding axes and fishermen holding fish looked weathered and old, much older than they probably were. BJ looked hard at the faces of an Ojibwe family around their wigwam. Some of them looked familiar to him, but he couldn't be sure. Unlike Running Wolf and his friends, they were not smiling or laughing.

On a set of hooks next to the old photos was Russ's Paul Bunyan paraphernalia: a red bonnet, a wooden stem pipe, and, of course, the huge, double-bladed axe. BJ had always been fascinated by the axe. How much did it weigh? Its double blade sparkled silver as if it had been sharpened that morning. BJ's eyes wandered down the thick wooden handle, then stopped at an emblem or symbol of some sort that had been burned or scrawled into the handle, not far below the head. BJ had never noticed this before. A circle, just smaller than a tennis ball, was inscribed. From the center, eight pitchfork-like spikes protruded outwards.

Something about that symbol rang a bell in BJ's memory. Where had he seen it? "Almost finished here!" yelled Russ from the rear of the store. BJ tried studying it with one eye closed—his tracking trick—but that didn't help. He approached the axe and held his arm out straight, using his hand to block out all but two of the pitchfork-like marks. "Birds' feet," he breathed. The edges of the symbol matched the markings he and his father had seen on the object blocking the lens of the trail camera. Russ had blocked his dad's trail camera so that he could empty the trap and keep the wolf from getting caught!

"How's the coffee?" Russ towered over BJ.

BJ spun. "Good! Um, I mean, I still don't... I mean."

"Say, would you be interested in looking at my music system?" Russ motioned toward the rear of the store. "I've got a router and the computer, but these new iPhones are weird, and I can't seem to make them work together. I like Prince, and I like the French-Canadian stuff, but Lenny Kravitz has disappeared from my playlist. I don't understand how this stuff works."

"I, uh... gotta go, Russ. Another time, maybe." There was a honk outside. Molly was in the Civic, waving. BJ practically leaped from the doorway and climbed into the car.

"Angie said you'd left, and I figured I'd find you here," said Molly. "Hey, Russ, Mark says he could meet this afternoon."

Russ nodded and waved. Molly put the car into gear. Before they drove off, BJ distinctly saw Russ taking down the axe and leaning it against the counter. "Mom, where's Dad meeting Russ?"

"Reservation Road, I think."

"What about?"

"I don't know. Russ wanted to tell him something, I guess."

BJ's mind raced. Russ had denied that a wolf was the source of the killings. And now it appeared that he knew much more than he had been letting on. Why had he blocked the lens of the trail camera and sabotaged the wolf trap? What else was he hiding? Mark's truck was parked in front of the co-op. He was leaning against the hood, visiting with Keanu. "Mom, pull over! I want to talk to Dad!" Molly gave BJ a quizzical look, but she stopped the car behind the truck. BJ leaped out. "Dad," he wheezed, "can I talk to you?"

"Not now, BJ."

"But Dad, there's something important I…"

"Sorry, BJ, but I'm in the middle of something. It will have to wait." BJ waited for an explanation, but none came. His father's blue eyes were as serious as BJ had ever seen them. This was his dad's game face. "We can talk tomorrow," Mark said with a single nod to his son. "And make sure you stick close to home. Don't go bothering Todd Sourmeister or anyone back in the woods." Mark walked BJ back to the car and helped him in through the door with his hand on BJ's head as if he were being arrested. "Keep your sister and mother out of trouble." Molly rolled her eyes. Mark closed the door and tapped the roof twice with his hand.

BJ rode home in silence. So many things were happening at once. His father was getting ready for something serious. But, thought BJ, if that was his dad's game face, what was the game?

At home, Charley was sitting cross-legged beneath the bird feeder in a pretend yoga pose. She didn't react when the Civic pulled into the driveway. Max gave two, three, four thumps of his tail but remained lying on his side on the back deck. Molly turned off the engine but didn't get out. Neither did BJ. Instead, they watched Charley. Birds ate all around her. A red squirrel dug into the grass an arm's length away from her. BJ watched his mother watching Charley. Molly wore the same smile. The paisley blue headband kept her dark curls away from her eyes, showing off a constellation of freckles that stretched from her nose down to her sun-tanned, muscular shoulders. BJ was struck, maybe for the first time in his life, by how beautiful his mother was. "Maybe," he joked, "we should move Charley's bed into the yard and save her the trouble of coming inside."

"Actually, she slept there last night," said Molly. "She insisted on it. Max curled up with her, and I checked on them a couple times throughout the night." Molly was quiet for a while, then said, "You know, Charley's been sitting out there, watching and listening, since she could crawl. She always wanted to be near the birds, so we moved the feeder across the yard to that area because it was a comfortable grassy location. It's her little sacred place."

BJ blinked. "What was that?"

"I said she's been there since she could crawl."

"No, after that."

"Oh, um, I said it was her special place."

"No," corrected BJ, "you said her 'Sacred Place.'"

"Did I? Well, 'special place,' 'sit spot,' 'sacred place,' whatever. It's all the same."

BJ sat back in flabbergasted silence. His sister's Sacred Place. Stalking Bear had said that some kids had their Sacred Places off in the woods while others had them near the edge of camp. Charley, like his friends from the past, had been sitting, exploring, watching and learning for years. For years, in their very own yard! BJ rubbed his cowlick at the realization that he had needed to travel back in time, meet a crazy magic man, dodge arrows, nearly eat a grouse head, and have poop thrown at him to do what his sister had been doing mere feet from their back door. Had she been visited by a warrior or a protector?

At length, they got out of the car, scattering the birds and squirrel. Charley gathered her bag and pillow and came inside for grilled cheese sandwiches and tomato soup. The sandwiches were not burned. BJ cleared the table and then announced that he wanted to go visit Elmer for a while.

"Have you thanked him for the journal and books?" said Molly.

"What journal and books?" said BJ.

"Your nature journal. He got that for you. And the bird and tree field guides are his for you to borrow, he said. Didn't you see them?"

"I, um, thought they were from you and Dad," said BJ.

"Nope. Elmer."

BJ left his mother in the garden and Charley scowling at him in the yard, and walked down the road to make it look like he was visiting Elmer, then cut into the woods and looped back north in the direction of the cave. Soon, he came upon the first No Trespassing sign. Some thirty paces beyond that was Todd Sourmeister. Why was he here when it wasn't yet their land, BJ wondered. Todd was staring at his phone, and BJ slipped around him with ease. His route brought him through his sit area, and for a while he stood still and watched.

Over the past few months, he had certainly gotten to know the area intimately. How much more would he learn if, like Stalking Bear, he spent seven full years there? Still, there was much he knew. Ref was probably denned up for the day. The family of red squirrels had mostly moved on. There was still one youngster in the area, chasing his mother around, looking for bits of food. They would be about fifty yards to the east, in the cavity of an old poplar. The pine marten that came through every couple of days had not discovered them yet. BJ hoped he wouldn't. He liked these red squirrels.

A large drop of water, which had been clinging to a birch leaf, fell and landed squarely on a puffball, sending a yellow cloud of spores into the air. A robin tutted. A whisky jack sat still on an outstretched branch, staring down. BJ followed its gaze—and found himself looking into the eyes of the largest deer he had ever seen. It was GW. Gichie Waashkesh, the Great Deer, was standing still, ears outstretched and magnificent. A huge set of antlers shone in the colors of a rainbow as the sunlight struck his waterlogged, velvety hairs. BJ felt a warmth spread throughout his whole body from the deer's gaze. There were only two things in the entire world: BJ and the deer. Eventually—it could have been a minute or an hour—GW turned and walked away.

It was then that BJ saw it. GW walked so slowly and carefully that his rear feet landed well before his front feet left the ground— and many inches behind them. BJ instantly knew what he was seeing, and he shook with excitement. This is what Elmer had been hinting at. This deer had not gotten that big by accident. GW had managed to avoid wolves and hunters by being the most careful animal in the woods, walking slowly, methodically, invisibly. BJ had only seen him because the deer had let him do so. For all he knew, the deer had been watching him all summer. He probably knew BJ's habits better than he knew them himself. BJ studied the ground where GW had stood. Sure enough, front feet first, then rear feet well behind. BJ took in a deep breath, filled with the tremendous satisfaction of having solved one of the forest's mysteries. He felt both proud and thankful.

A cocktail of emotions was still swirling in his chest when he got to the cave. Inside, he tossed his shorts and T-shirt into the corner, then stood before the red hand. He raised his right hand to touch the mark but stopped. Was that a noise outside? BJ scrambled back up through the hole just as his sister appeared at the rim, walking in her cow slippers and holding a pillow and blanket. "Charley, I..." He almost said he didn't want her to come, but it would have been a lie. BJ almost always wanted his sister to come with him, though he never really came out and said it. Instead, he said, "Did you see Todd?"

"He was asleep."

BJ thought he sensed a hint of mischievousness in her tone. "Charley, did you do anything to him?"

"I only tied his shoelaces together."

Well, it was better than a kick in the nuts. "Okay, stay alert, all right? Keep a sharp lookout, please. I don't know how long I'll be gone."

Charley yawned and began to spread her blanket on the ground below. BJ climbed back into the cave with a tiny knot in his stomach. Charley would be fine. After all, no one knew about this place. No one at all.

Chapter Thirty-Five

For a long time, BJ stood still, surveying the bare wooden racks, silent wigwams, and dark fire pits. He felt empty. A cool breeze blew through the lifeless village like wind through the ribs of a skeleton. Needles from the pine trees in and around the camp floated through the air, covering the ground in a yellow haze. It was the end of the growing season, of warm water, of long sunny days. Like the summer camps and cottages of the future, this place would sit still beneath needles, snow, and ice for months while their inhabitants survived the winter elsewhere. BJ meandered through the village, past the place of the arrow-maker (seven roughed-out, discarded shafts on the ground). A tiny fish fillet, hard and brown, clung to the corner of a drying rack. A bundle of basswood bark. Running Wolf's fire pit sat silent and dark.

What would happen to this place if, for some reason, they never returned? What then? BJ supposed the needles, snow, and rain would continue year after year until the buildings fell to the ground to be covered with leaves, dirt, and time. Would their songs and laughter be remembered by the trees and the earth?

BJ wandered to the northern end of the village where ceremonial buildings sat, some long and smooth, others narrow, bullet-shaped. On several occasions, Running Wolf, along with many elders, and most of BJ's young friends had come here for some type of ceremony, but BJ

241

not been allowed to participate or even observe, and this had stung him. Why was this forbidden? He was briefly tempted to go inside the buildings and explore, but it felt wrong, so he didn't. Maybe this was just not part of the Vision. Maybe some things were not meant for him. Well, his Sacred Place certainly was. He headed into the forest.

Minutes later, BJ stood before the great red pine, running his hand up and down a smooth section of bark. How many fires or storms would this great tree see and survive in the next few centuries before growing old and falling to the earth? How many generations of blue jays, squirrels, and martens would grow up among its branches? How many people would lean against its trunk? BJ felt the heartache of looking at a friend for the last time. BJ let his forehead touch the bark. It would be the last time he would see many things.

"Not bad, Pale Butt," said a voice next to him. And there he was. That man. Handsome, vibrant, impish, sitting cross-legged on the ground as if he'd been there his entire life.

BJ considered him for a long while before speaking. "Is it you?"

"The Red Face Warrior?"

"Red Hand Warrior."

"Oh right, Red Hand Warrior. Nope, not me."

BJ wanted to yank the cowlick from his head. "Then why am I here? The book told me to find him. You told me to find him! That's what the Vision thing is all about, right? Sit here for a long time, and he would show up. So, where the hell is Red Face…"

"Red Hand."

"WHATEVER! If you're not him, then who are you?"

"You'll figure it out. Also, I'm pretty sure you've met the red-hand guy."

"I… what?"

The man stood and stretched. "Gotta run. I ticked off my brother, and he's mad as a moose in October." He pointed at BJ. "Now, you get out there and kick some ass. Oh," he said, remembering. "Tell Paul I send my regards."

"Paul?" frowned BJ, "Paul who?"

The man shook his head at BJ. "Ask your sister. That girl sees everything!" Then he broke into a huge white smile, a smile worthy of a toothpaste commercial. He winked at BJ, then disappeared, leaving needles and leaves swirling in the air where he had been standing a second before.

"Nanabojo," whispered BJ. "YOU'RE NANABOJO!" And, just then, he felt something wet and slippery squirming around his crotch, and he leaped up and screamed like he'd been struck by lightning. A frog had appeared in his breechcloth. A large one. BJ yelped and danced in a circle until it fell out onto the ground and hopped away. He shook his fist at the sky, "That wasn't funny!" Then, when he'd finally caught his breath, he said, "Okay, it was a little funny." Nanabojo, the Trickster. Nanabojo, the Manitou. BJ shook his head and began to laugh in spite of himself. Just when he thought things couldn't get any more nuts.

A voice sounded from the direction of the village. BJ held still to listen. More than one voice. The others had returned! He stepped in their direction and felt something hard beneath his foot. He reached down, scraped away a few needles, and picked up a small flat rock about the size of a golf ball. BJ rubbed it against his breechcloth, and then blew on it, revealing a hole on one end about the size of a pea. Aside from this hole, the rock would have been a good skipping stone. Easily a Kennedy. BJ curled it in his palm, gave one last glance to the red pine, and headed to camp.

Stalking Bear was the first to notice BJ standing at the Cannonball Rock. He ran to greet him, putting both hands on his shoulders.

"Where is everyone else?" asked BJ.

"They are preparing for the ceremony. Hasn't Running Wolf told you? He is going to give you a name tonight!" BJ was stunned. A ceremony for him? A name? What did that mean? Stalking Bear gestured at the empty wigwams and silent fire pits. "The others have gone on to their own winter camps until spring. Normally, we would have gone to ours directly from the ricing lakes, but we wanted to come back to see if you were here so that we could do your ceremony."

BJ felt a rush of excitement as they walked down into camp. Would the warrior show up when BJ got his name? Running Wolf's camp was busy. Little Otter was stacking wood by the crackling fire. Morning Flower was separating leaves and stems of various plants for Runs Swiftly, who added them to a stew. Running Wolf was pounding a mixture of herbs into a wooden bowl with a pestle, adding bits of water and earth. All of them paused in their work and stood to greet BJ with pats and caresses. Shines Bright went back to a hand drum he had been tapping with a bent stick. Bent Nose was nearby, looking pensive. "You guys are working hard!" said BJ.

"It is ceremony," said Shines Bright. "And Stalking Bear took a caribou before we arrived. This is a great sign!" BJ looked at Stalking Bear with wonder. His friend was not only fighting off invaders, he was also hunting for his family, for his people. He couldn't be more than fifteen…

Morning Flower handed the last of her plants to Runs Swiftly, then strode to Running Wolf's lodge and ducked inside. BJ watched her every step. The others moved about, absorbed in their work, but Shines Bright sat with BJ. "You have not told us about your family other than your father, who is a protector of the earth," he said.

BJ loved this description of his father's job. It sounded a lot cooler than conservation officer. "I have one sister. She is small but extremely tough."

"Hmmm. Tough girl, like Runs Swiftly!"

"Yes, but gentle, too. The birds and animals like to be around her."

"What a great combination! Like Runs Swiftly and Morning Flower combined, maybe." BJ found this a rather sweet comparison. "And your mother?"

BJ enjoyed the questions. They made him appreciate his family. They made him thankful. "My mother is also very strong," said BJ.

"She is a good runner. She grows plants. She takes care of the food. I suppose she's kind of a medicine woman." Do essential oils and herbal rubs count? Yes, he reckoned they did.

Shines Bright watched a group of blue jays caw their way from one end of the village to the other like a rowdy gang. "That sounds like a nice family. Will your sister get married soon?"

BJ laughed. "Oh, gosh, she's just a kid!"

Shines Bright indicated Morning Flower, who was walking towards another wigwam, a tool in one hand. "She will be married to Stalking Bear in a couple of years, I think."

BJ's heart went straight to his throat. Could that be? Morning Flower getting married soon? She was his own age, and he was just going into tenth grade! A combination of sadness and jealousy crept into him, and he felt ashamed. Did he think she would return with him and that they would marry after high school? Or that he would stay here and be with her for the rest of his life? BJ had been so busy playing and exploring with everyone that he had not noticed that his young friends were, indeed, on the cusp of adulthood—at least in their culture and time. Yes, they had the freedom of a childhood in the wilderness, and they spent the days playing. But when they were not with BJ, they worked. They performed duties like any member of the village. BJ had seen this. It was true that, in the old days, thirteen or fourteen could be a marrying age for girls. The pairing of Morning Flower and Stalking Bear shouldn't come as such a surprise, really. She could hardly pick a better companion. There was some comfort in knowing that two of his favorite people would be together.

"I would have thought about marrying her," continued Shines Bright, "but we are both of the same clan, so that is not possible. Maybe I will end up marrying Runs Swiftly and spend the rest of my life getting bossed around!"

They both laughed.

The ceremony did not take place in the traditional corner of the village, but around Running Wolf's fire. Still, it was a powerful event.

The sweet smell of burning sage, the taste of seared caribou, boiled wild rice with juicy greens. The hand drum. These things pierced deeply into BJ's heart and soul. Running Wolf sat cross-legged at one end of the fire, an animal skin laid out before him. On it was a pair of wooden bowls, one smoldering, the other filled with a dark liquid. After they had eaten, he picked up the burning bowl and handed it to Shines Bright, who held the bowl with one hand and waved the smoke onto his face with the other. He passed it clockwise for the others to smudge themselves. When the bowl returned to Running Wolf, he set it down. "Before we begin, it is right and appropriate that we give thanks for all the gifts that we have." There were grunts of affirmation. "We will begin by thanking the earth for nurturing us throughout our lives. She is our mother, and she is fulfilling her original instructions in this way."

Some nods. The edge of the full harvest moon broke, deep orange, over the eastern horizon as Running Wolf spoke. "We further are thankful for the waters of the earth, which cleanse us when we are dirty and quench our thirst when we are dry. The songs of the waters as they move down the mountain and into Gichigami are as beautiful as any song on the earth. They bring us much joy. Without clean waters, we cannot live. Water is life!"

"Ahaaw," said Shines Bright.

Running Wolf indicated a basket of rice. "The Plant Nations have been particularly generous with us this year. They have given us much food, medicine, and color. We are thankful for their gifts, for they are also fulfilling their original instructions." Running Wolf continued in this way, thanking each group of living things—plants, animals, trees, birds, even the sky; the winds, rains, moon, sun, and stars. He concluded by thanking their ancestors and the Creator for the lives they were all given. BJ realized that he was hearing the thanksgiving prayer that Elmer spoke of. He wondered if it would reach Elmer unchanged or if it would evolve over the centuries. It probably didn't matter. There was something deeply sacred about the words. Just hearing them made BJ feel as if light were being poured into his soul.

Running Wolf connected the stone pipe bowl to the long wooden stem with slow, methodical movements. He stood, holding the pipe aloft to each of the four directions. Morning Flower held out a bowl of tobacco. Running Wolf took some and pressed it into the pipe. Stalking Bear handed him a thin, burning stick. Running Wolf lit the pipe. He puffed and blew smoke. He turned the pipe clockwise once, then handed it to his left. Shines Bright took the pipe, smoked, spun it, then passed it on. When the pipe came to BJ, he took some smoke into his mouth and blew it out. It tasted bitter. Running Wolf then placed it back on the blanket. The flute-like trill of a vireo echoed a goodnight call from the forest.

Running Wolf indicated BJ. "Our friend was sent here through the Spirit Cave four moons ago." He motioned to the items on the blanket. "We have four sacred herbs." He held his hands in the air. "We have four directions." He gestured around them. "We have four seasons. This is his fourth visit to us. We pray to Creator and all our ancestors that his time here will be full of meaning and that good memories will be with him as he walks his path."

More nods.

BJ felt a lump form in his throat. He was a ninth-grade boy from Grand Marais, Minnesota. They didn't have to do this for him. They didn't have to do *anything* for him. They had returned to camp to help him out. And when it was done, they would never see him again! It was massively humbling, nearly overwhelming. BJ lowered his gaze, not wanting anyone to see his eyes.

"Beejay has shown us much love and friendship," said Running Wolf. "I hope that we have done the same for him."

BJ nodded. A tear struck his lap.

Then, the tone and volume of Running Wolf's speech changed. "I have been watching our young friend carefully since he arrived. I have spent some time thinking and dreaming about his gifts."

Gifts? What gifts? What about the red-hand guy?

"There are many things that the Anishinaabe find important to live life in a good way. We have seven teachings of the Grandfathers. Among these are respect, truth, bravery, wisdom, generosity, and humility. I have seen Beejay display all of these during his time here."

That was only six.

"Beejay also has a very sharp eye." Running Wolf smiled easily. The story of BJ winning the doll-taking game had been told many times. "But I believe that it is the seventh teaching of the Grandfathers that Beejay embodies more than all of the others."

I'm just a ninth-grader from Grand Marais.

Running Wolf picked up the second wooden bowl from the blanket. Light from the fire and the full moon highlighted the wrinkles on his forehead and around his eyes. He looked older, ghostly almost. "Like many of you, Beejay is becoming an adult. He is learning to care for his own family and village. My dreams have helped me to see his gift." Running Wolf held the bowl to the heavens and declared, "Beejay has been waiting for his warrior. He has been watching and learning. He has been patient. He has been full of love and kindness for all the people and things around him." Running Wolf returned the bowl to the ground. "After today, he will be known to us, and to the spirit world, as Great Heart." A jolt of energy coursed through everyone.

Great Heart? My name is Great Heart?

Running Wolf handed the bowl to BJ. "Take this and leave your mark in the Spirit Cave. Your warrior will be there." He looked to the stars again and spread his arms wide. "We ask the spirits of our ancestors to watch over Great Heart and bless all that he does. Great Heart will be a warrior for his people." Running Wolf picked up the pipe, separated the bowl from the stem, and placed the two pieces back on the blanket, ending the ceremony. There was no clapping. No cheering. No back slaps. Running Wolf stood and retired to his lodge. His face was shiny with tears. One by one, the other adults did the same, followed by all of BJ's friends.

Great Heart. My name is Great Heart! BJ felt humbled beyond description. His warrior would meet him in the cave? The moon was over the trees now, its color having gone from red to orange to light blue. BJ stared into the fire, then at the bowl of liquid, then back into the fire. He felt glued to the ground, unable to stand, afraid to move. Once he got up and walked away, that would be it. No more Running Wolf, Stalking Bear, or Morning Flower. By the time he got home to Grand Marais, they would be gone from the earth for centuries. The pain of this thought pierced him like a knife. But he had to go. He had to meet the warrior and bring him back. For his family. For Grand Marais.

BJ pulled himself from the ground. As he did, he remembered that he was still holding the little flat rock. He held it up and looked at the moon through the little hole. An idea came to him. He found the bundle of basswood bark he had seen earlier, pulled off a strand, threaded it through the hole in the rock, and tied the ends in a knot to form a necklace. He set it on the stump where Morning Flower always sat at the fire. Would she find it? Would she know it was from him? He hoped so. It was all he had left to give.

There were 1,237 steps on a direct walk back to the cave, but BJ didn't remember counting them that night. Soon—too soon—he was standing at the lip of the hill, the bowl of thick liquid cupped in his hands. *Don't forget! Don't forget anything!* BJ studied the great tree, trying to burn the image of its trunk and branches into his mind. Then, a prickly feeling made him turn towards the river.

Standing together on the Tabletop, illuminated by the moon, were Runs Swiftly, Shines Bright, Stalking Bear, Little Otter, and, in front of them all, Morning Flower. They had come to see him off. What do you say when you know you will never see someone again? Not goodbye. There are no goodbyes. *We will see each other again.* BJ raised his right fist high in the air. The others did the same. They stood, united, cementing a bond of friendship and love in defiance of space and time. BJ took a deep breath and climbed down through the hole.

The moon cast more than enough light into the cave. "Hello?" BJ scanned the corners of the cave. There was no answer. How long should he wait? Was it one of the kids? Was he sneaking to the cave right now to greet him? BJ stood in perfect silence for five, maybe ten minutes, listening to his own breathing. His own heartbeat. Maybe he should make his mark while he waited. BJ picked up the bowl and scanned the wall. What should he draw? Maybe a heart or something symbolizing his new name? BJ didn't have a paintbrush. He had never been good at drawing. Charley was the artist in the family. The last thing BJ wanted was for some dumb painting to stand out among all the cool ones. He needed something simple and clear. Something that he wouldn't screw up. Something that wouldn't get in the way of—

And then, like a sledgehammer, it hit him. The hand. The red hand belonging to the brave warrior. The young scout. The mysterious hunter.

The hand was his own.

BJ trembled as he set down the bowl and shoved his right hand into the paint. He held it aloft, letting the liquid drip down his wrist. The book, he now remembered, had not said to find the Red Hand Warrior. It had said to find the warrior *with the red hand*. BJ had stood here and wished to know the age of the person who had made the print. He had wished to know what the world was like when the mark was made. He had wished to know his name. BJ pressed his hand hard against the rock and closed his eyes in gratitude. When he opened them, the room was filled with light—sunlight. BJ stood naked, his hands dry, the bowl of paint gone. The red hand on the wall before him was… ancient. It was the hand of Great Heart.

BJ's spirit was soaring as he climbed out of the cave. But the sharp bird alarms sounding across the hill and the strange smell in the air brought him quickly back to earth. Charley's pillow lay by itself in the middle of a torn and shredded mossy floor. One of her puffy cow slippers was nearby, the other halfway up the opposite slope. BJ leaped from the boulders and looked at the ground. Two sets of large bootprints were plainly visible in the moss. Two men. Two unknown men had come into their little room.

And they had taken Charley.

Chapter Thirty-Six

The realization that Charley had been kidnapped struck BJ with such force that his knees buckled, dropping him to the ground. His breath was rapid and shallow, making him light-headed. He placed his hands on the moss and fought the urge to throw up. *This is my fault! I should have made her go home. I shouldn't have let her stay! Focus now!* said a different voice in BJ's head. *Stay present! First things first: What had happened?* Yes, that was it. BJ could do nothing until he knew what had occurred.

He forced himself to his feet and scrambled to the lip of the hill, then back down, studying the ground with care. Then he did it again. Here is what he was able to learn: two men, walking from the north, happened across the upper rim of the hill and spotted Charley. They charged down and leaped on her. This struck BJ as nearly impossible, but then he remembered how tired she had been. Charley must have fallen asleep. By the looks of the ground around her pillow, she awoke quickly and put up a tremendous struggle, but they subdued her and carried her off.

BJ's fear turned to anger, then a fiery hatred. A direct attack on his sister. On his family. On his people. Two thoughts bubbled to the surface of BJ's furious mind. Get her. Then, get them. In the moss next to Charley's pillow was the impression of a large adult, arms and legs spread out wide. "The Blast," BJ whispered. Charley would have been nose-to-nose with him when she screamed. BJ nodded, then began to follow their trail. It was not difficult, even for a beginning tracker. It looked like a tractor had driven through. Broken branches. Torn ground. Shredded bark and leaves. Charley was putting up a hell of a fight.

A sound, far away. From home. BJ listened, nearly breaking into tears when he recognized it: the bell. Insistent. Scared. His mother had discovered their absence and was trying to call them back to the house. Clang-clang-clang! There was no time to return. BJ didn't know what was happening to Charley. Within an hour, there would be law enforcement all over the hills, but by then, it could be too late. He had no choice but to find her as soon as possible. By himself. He pulled out his phone, punched 911, then placed it on the ground. "I'm sorry, Mom!" he sputtered, then ran up the mountain.

BJ made his transformation on the fly: A smear of mud from a wet depression. A swipe of charcoal from a burned stump. Clay. Needles. Leaves. All of it done with barely a pause in his stride. As he ran, his summer—and his vision—began to come together like pieces of a puzzle. The hiding games. The tracking. The stalking. The awareness. All the adventures he had experienced with his friends and at his Sacred Place, all added up to the perfect bundle of skills for the mission at hand. But instead of going after a birchbark doll, it would be his own sister. Within minutes, BJ was fully camouflaged and focused like a goshawk.

Get her. Then, get them.

BJ ran on, then stopped abruptly at an alarming sight on the ground: Hair. And blood. It was not Charley's. BJ squatted to study the scene. Lying in the middle of the bloody mess was what looked like a piece of a human ear. "Wolverine," said BJ. "You guys grabbed the wrong girl." He continued, loping up the hillside, through brush, around trees. The ground evened out. BJ leaped over a birch log and skirted around a moss-covered boulder, then skidded to a halt. That log. That boulder. They were from his dream. The rest of the vegetation was different, but those two things he had seen. In fact, he realized, this was where he had been with Morning Flower before their friends ambushed them. The boulder had not been as moss-covered, and there had been no birch log.

BJ thought back to the walk with Morning Flower that day, and he could smell the warm breeze rolling up the hill across the blueberries and bunchberries as the summer neared its end. The scent of cedar was still here. And it was then that he knew. BJ knew where they would be. He rubbed his cowlick in thought, then began searching the ground. After a minute, he found what he was looking for—a piece of ironwood, smooth and barkless, about the length of his arm and as thick as his wrist. BJ seized it and slapped it into his left palm like a baseball batter. Dense and sturdy. A good throwing stick.

Or a fighting one.

BJ returned to the boulder and put his hands into a crack near its base. He worked a loose section of rock back and forth until it separated. Then, covering his eyes with one hand, he slammed the piece against the boulder, shattering it into a dozen smaller shards. He sifted through these until he found a sharp one about the size of his palm. A knife. BJ shoved it into his shorts pocket and ran on, eyes open, head up, like a wolf. He was sure of his destination. The trees began to thin. Flecks of migrating birds dotted the sky above the lake—geese, hawks, robins, their dark forms soaring back and forth among the cumulous clouds across the face of the sun. On any other day, such a view would have filled him with delight and wonder. How could something so terrible happen on a day like this? How could anyone steal a child?

Who will help your people?

Before BJ knew it, he was there, feeling the goosebumps on his arms, just as they had when he first stumbled into this place. The birds did not sing here among the sharp, lifeless cedar limbs. The deer did not browse on their withered and bitter leaves. The sunlight did not reach the ground. It was the place of darkness. The place of bad spirits.

BJ stared at the tangle of dead and dying trees and remembered the promise he had made to Morning Flower to never again enter this place. It was a promise that he would have to break. Charley was inside. BJ was as sure of it as he was of anything. But why had they taken her here? Who would choose to be in this place? Cold, dark fear began to seep into BJ's chest, working to extinguish the fire of anger and bravery that he had kindled and nurtured for the past hour. His shoulders sagged. He wished that Stalking Bear and Running Wolf were there to help him. Even Nanabojo. BJ did not feel strong or powerful. He did not feel like the warrior he had imagined the maker of the print to be.

The ancestors will help you along your path.

The words of Running Wolf sounded as clearly as if he were there on the hillside with him. The ancestors. Whose ancestors? BJ's? Elmer's? What could they do? BJ faced the lake and dropped to his knees. *Help me. Please help me! Grandfather Running Wolf, I need your strength. Stalking Bear, I need your stealth. Runs Swiftly, I need your speed. Morning Flower, I need… I need your courage. I need your sisu!* This prayer was one of the first acts of Great Heart. Its sincerity and its purity set the spirit world astir. Far below, a blanket of fog appeared very suddenly over the lake. It began to creep towards the shore, unfurling like a great white carpet. Up the hill it rolled, obscuring everything within it. Somewhere in the distance, a drum began to beat.

Boom-boom, boom-boom, boom-boom.

The white enveloped BJ. Voices sang with the drum. They were the same voices BJ had heard when he and Charley discovered the hill and the cave at the beginning of the summer. Chanting. Singing. Drumming. The images of Running Wolf, Stalking Bear, Shines Bright, Runs Swiftly, even Little Otter and Morning Flower, formed within the white. Images of his own great-grandparents, whom he knew only from photographs. They were dancing. They were singing. To him. They spun and swirled with the sound of the drum. After one full circle, they stopped. They glared at BJ, raised their fists to the air, and let loose a great war cry. The mist dissolved, and so did they. BJ was left staring out onto Gichigami. His call had been answered. He was not alone. The spirits were with him.

BJ stood, clenched his jaw, and walked into the darkness.

Chapter Thirty-Seven

The ground was cold, black, and bare. Nothing lived here except for the things that slithered out of holes, spun webs, or crawled with a thousand feet. Charley arched her back and twisted her torso, trying to find a comfortable position—a task made difficult by the duct tape around her ankles and wrists. A brown spider the size of her thumb nail crawled from one side of Charley's foot to the other, then made its way out into the open part of the floor, where it was stepped on by a large, black boot. Loose-fitting camouflage pants tied with a yellow length of rope covered the legs. The handle and cylinder of a six-shooter protruded from his back pocket and was tapped frequently by a bandaged right hand. The man's left arm was secured in a makeshift triangular bandage. A gray T-shirt was wrapped around his head, leaking blood at the right ear. He paced in the small space like a lion in a cage. His expression was vacant. His eyes hollow. This was not a face that made you think of songbirds or flowers or apple strudels. Troy Gustafson looked like he had fallen headfirst into a woodchipper.

In a sense, he had.

Troy paused to kick an empty beer can, then resumed pacing between Charley and a green cooler, which sat next to a hunting knife and a box of .38-special bullets. The hideout reeked of cigarettes and beer. A Coleman lantern hissed from one of the sharp tangles of branches that formed the natural ceiling. Troy's shadow grew and shrunk as he moved. To Charley's immediate left was a card table with an assortment of canned foods. To her right, two camping cots, each with a sleeping bag and some clothing. A pair of muddy boots lay discarded beneath one of the cots. On the other sat a man with long dark hair. He sat still, holding his head with both hands. Next to him was a .22 caliber rifle and scope. Beyond this, a black hole among the tangle of branches gaped like a great mouth as if it wanted to suck the three of them—and everything else—into oblivion.

Troy's voice cut through the thick air with a voice that sounded like gravel. "Archie, did you see what she did to me? Did you *see* this?? HALF MY EAR IS GONE! ARCHIE!"

Archie winced as if struck, then whispered, "I can't hardly hear nothin'. I think my eardrums are blown. My head is killing me."

Charley smiled from beneath the duct tape.

Troy glanced towards the hole. "Where is he?"

"He's in there. He'll take care of us. Said he would. You shouldn't a brought the girl here."

"What was I supposed to do, leave her there sleeping? I knew it was Maki's kid. I wasn't wasting a chance like that!" A wolf howled from somewhere outside the hideout. Troy's hand dropped to his revolver. "Did you hear that?"

"Hear what?"

"Never mind!" Troy limped to the cooler and sat down.

Charley's eyes remained on the two men, but her shoulders were moving back and forth in tiny, regular motions. She was working to free her wrists. The mosquitoes buzzed. The lamp hissed. Archie moaned. After a while, her shoulders stopped moving, and her eyes settled on the space where the .22 rifle was—or had been. It was no longer there. Soon after that, her eyes narrowed as she noticed that the boots from beneath the cot were gone as well. Troy was fighting against sleep, nearly falling off the cooler. Archie had collapsed onto

260

the cot and was snoring loudly. An hour more and the hunting knife and bullets had also disappeared.

BJ had been watching the men for more than an hour before he took the rifle. By then, he had counted every object in the hideout and knew where Troy and Archie directed their attention. Taking the gun and the boots was not very difficult. The knife and bullets, however, were on the ground at Troy's feet, exactly five hand lengths into the open. It had taken him half an hour to ease his way to it and another half an hour to ease his way back into the tangle of cedar branches. During that time, he was partially exposed for some fifteen minutes, but he moved so quietly and carefully that he looked like another dirty log. He assumed that his sister had noticed him by that point. The men had looked past him just as BJ had looked past Stalking Bear when he had snuck to within touching distance of him so many times.

BJ painstakingly worked his way around the outer edge of branches. He could see his sister keeping track of him. Good. He wanted her to know he was there. Moving through the sharp tangle of brush was not simple, but it wasn't difficult, either. BJ had spent so many hours and days stalking and sneaking through otherwise impossible terrain with Stalking Bear and Morning Flower that it had become almost second nature.

When he reached Charley, she had nearly freed her wrists from the duct tape, and it took only a small cut from his stone knife to finish the job. BJ squeezed her hands, then slipped around to her side and began to work at the tape binding her ankles. He had been at this for less than a minute when Troy startled awake and stared groggily around the room. He stood uneasily, limped to Charley, and forced a smile. His front row of upper teeth were all metal. He pointed at his mouth. "I owe your dad for these," he said, then pointed to the bloody spot on his head bandage. "And I owe you for this. I wonder"—he leaned close to Charley—"how I can pay you both back?"

BJ could practically feel the hot wolverine anger emanating from his sister, and he tensed his body, ready to react in case something happened. After a moment, Troy blinked, straightened up, and returned to the cooler. He never perceived that the muddy chunk of wood at Charley's feet was her brother's head. BJ resumed his work more slowly since Troy was now awake. Within a few minutes, Charley's ankles were free. BJ left the strip of tape in place to make it appear as if they were still bound. Charley began to subtly flex her leg muscles and point her toes. She would know she was going to have to make a break for it soon.

Then came the voice. A voice that made BJ feel like ice water had been poured over him. Hollow, dark, and deep, it issued from the black hole and sent a shudder through the hideout. Archie shook awake, and Troy stiffened. "I am here," it said. "Did you find if the man has a family?"

"Um," mumbled Archie, "Sort of. We didn't get to the house."

"You were to go to the house."

Neither of the men faced the hole directly. Instead, they tilted their heads and spoke to the side like a lesser wolf might address the alpha male in a pack. "We found his kid. We got her here," rasped Troy.

"You have taken the child of your enemy and brought her here? No one can know about this place. She must never be allowed to leave."

Troy cleared his throat. "Yeah, I guess not."

Lips smacked and the voice grew closer. The men shrunk away from the hole. "It is just as well. I am growing weary of your food." A pair of large, yellow, reptile-like eyes appeared in the darkness. "Where," it hissed, "is the girl?"

"She's right…" Troy turned, pointing towards the base of the cedar tree, but stopped in mid-sentence. Only two pieces of duct tape lay on the ground.

The kids had not quite reached the sunlight when a voice like a thousand snakes screamed from the darkness. "SHE WILL BRING

BACK THE OTHERS! SHE WILL BRING HIM HERE! STOP HER NOW!" BJ yanked Charley through the last of the cedar branches and into the open. They ran wildly, bounding down the hill like panicked deer. Confusion and swearing sounded behind them. They must have discovered the missing boots and weapons. A shot. Someone fired the gun! BJ and Charley dove to the ground.

"Watch what you're doing!" screamed a voice.

"It just went off! Shut up and get her!"

The kids barely had a head start. They fled, with BJ hoping that with everything he had, they could stay ahead of the men all the way home. Troy and Archie were injured, but they sounded desperate and would likely pursue them all the way into their backyard. "There's two of them!" yelled a voice. BJ turned to see Troy leveling and firing his gun. BANG! The bullet struck a tree no more than an arm's length from Charley. The kids bolted through the brush, zig-zagging back and forth down the hill. Another shot. Troy had completely lost his mind.

BJ rounded a crest and came face to face with six wolves. At their head was a large black male BJ instantly recognized from the footage on his father's trail camera. BJ raised his stick in self-defense, but the wolf ran past him in a blur. Archie burst through the brush and was flattened by the animal. It pinned him to the ground, lips and nose curled back, bearing a set of gleaming white fangs an inch from his face. Archie froze as if turned to stone and whimpered like a puppy.

Troy arrived, shooting wildly. BANG, BANG! He was screaming nonsense, sputtering almost. "Come on!" Charley yelled to BJ. Again, they ran. Behind them, there were barks, snarls, and another shot, but they did not look back.

They reached a heavy thicket of alder brush, and an idea struck BJ. "This way!" He led Charley through a patch of mountain maple and into a thinly wooded area dominated by fern, birch, and poplar. The river bubbled in the distance. They were maybe a ten-minute dash from home, but BJ had decided that he would not lead Troy into their yard. Instead, BJ led their pursuer into his Sacred Area.

His Sacred Place. If ever there was a home-field advantage, it would be here. *Enough sprinting like whitetails. Enough panic. This is my home. This is my family, and you are on my turf!* A familiar hollow log came into view, giving BJ another idea.

A minute later, the kids were well hidden when Troy came crashing through the brush, swearing, nearly frothing at the mouth. His left arm had pulled loose from the triangle bandage, and his sunken gray eyes were wild with fear and madness. "Kiddos!" he sang, weaving his head back and forth and waving his pistol. "Where are you? I heard you down here somewhere. Come to Troy! Come out and play!"

The wolves reappeared, streaming in and out of the trees like shadows. Troy fired at them, forcing a partial retreat. Troy turned back around. "Come out, come out, wherever… wait a minute." His eyes locked on Charley's pink and white jammies, just inside the hollow end of a log. "He-lo," purred Troy, like a cat that has just cornered a mouse. He straightened up and swaggered as best as he was able to the end of the log and dropped to his knees. "Come… to… TROY! AAAARRRRGH!" Maybe it would have been different if Troy had moved slowly or not shouted. Or maybe if BJ had not thrown the jammies in the hole so hard. Who knew? Either way, Ref was not very pleased when Troy shoved his face in after the jammies and yelled, and that is how Troy got blasted squarely in the face from a distance of no more than six inches.

BJ and Charley watched from the brown and green ferns nearby as Troy's body convulsed. He struck his head against the top of the log, fell back down, and got sprayed again. His gun went off, firing into the ground. Ref burst out the far end of the log and disappeared through the ferns. Troy was writhing on the ground like a poisoned animal. "I can't see! I CAN'T SEE!"

"Let's go!" said Charley, pulling at her brother. But he stood firm, just as she had when confronted by Eddie Sourmeister. BJ inhaled a deep breath and thought of Morning Flower and Stalking

Bear and Running Wolf. He remembered them defending their village at the start of the summer when the ferns were just beginning to curl up from the ground and then again at the end when they were shriveled and brown. BJ inhaled deeply and curled his toes into the earth. Still gripping the ironwood in his right hand, he strode to Troy and looked down at him.

"BJ!" pleaded Charley.

Troy spit and blinked and coughed until he realized that someone was there. Eventually, he straightened to his knees and squinted upwards through greasy bangs. His eyes were swollen and red. The forest fell silent as BJ and Troy faced each other. Then a sound, raspy and hoarse, began deep in Troy's throat, at first sounding like another coughing fit but turned into a laugh. Not an easy laugh—it came in spurts and gags—but still a wicked, evil, mindless laugh. This was not the sound of a man who had been defeated. It was the sound of someone who was not yet finished, someone with a trick up his sleeve. The reason for this became clear when Troy raised his bandaged right hand, still holding the revolver. "Gun," wheezed Troy, "trumps stick. What do you (cough!) say to *that?*"

BJ glanced at Charley and saw the fear in her eyes. His warrior sister who had defended him on so many occasions. His little sister. He turned back to the man who had taken Charley and tried to harm her. BJ squared his feet. "Six."

Troy laughed again, this time in a clear, hollow voice. "Six? I'm going to shoot you, and that's all you got to say? Six? Ha!" He cocked the hammer back and steadied the gun. "Six what?"

"Six shots," said Great Heart, his knuckles turning white on the beam of ironwood. "You're empty."

An instant of comprehension showed on Troy's face before the stick slammed into the side of his head. He folded to the ground like a marionette whose strings were cut. BJ tossed the stick onto the unconscious form. "LEARN TO COUNT!" He ran to his sister and hoisted her up in a full embrace, nearly squeezing the air out of her. Charley wrapped her legs around his back and held on tight, and they stayed this way for a long time. "Let's go home."

BJ had not yet set her back down when a sound turned their attention to the alder thicket. Archie? The wolves? But it was neither. Instead, two giant, impossibly large gray hands with pointed black nails parted the brush and out stepped the most terrifying thing either BJ or Charley had ever seen or imagined. A giant, twice as tall as a grown man, leered at them with reptile-like eyes, as a T-Rex would to a fawn. Everything on its thin frame was angular and hard, from the triangular ears to the sickle-shaped fingers. Its back was slightly arched, showing each vertebra beneath the taut, gray skin. It kicked Troy's unconscious form to the side and smiled, revealing a set of black, dagger-like teeth. "I," it declared, "am Windigo." It was the voice from the place of darkness.

BJ and Charley reeled. "You!" said BJ, his mind a whir. "You killed those animals. You killed that man!"

"Indeed," said Windigo, stepping forward, "and there would have been many more, but your father is not the only one protecting the mountain." Suddenly, the wolves were there. In a flash, they were on the monster, snarling, biting, tearing. Windigo arched his back and hissed a scream of fury that made BJ and Charley cover their ears. It threw the animals like rag dolls. BJ and Charley fled once more, this time towards the river. "Run children!" teased the monster from behind. "Run from Windigo!" They flew through brush and branches as if they were made of tissue paper. Branches tore and cut at their cheeks and arms, but they hardly noticed in their panic. Behind them, trees crashed, and the earth pounded as if a steamroller was bearing down on them, crushing everything in its path. Then they were at the river. BJ chanced a glance backward—at exactly the wrong time. He tripped over a protruding root and fell, sprawling to the ground. Charley fell with him.

In five strides, Windigo was upon them and plucked Charley from the ground in its great gray hand. "Humans!" he shrieked. "Tiny, weak, shallow humans! There is no running! There is no escaping! Hiding from me"—it leaned down—" would be like hiding from yourselves! I am nowhere and I am everywhere! I am one and I am a thousand!" It's eyes glowed yellow. "I have watched. I have learned! You are not so different from before. Gluttonous, greedy, pathetic humans! The more you fight and take and destroy, the stronger and more numerous I become! Your people have become the living dead, walking without seeing, listening without hearing!" It smiled an impossible, grotesque smile. Its black dagger-like teeth glistened. "You live in a fantasy world, distracted and divided. I will do what I have always done—take!" It smacked its lips, opened its jaws wide, and held Charley aloft.

BJ turned away, unable to watch, and found himself looking at a pair of huge brown leather boots. BJ's eyes moved up a set of tree trunk legs to a red-and-black flannel shirt and... Russ! Eyes blazing, nostrils flaring, he held the great axe in his right hand. The mysterious symbol on the handle was glowing. The expression on Russ's face was terrible. "You," he said, stepping over BJ, "don't want to be the one to touch my goddaughter."

The Windigo dropped Charley as if it had been struck. "You!"

"Me." Russ leaned the axe against a tree and began to roll up his sleeves, revealing a twisting set of veins bulging like swollen garden hoses. He seemed, if possible, even larger than before. Taller. Thicker. Not quite the height of the Windigo, but easily twice as heavy. The air around him was electric. "Kids." Russ's eyes stayed locked on the monster. "You go back home now."

Windigo grinned. His teeth glistened. "The people are still greedy."

"The people are still good," countered Russ.

"They will help me destroy."

"I will help them rebuild."

"They think of themselves only. They have blackened souls."

"They have great hearts."

"I will not be alone. I will—"

Russ struck like lightning. One moment, the Windigo was speaking, and the next, it was hurling backward, breaking full-sized trees off as he flew. He landed in a heap thirty yards in the distance. Russ shook his right hand. "He always talked too damn much."

Windigo stood and stretched out his arms, opening his claw-like hands. He bent forward and contorted his mouth into a nightmarish, ice-water scream. The sound filled the entire forest, freezing BJ and Charley in place. Charley covered her ears. Russ squared his feet, readying for round two. And then the dark wolf was back, standing between Russ and the kids. "Run home!" it said. "RUN!" shouted the wolf.

BJ and Charley leaped to their feet and fled. They had just reached the red pine when the shock wave from the collision of the two giants sent the birds flying from the treetops in rings. The thunderous roaring of Russ and the pitched screams of the Windigo sounded like a battle between the gods upon Mount Olympus.

Chapter Thirty-Eight

BJ could not feel his legs when he and Charley arrived at the top of the yard and leaned against the Cannonball Rock. The wolf accompanied them partway back, then disappeared. Down in their yard, squad cars, fire trucks, an ambulance, and even a pair of horses were gathered. People in uniforms and badges stood in clusters, leaning over maps and barking into radios. Molly's voice shouted from the center of it all, "There they are!" She charged up the hill to greet them among a torrent of "Where have you been?" and "We were so worried!" BJ hugged his mother. BJ could barely see straight. He just wanted his family. He was helped down the hill by Sheriff Mike while Molly held on tight to Charley, whose legs were wrapped around her mother.

It was many minutes before BJ could compose himself enough to answer the dozens of questions being hurled at him and his sister. He gave a brief description of Charley's capture and rescue, while skipping over the Windigo, the wolf, and Russ. Gasps were issued and hands covered mouths. Sheriff Mike said, "we can add kidnapping and attempted murder to the other charges."

Molly swooned. BJ and Charley both wrapped their arms around her. "We're all right, Mom. We're okay." BJ looked around. "Where's Dad?"

"Somewhere between here and Reservation Road, looking for you guys," said the sheriff. "Half the Search and Rescue people from the county are up on the mountain. Steve!" he barked. "Radio Mark and tell him the kids showed up!"

"Already done. Sounds like he's already got the two suspects. He's heading back with them now."

They all cheered like they'd scored an overtime goal. Molly kissed and hugged BJ and Charley again, refusing to let them go for a long time. When she did, BJ said to the Sheriff, "So, Dad has Troy and Archie? What were the other charges, then?"

"Poaching and vandalism. We almost got them a few days ago. Your dad had been keeping very close tabs on that entire area since that bullet went through your window. He's the one who figured out they were there. He got a video of them breaking into a home, so we set up additional patrols. We had a general idea of where they were hiding out but weren't sure. Tribal law enforcement couldn't find them, and your dad reckoned they'd moved their hideout into the national forest. He had figured out their pattern: breaking into homes every few days to steal food and other stuff. He was staking out Reservation Road this morning, but they didn't appear, and when you guys didn't show up, we got worried. Then we got your 911 call and knew where to go. Mark and a few other officers came through the National Forest from the north. We set up a command center here and were just getting ready to head up from the south to meet them."

As if on cue, Mark arrived at the Cannonball Rock with a shotgun over his shoulder, prodding Troy and Archie forward. Both men wore handcuffs. They were beaten, bloody, and miserable. "Monster," Troy was babbling. "You gotta believe us. Tell him, Archie. ARCHIE!"

"What?"

"Oh, shut up!"

The smell that accompanied them made everyone grimace and wave at the air. "What did you do, Mark, shoot him with a skunk?" There was a chorus of laughter.

Sheriff Mike said, "Don't put them in my car!"

Mark motioned to the deputy. "Put them in the federal vehicle. Larry could use the company."

An agent with a badge on his belt opened the back door of an unmarked car and helped Troy into the back, where Larry Sourmeister sat, looking deflated and defeated. He began to cough and sputter almost immediately. "You know, man," said the agent, "organic tomato juice is the best for skunk spray."

BJ's mouth fell open. "Keanu?"

"Hey, little dudes!"

"You're a cop?"

"If you're surprised," said the sheriff, "welcome to the club."

"FBI," said Keanu. "No one knew except for your dad. I came to help investigate some possible wolf poaching by Larry here, but that morphed into tax evasion and money laundering when you gave me that tip, Charley."

"Huh?"

"The phone number."

BJ thought back. "The Milwaukee number?"

"Right, except it wasn't Milwaukee. That extra digit you remembered was no mistake."

"414-458-932-56" said BJ.

"Holy cow," said the sheriff, "you are good with numbers! Give that kid a job, Keanu!"

Keanu beamed. "We sure would! So anyway, it's not 414. It's 41-44-589-3256, which is Zurich, Switzerland."

"I don't get it," said BJ. "How did you figure that out?"

"I didn't. Francisco Gonzales did when he came by the table and saw it written on my clipboard. I guess he used to have friends in Zurich."

Mark explained, "That's where a lot of the Swiss banks are, BJ. Banks that are used by the Mafia, cartels, tax evaders, and money launderers." He glanced in the window at Larry, who was looking very pale. "Larry's got a lot of creative financial transactions to explain. He'll be out of the development business until he does!"

"What about the land he bought back there," said Charley, pointing towards the woods.

"Today was the deadline," said Mark. "And I'm thinking he's not going to make that meeting." BJ nearly cried with relief. The mountain was safe.

"Took us a while to trace his phone calls," said Keanu, "because he had a Tracfone he used for his dirty work. Once we got ahold of that number, we saw the communications with Troy over there."

BJ glanced at Troy Gustafson, who still looked like a beaten dog. "So they know each other?"

"Sure looks like it," said Mark. "That might explain why the homes were getting vandalized and how Larry was able to snatch them up so fast."

Russ arrived, scratched and bruised but smiling. Charley ran to him and was scooped up into one arm. He walked into the melee and held out a thick fist for BJ to bump.

Molly held her hands to her cheeks. "What on earth happened to you?"

Russ wiped blood from his forehead. "I'm such a klutz! I peeled off from the search party and ended up tripping down a slope and landing on a pile of rocks."

Mark narrowed his eyes. "How many times?"

"Well, Russell Christiansen," Molly gushed, "I've got just the thing for those scratches!" She turned towards the house and nearly ran into Elmer in his Twins cap and worn flannel shirt.

"You look as tired as I feel," noted Mark.

"Dog tired! What did I miss?" He received a collective groan in response.

"All right then!" declared Mark, throwing his hands in the air, "that's about enough excitement for one day. I, for one, am looking forward to being back to normal…" He was interrupted by the blaring of the alarm from inside the house. Smoke began to curl out of the kitchen window. The firefighters straightened up, looking eager.

Molly clenched her fists, red-faced. "Oh…" she said, trying to compose herself.

"I'll have two, whatever they are," teased Elmer.

"Oh…" Molly marched to the deck.

"The water tanker's ready if you need it," grinned the fire chief.

"Oh… SHIT!" Molly flung open the door and stormed inside. A moment later, a cast-iron frying pan flew, end over end, into the middle of the yard, scattering the group like grouse. "That," Mark nodded at the smoking ruin, "Ah yes, back to normal—didn't take long at all."

Chapter Thirty-Nine

For most Native peoples, fall was a time to celebrate the harvest and prepare for the arrival of winter. Foods were gathered and stored. Feasts were prepared. Time was taken to be thankful for the bounty provided by the earth. Hunters and gatherers did this. Farmers, too. So did the Ojibwe.

Running Wolf and his people spent every fall of their lives ricing and drying as much meat, fish, and plants as they could—as their elders had taught them to do. They passed these and other traditions down to their children and grandchildren. This was the way. Over time, some traditions evolved or disappeared as the environment changed or newcomers arrived. Other traditions survived, more or less intact.

On this early September morning, Elmer was doing his part to see that one of them continued and was shared beyond the Ojibwe Nation. After all, he said, everyone needs to be connected to where they live.

The blue Chevy truck rattled to a stop near the water's edge. Elmer and all four Makis climbed out. "This is one of the lakes my ancestors came to during *manoominike-giizis*, the ricing moon." A thin blanket of mist covered one end of the water, obscuring a group of feeding and splashing mallards. Another shoreline shone bright yellow where the morning sun struck the thick beds of rice.

The Makis unloaded the canoes from the top of the truck, then put one long pole and a pair of ricing sticks, each about two feet long, into the boats. Charley added water bottles, a small cooler, and her Dora the Explorer backpack.

Elmer knelt at the water's edge and sprinkled tobacco in prayer. He stood and grinned. *"Mino-giizhigad noongom!"*

BJ nodded. It was a good day, indeed.

"Thanks for taking us along," said Molly, tying her hair back in a puffy ponytail. "We haven't riced since BJ was born."

"Is there rice in Bemidji?" asked Charley. BJ wondered the same. It was going to be strange to leave Grand Marais.

"Tons!" said Elmer, motioning her into the bow of the canoe. "There's not as much as there used to be before they dammed up many of the lakes there, but there's still plenty." He climbed into the middle. BJ shoved them off, hopping into the back at the last moment. Elmer turned towards Mark and Molly, who were already in their boat. "Why don't you two work along that shore while the kids and I look over here? Let us know what you find." Mark poled their boat into the reeds and disappeared.

Elmer sat back on his haunches and pointed his knocking stick forward. "Manoominike-daa!"

Standing just behind him, BJ jammed the knobby end of the long pole into the mud, twisted his torso, and worked his hands to the top, propelling the canoe forward like a gondola. Charley sat at the bow, facing them, her backpack at her feet.

After a few minutes, they came to a suitable patch of rice. Elmer reached a knocking stick out to his left and bent a group of rice stalks over the canoe, which he struck with the stick held in his right hand. A shower of rice grains sprinkled into the boat. BJ yanked the pole from the water and lifted it into the air by walking his hands towards the bottom. He jammed it back in the mud further up and propelled them forward by running his hands back up its length. The rice bed was thick, and propelling the canoe forward required a certain level of force. Elmer reached out to the right side and repeated the process, reversing hands. It took some work for BJ to get the hang of advancing the boat at just the right speed, and changing direction was tricky, but eventually, he and Elmer fell into sync, and a gentle cadence was established. Swish. Whack. Sprinkle.

BJ breathed in the morning air with relish. He felt like he could run a marathon, maybe even keep up with Stalking Bear. The mornings had been cool for a good ten days, and the mosquitoes had almost completely disappeared. Mark was visible in the distance, propelling their boat forward. Mallards quacked and dabbled ahead of them, flushing loudly into the air each time the boat got close.

Charley hummed, letting her fingers drag in the water.

BJ nodded at an eagle watching them from the top of a snag. *Great Heart. My name is Great Heart.* Swish. Whack. Sprinkle. After the rescue and arrest of Larry, Archie, and Troy, the waning days of summer had been spent having tea with Elmer and Tío Francisco, playing Capture the Flag with Tony, David, Charley, and, of course, spending time in his Sacred Area. So, it had been Nanabojo who had guided him into the past. Well, "guided" was a bit of a strong word. He had sort of pointed the way, helped a bit, then wandered off. Had he been responsible for the face in the cliffside and in the hollow tree? Had he changed the words in the history book? Was he the coyote standing out on Lake Superior, staring at him during gym class? BJ twisted his torso, turning the canoe towards a promising bed of rice. "Hey, Elmer, do you think Nana—" He caught himself. "Do you think the man—that man—is still around?"

"Dunno. The Manitous are unpredictable, especially him. He could disappear for another century, for all I know. But if he decides to really come pay Grand Marais a visit, then buckle up."

BJ tried to imagine what that might mean. "Hey, you know what he told me?"

"What?"

"He said to give his regards to Paul. Who's Paul?"

"Probably talking about Russ."

"What's Russ got to do with it?"

Charley was leaning back, gazing at the sky. "He's Paul Bunyan, you know."

"Right," said BJ. "I know he looks like the statue and likes to dress up and all that, but—"

"No," said Charley, "Russ is Paul Bunyan."

"What are you talking about?"

Elmer rested the knocking sticks on his lap and turned his head partway around. "BJ, Russ doesn't look like the statue. The statue looks like *him*."

BJ came dangerously close to falling out of the canoe. "Hold on. I know people like to call him that, but how can he be Paul Bunyan? ARE YOU TELLING ME PAUL BUNYAN IS A REAL GUY?"

Elmer resumed ricing. "He's not a guy. He's a Manitou, a spirit, like the Trickster. He's been on the earth forever. He has lived under a thousand names. The Sami in the Arctic called him Kalevanpoika. He's a Warrior Spirit, you know. That axe is the real deal."

BJ stood stunned for a full minute until Elmer pointed with his knocker and said, "Ho!" BJ had let the boat drift out of the rice bed. He shoved the pole down to the bottom and torqued his upper body to reorient them, his mind still on Russ. "Elmer, do you know about the mark on the handle?"

"On the axe? Yeah, I was curious about that, too, but Russ doesn't talk about everything. I looked it up. In English, it's referred to as the 'Helm of Awe.' It's a symbol of strength and war. I'll tell you one thing: if things get dicey, you want Russ on your side."

"I noticed," said BJ.

"Thing is," continued Elmer, "Manitous can't just stick around. They've got their own lives and their own business. Also, if they just settle down in one place and everybody knows about them, people start to get stupid and worship them, and things get really messed up. We have to be careful with Russ because if too many people find out about him, he'll leave and not come back." Charley's face drooped when Elmer said this, and BJ felt the same way. The idea of Russ leaving Grand Marais forever was sad and kind of scary.

BJ straightened the canoe out in a bed of rice and resumed poling. "Elmer, do you know why Russ might have covered up my dad's trail camera and closed the wolf trap?"

"Because I asked him to. Hey!" BJ had flinched so hard the canoe almost swamped. "Remember, BJ, everyone, including your dad, thought that a wolf was responsible for those killings. I knew it hadn't been a wolf, but I couldn't come out and say so. I was worried a Windigo was around, but couldn't believe it, really. I'd never seen one. Anyway, it would have been tragic if an innocent wolf had been destroyed because of that monster."

Swish, swish, whack!

They continued ricing at a steady pace while the sun rose into a clear blue sky and flocks of geese passed by high above on their way south. Elmer explained that Russ had followed the Scandinavian immigrants to America, disguised as a logger, but he became close with the Anishinaabe people because they reminded him of the Sami, far in the Arctic. When he saw that the logging was not only destroying Ojibwe land and culture but also that some Natives were being forced to work in logging camps themselves, he stopped. He did what he could to rid the area of Windigos, which had been terrorizing the villages. They gave him a remote end of the reservation to live on when those borders were drawn up in exchange for keeping an eye out for Windigos and illegal logging operations. The colonizers only knew the first part of his story, so they built the statues to celebrate the logging part. And, of course, made him whiter. "There are still a couple of Native elders who know his real story, but not many."

"Like Audrey?" said BJ.

Elmer stopped knocking to laugh. "She's always had the hots for him. Poor Russ!"

BJ thought of another question. "So what did Nana—I mean, you know who—mean when he said give him his regards?"

"Yeah, I forgot about that part. He's messing with him. Apparently, the Trickster was around during those settlement days," said Elmer. "He used to absolutely torture Russ, playing all sorts of jokes on him. Loosen his axe head so it would fly off and land a mile away, steal his clothes at night, and so on. He really knew how to press Russ's button. Russ would come roaring after like a raging bull, but he could never catch him." Elmer chuckled. "By the way, I think he's the reason Russ's music player has been acting strange."

"You mean all the random songs coming out of George? You're kidding."

"Would I kid you?"

"Yes."

"Okay, you're right, I would. But I bet you it was him. Hey!" Elmer pointed with a knocker. "Keep us in the good rice, eh?" BJ had let the canoe drift again.

"Sorry!" They worked in silence for another hour. It was hard maneuvering the boat with the pole, especially as it gained weight with the accumulating rice, but BJ enjoyed the workout immensely. A kingfisher dived into the water, then flapped up into a tree with his catch. Thin, long-legged spiders weaved strands of silk back and forth between the gunwales with incredible speed. Bugs sprang up and down from the rice with little popping sounds. Elmer had taped the cuffs of his jeans tight to keep critters from crawling up his legs, but BJ didn't mind the occasional tickle on his bare legs. Ricing was not for the squeamish.

Charley rode in silence, watching the shoreline pass by and sometimes examining the rice kernels and bugs. "Did Russ kill that Windigo?" she said.

It took a minute for Elmer to answer. "I don't know. The stories are that Russ used to pound them into oblivion, and they'd sort of disintegrate, but they would reform somewhere else later on. My grandmother used to say that only one type of person could actually kill a Windigo for good." BJ waited for the answer, but it didn't come. If Russ couldn't kill one, then who on earth could? "The Windigos are smart and sneaky," continued Elmer. "They are shapeshifters. If they come back, we are going to need all the help we can get—not just Russ, but young, old, Indian, Mexican, white. We all have a role to play in defending and protecting our community. Everyone is important. There are many shades of a warrior."

Swish. Whack. Sprinkle.

At the end of the day, they met Mark and Molly back at the launch, each boat nearly overflowing with rice. There were groans as they all climbed out and stretched. After loading the rice into a dozen burlap bags, they tied the canoes onto Elmer's truck. Mark was standing still, staring at his phone.

"What is it?" said Molly.

"I missed a call from St. Paul. There's a message." BJ's shoulders slumped. Probably a call to tell them when they were moving. Mark punched the button and listened, with no expression on his face, to what seemed like a very long message. When he was done, Mark put the phone back in his pocket, folded his arms, and allowed a small grin.

"Well??" said Molly.

"I guess we're staying," said Mark.

BJ and Charley leaped in the air as if they'd won the Stanley Cup.

"The woods are full of you guys, but I'm glad to hear it," said Elmer, winking at BJ.

"The commissioner resigned," said Mark. "He is in really hot water on the land swap deal between the Feds and Larry. Looks like there were some shady financial transactions involving that Swiss bank, and the governor might even be involved."

Elmer gave a low whistle.

"Okay," insisted Molly, "but what's that got to do with your job? The DNR is still short thirty-something Conservation officers, and the Legislature won't get off its ass to supply the funding, so is your position here secure or not?"

Mark removed his maroon ballcap, ran his fingers through his blond hair, then put it back on. "Yeah, that's a funny thing. Apparently, just yesterday, someone backed the department into a corner by donating two million dollars, which they said could only be used for the preservation of my position here in Grand Marais.

This news stunned everyone. "Your position, specifically?" said Molly. "Who on earth could have done that?"

"A couple of wealthy old gals from Williston, North Dakota. Any of you ever heard of an Eva and Olga Kern?"

The first day of tenth grade was uneventful in that there were no coyotes walking on water, no textbooks with insane messages, and Charley didn't punch anyone in the nuts. There were, however, two new teachers: Ms. Rubenstein, a recent graduate from somewhere on the east coast, was hired to teach English; and Madame Bouche, the alarmingly pretty ex-wife of Mr. Davis, joined the staff to teach French. At lunch, BJ caught up with the gang. David had gone to the ceremony in Luck, Wisconsin, which he said was pretty cool. Tony reported that Tío Francisco had eaten with his family in the main house for the first time in nearly a year and offered to take Tony camping.

When the final bell rang at the end of the day, BJ headed down to the main office to say hello to Mr. Olafson. The principal was sitting in his chair, staring at the lake trout on the wall. BJ knocked. Mr. Olafson spun his chair around, and when he saw who it was, his right eye began to twitch violently. "Already, BJ? Day one, and you've been sent to see me? What did you do now?"

BJ laughed. "I didn't do anything. Just came by to say hello and see how your summer was."

Ryan's eye stopped twitching. "Oh… sorry. I, uh, the summer was really great. I fished. A lot. Thank you. Time sure flies by."

"Tell me about it. See you later!"

"Bye, BJ."

Charley joined him outside the east exit, and together, they headed down the sidewalk towards the Paul and Babe statues. Audrey was there, with a rock for each of them. BJ opened his backpack and pulled out a bag of rice. Audrey's eyes sparkled. "Where you get dis?"

"Ingi manoominike geget!" said BJ. He had made Elmer teach him the sentence for just this moment.

"Howah, you guys riced!" Audrey laughed, and it sounded like bells rolling down a granite slope.

They walked past Ida's Bakery (three apple strudels!), then crossed the street towards the bait shop. Russ was out front. They had just arrived when a big white SUV pulled up, and Angie leaned out of the window. "Hey, guapo, when can I bring this muchacho over?" Tony was in the back seat, his thumbs working furiously on his phone.

"Saturday works," said BJ. "Maybe we'll play the doll-taking game."

Tony looked up. "Huh? What's that? Dolls?"

"He'll be there." Angie winked and drove off.

Russ grunted. "Watch out for their dog."

"Will do," said BJ. His eyes were on a girl in a black hoodie gathering rocks on the beach. Long black hair ran down her chest and nearly touched the ground each time she bent over. BJ had seen her at lunch, eating alone, the hoodie covering her face as if she didn't want to be bothered. BJ motioned at her with his head. "Who's that?"

"That's Elmer's niece, who just moved down from the rez. You know you might—"

BJ was already across the street, walking towards the beach. Something about the girl was familiar. When BJ was no more than an arm's length from her, she turned around, and he nearly collapsed from shock. She was the spitting image of Morning Flower. "What?" she shot defensively.

BJ gaped at her. "I…"

"What?" she repeated.

"Sorry! I'm sorry. I thought you were somebody else," sputtered BJ. Of course, it was not Morning Flower. How could it be? But the resemblance was uncanny.

"Wait," she said, eyes narrowing. "Are you BJ?"

"I…"

"I'm your neighbor," she said.

"I know. I mean, I knew. Or, I just knew now. I mean…"

"I'm Amy." Her eyes were big and brown.

"Right," said BJ, still feeling dumb. "I'm BJ. You knew that, though." It felt surreal to be having a conversation with what amounted to Morning Flower in a hoodie. "Um, what classes do you have?"

"I'm in math with you."

"Oh." BJ hadn't noticed her. He sat near the front. "So, do you ski?" Most of BJ's interactions with girls were on the cross-country ski team.

"Uncle Elmer wants me to start."

BJ cleared his throat. "I'm on the team. You get good pretty fast if you're on the team."

Amy bent down to pick up a rock, and it was then that BJ noticed the necklace dangling along with her hair. A beaded white, red, black, and yellow string held a pendant, a flat rock about the size of a golf ball, beige, smooth—and with a hole on one end. Could it be? "Where," BJ pointed, "did you get that?"

"This?" Amy held up the rock. "My grandmother did the beading, but the stone is really old. It came down from my ancestors."

"Yeah," said BJ, transfixed. "It sure did."

Amy gave him a curious look, then jutted her head at the water. "Can you skip?"

BJ snorted at her. Could he skip! He mustered an insulted expression. They gathered a handful of stones and squared off. BJ felt his courage returning. "Think you can get a twelve?"

Amy glared at him, then blew on a Kennedy. "Watch me."

Afterword

This book took me to unexpected places. The story was initially conceived as a bedtime tale to inspire our children to spend more time outdoors. As it evolved, so did the opportunity for lessons. If my main character is going to learn about nature and the Earth, and he lives in northeastern Minnesota, then the best people to mentor him would be the Ojibwe. This introduced an obvious need to teach some colonial history (treaty issues and boarding schools), along with some basics on culture, much of which I have learned through stories and participation in ceremonies with my Native friends in Bemidji. While many of my own mentors are from Lipan Apache, Akamba (Kenya), Ojibwe, northern European, and Lakota traditions, there are common denominators among most Earth-based cultures that I have included in this story: the art of sitting still, the concept of trial-and-error learning, and the playing of games are a few examples.

There is plenty of humor in the Native world. When the Trickster, Nanabojo (sometimes known as Winabojo or Nanabush), showed up, the tale began to take some wild turns, making me feel like I'd lost control of the steering wheel. I discussed this with Larry Aiken, a local Ojibwe Elder and healer (who has since walked on), and he said, "If he knocks on the door, you better let him in." In the end, it's my hope that this book series will be the literary equivalent

285

of a tale around the fire, one that makes the listeners at first double over with laughter, then, later, inspires them to develop deeper connections to the natural world and to their own communities, eventually leading them to become defenders and protectors of the Earth in their own right.

Acknowledgments

Without the continuous and loving encouragement of my family, this story would have remained a simple bedtime tale. Thanks to Tom Brown Jr. and Jon Young for their teachings in tracking, wilderness survival, and a spiritual approach to the Earth. Thanks to Anne Dunn, Larry Aiken, Erika Bailey Johnson, Anton Treuer, Rob Loiselle, Duane Ootholdt, and Kim Shelton for graciously sharing stories, culture, food, and laughter with me and my family. Amy Rutten, my first writing buddy, has been a fantastic reader and cheerleader. Paul Kivi and Dan Alloso provided great insights and support. Lenny Golay, from her perch in Manhattan, read, critiqued, edited, and encouraged me every step along the way. My amazing editor, Erica Ellis, held my feet to the fire, pushing me to make this story better, paragraph by paragraph, line by line. Finally, my great thanks to Ian Graham Leask and the team at Calumet Editions for their faith in me and in this story. I am grateful for their endless polishing and patience.

About the Author

Robert is an educator, writer, EMT/first responder, storyteller, coach, actor, community volunteer, and stay-at-home father. He has picked tomatoes in Mexico, danced flamenco in Seville, and played rugby in southern France. He speaks fluent French and Spanish and is conversant in a few other languages, including Ojibwe. He has fallen in love with every culture he has ever known and has taught Native and non-Native youth everything from foreign languages to wilderness survival skills, native plant harvesting, and self-defense. He enjoys family and friends, travel, tracking, hunting, and practicing primitive skills. Robert lives in the North Woods of Minnesota with a dozen chickens, two big dogs, and one small wife. Their three children are out in the world making it a much better place.

Made in the USA
Monee, IL
12 April 2024

56447072R00173